For Donna Mello

My editor, my cheerleader, my fan, my friend

I could not have completed this book without her encouragement, insight and direction

and

For Hardy

My greatest fan

Always by my side to understand and encourage.

HAUNTED IN PARADISE

IN PARADISE, SOME THINGS NEVER STAY BURIED

SUSAN E. ROGERS

ISBN: 978-1-960534-36-1(Paperback)
ISBN: B0FQ9CBTF5 (Ebook)

Written by Susan E. Rogers
Edited by Kaily House
Cover art by Susan Russell

Published by Grendel Press LLC
www.grendelpress.com

CHAPTER ONE

The pelican was stalking me. The oversized gray and brown bird cruised by me as I walked toward Fisherman's Pass. Its long neck hunched down into the shoulders of its chunky body, crooked wings outstretched three feet on each side, and its pointy beak aimed straight ahead. It was following me.

A funny tingling began at the nape of my neck, the signal that something psychic was about to happen.

I looked over my shoulder at the stretch of beach behind me in the direction of my house. The tide was going out, and the sunken impressions of my footprints marked the saturated sand near the waterline. The bird circled back and came toward me again. I turned forward and quickened my pace. The pelican flew at me from behind and buzzed a foot above my head. Jerking away too quickly, I lost my balance and landed on my hands and knees.

"What the hell," I muttered, brushing the sand away as I stood. It wasn't like a pelican to fly so close to a person.

The bird landed on a huge boulder at the end of the jetty, not more than thirty feet from me, and squatted there with its head turned to the side, one silver and black eye glaring at me. I stared right back with my mouth set, not afraid. While I watched, the pelican turned its head forward and aimed that long beak straight up in the air, never breaking eye contact. He opened his beak and his squawks unmistakably transformed into words.

"Beware! Be warned!"

My head jerked around. "Some kind of crazy spirit trick," I whispered to myself.

The pelican lowered its beak close to its chest and then slowly brought it back up and pointed the tip directly at me. There was no mistaking the purpose of the movement. I hoisted myself up, one foot at a time, onto the wet and slippery boulders of the jetty, careful of my footing as I scrambled to the next one, arms outstretched to keep my balance. Once I was steady, I glanced at the pelican. He was frozen in place and hadn't moved a muscle. Now that it had my attention, it took off abruptly, darted straight up in the air and flew directly over my head toward the beach.

The bird landed on a wooden piling near the far end, and I let out a sigh of relief. It tilted its head, opened its beak wide, and repeated the squawks.

"Beware! Be warned!"

My whole body shuddered and I slipped, taking a few steps backwards to regain my balance. The pelican spread its wings, blinked, and took off. I retraced my steps over the jetty and sank down on the sand to regain my composure. Three more pelicans headed my way over the water from the other side of the Pass. I scrambled to my feet and jogged off in the direction of the house. I was done with pelicans for the morning, no matter how benign or indifferent their behavior might be.

When I got inside, I locked the back sliding glass door behind me and leaned against it. After a few deep breaths, I headed to the bathroom. A long hot shower relaxed my tensed muscles. Too bad it couldn't do the same for my brain. The bird's warning played over and over through my mind.

My cell phone rang just as I started to dry off. I wrapped the towel around me and headed for the kitchen where I had left the phone on the counter. Too late. The chirp told me I had a voice mail. I dialed the number and listened.

"Hey, Sharon. It's Jimmy. Just landed at Tampa airport and I'm on my way over to Gulfside. I can't explain now but I have to see you right away. It's really important. Call me back and let me know where we can meet. Love ya. Bye."

His tone was intense. I didn't even want to guess what circumstances might have prompted my stepson to come to Florida.

It was only midmorning and already my psychic intuition was zinging at warp speed.

"He's dying."

A tear glistened in the corner of my stepson's eye. He blinked, refusing to let it fall.

"I'm not surprised. When I had my Tarot cards read a few years ago, they said he would be gone in five years," I said.

"You know I don't believe in that stuff." He quietly sniffed.

"I know, but I do." I was trying hard not to be snippy but I simply couldn't help myself when the discussion was about my ex-husband. "Besides, everybody in his family had a bad heart. I don't think a single one of them lived beyond seventy."

I sipped from my glass of Michelob and ran my fingers through my shoulder length auburn curls to push back what the wind had blown in my face. This was my paradise, I thought as I looked across the sand and water at the horizon. When I took early retirement from my job three years ago, I had already decided this was where I was going to spend the rest of my life. I had been coming to Gulfside since I was a kid, ever since my parents discovered it and decided it was the perfect vacation place. Every year they made their faithful trek in October, driving twenty-four hours straight through from Rhode Island. I didn't come with them every time but often enough over the past forty-some years that I continued to visit even after they passed. I always felt comfortable, like it was a second home. Now it was my only home, and it embraced me like a warm breeze. I belonged here.

Jimmy and I were seated at a small high-top table on the deck of my favorite beachside tiki bar. The Jolly Pelican was a local hang-out right on the beach, tucked away at the end of a dead-end side street where most out-of-towners didn't bother to go. It wasn't flashy or pretty, just an every-day bar and grill with weathered boards on the walls and worn vinyl cushions on the barstools. They offered a menu of fried seafood, burgers, and cheap beer. I happened upon it one day soon after I moved into my house as I explored what my new hometown of Gulfside had to offer. It was the perfect social place for me. I popped in once or twice a week and had become acquainted with some of Gulfside's permanent residents here.

I looked back at Jimmy, who seemed lost in thought. I hadn't seen him since I left Rhode Island. At forty-eight, he was starting to look older. Strands of gray mingled with his reddish blond hair and his close-shaved beard was almost all white. He had put on at least twenty pounds and looked brawny. He carried it off pretty well, though. Always a good-looking kid, he took after his father, who I'd divorced ten years ago. Jimmy was the only one of my stepsons I had any contact with.

Technically, he was no longer my stepson, but that was just a formality. Jimmy would always be a part of my life.

"He wants to see you." Jimmy looked up and tried to make it sound like an off-hand request but we both knew it carried lots of implications.

"That doesn't surprise me. What does he want—to kiss and make up? It isn't going to happen." I sighed and shook my head.

"No, I think he wants to apologize," Jimmy said. "For the way he treated you and what he did in the end. He wants to make peace."

"Right, so he can die with a clear conscience?" This time I couldn't keep the sarcasm in check. I slapped my flip-flop back and forth against the sole of my right foot that dangled above the floor. "I don't think so. It's not my problem." I shook my head again.

"Why not see him? You don't have to stay more than a minute or two. He'll be gone soon. It won't hurt you to let him go in peace, will it?" He gave me that wide-eyed begging look that he always used on me when he was a kid.

My Jimmy, he was the best of my ex-husband's three boys. He was the first-born and so a junior, named after his father, always called Jimmy to differentiate between them. Being the oldest, he naturally had adopted the role of taking care of everybody else. He protected his younger brothers from neighborhood bullies and took the rap for them with their father's strict rules. He did extra chores around the house, helping me with the housework and the gardening. He never said an unkind word against anyone, no matter how badly they treated him. I loved him since the day I met him when he was just seven years old. A snot-nosed little kid with cuts and bruises, scruffy hair and a belly that peeked out from too-small hand-me-downs. I tried not to play favorites over the years but I think I always loved him the most. It didn't surprise me in the least that he was here to plead his father's case. But it wasn't going to work, not this time.

"This is going to sound harsh, but I need to make you understand." I took another sip of beer and, with a big sigh, looked straight into his eyes. "I don't care about your father or what happens to him. It's been twelve years and I am completely done. He hurt me to the very core of my heart and soul. It took a long time to heal myself, but I managed. I don't hold a grudge. I'm not angry. I just don't care."

Jimmy flinched but didn't say anything. He just sat there and I could tell he was trying to make it fit with his own feelings. His father had treated him badly over the years too. Jim had ignored him most of the time but always held him to harsh standards that Jimmy couldn't quite meet. Jim never had time to go to his football games and never praised his good grades, but if Jimmy came home ten minutes late or didn't finish his chores, Jim didn't hesitate to lash out with anger and a far-too-severe punishment. Even though I tried to intervene, Jim wouldn't change his mind or his attitude. Jimmy never gave up trying, hoping that someday he would be able to do something that would make his father love him. Now he was running out of time. That someday was slipping away.

"Maybe he's different now. He sounded sincere on the phone." Jimmy wasn't one to give up easily. "I really think he's had a change of heart."

"Jimmy, I lived with that man for thirty years and I know him better than anybody else in the world," I said as gently as I could. "He isn't one bit sorry about what he did to me or how he did it. He's not going to change because he's dying. It's all for show."

"Ok. I get it." He held his hands up in surrender, then took a long drink of his Jack and Coke.

"What about your brothers? Are you taking care of this all by your-self?" I knew what the answer was going to be.

"Yeah, you know how it is." He sighed. "Danny just got mar-ried—again. This is the fourth, I think. I can't keep track of them all any more, between the wives and the girlfriends. He's still trying to keep that contracting business going back in Rhode Island, so he can't leave to come down here. He didn't offer to make any of the arrangements up there either." He took another drink and sighed again. "And Mike, I don't know where he is. I wish I did. Last I knew three years ago he was in Indiana, but when I tried to call him, the number was out of service."

I sighed too. There was nothing I could say. Little had changed in the ten years since I had seen those two. My ex-husband was married twice before me. Maybe that should have set off warning bells, but I was desperately in love. Jimmy and Danny were almost exactly a year apart and their mother was Jim's first wife. Mike was from the second marriage, two and a half years younger than Danny, and his father left before he was born. Jim named them all—James Michael Jr., Daniel James and Michael James—claiming possession of them right from birth. Yet they were three little boys emotionally abandoned by their father as babies.

Jim collected kids like he collected women and once he got hold, he never let go. His first two wives and an old girlfriend still called him regularly when we were married. It used to drive me crazy. The two older brothers barely knew the younger one until I came along, and they started to spend every weekend and a good part of the summer with us. I was the caretaker on those visits, and their father was as indifferent as the day they were born, except when they did something wrong. It looked good to the rest of the world, but there was no connection, no emotional bond. He claimed them but gave nothing in return. It was no surprise their adult lives were such a mess. It took me years to figure out how pathological my ex-husband's behavior really was and by then I had invested too much into the marriage and the kids to walk away.

We both sat there quietly for another few minutes. As much as I felt sorry for Jimmy having to tell his father I wasn't going to see him, I would not change my mind. I had always known this day would come sooner or later, and I made that decision long ago. I was glad it was going to be all over soon.

"So, are you good here?" Jimmy asked as he took another sip. "You seem happy."

"I am. Very happy." I nodded. "If you asked me years ago, I would have said I never wanted to leave Rhode Island. Things changed and I changed. This was the best decision I could have made, and I'm never moving back."

"I'm glad to hear that. I worry about you, you know." He put his beefy hand over my smaller one.

"I know you do and I appreciate that. I worry about you too. You'll always be my boy no matter what." I smiled and he smiled back. "I wish I saw you more often, but I know you're busy. Just remember, my door is always open. I do have a pull-out in the spare room. Whenever you're around, let me know."

I drank the last swallow of my Michelob, and he finished off his drink. We got up from the table and without saying a word walked together out the back of the tiki bar onto the sand. We both silently basked in the beauty of the scene for several minutes.

"It is peaceful here," he said finally. "I can understand why you like it—your little bit of paradise." He paused taking in the scenery of the beach once more. "Come on, I'll give you a ride home."

"No, you go ahead," I said. "I'm going to walk down the beach back to the house. It'll only take me twenty minutes. It's going to be a beautiful sunset. Are you sure you can't stay and watch it with me?" I wanted to persuade him to stay with me a bit longer, but I knew he wouldn't.

"I'd love to, but I can't. Next time, I promise."

He gathered me in his arms and I stood on my tip-toes to reach up to him. We gave each other a long hard hug, a mama bear and her cub kind of hug.

"Love you," he said as we broke apart and he kissed me on the cheek. "I'll call you tomorrow."

"Love you too." I kissed his cheek and patted him on the arm. "Don't forget."

"I won't."

Jimmy turned and walked back into the bar. I watched until he faded from sight, blending with the shadows inside the small building. I turned then and walked toward the water's edge. This really was my paradise. I loved living here, and I would absolutely not let my ex-husband, alive or dead, spoil it for me. Not now, not ever, not if I could help it.

CHAPTER TWO

The sun slid toward the horizon as I walked down the stretch of beach toward my house. The colors became more intense as the blazing orb neared the thin line where the water met the sky. I always loved the sunset. It brought me peace and contentment as another day ended and night claimed its ancient right.

An unwanted memory barged its way into my consciousness and tarnished the moment's peace. Four years ago, Jim moved to Gulfside bringing his girlfriend with him, at the same time I was making my retirement plans for a future move here. When I found out, I was livid. I was the one who first brought him here after we were married. He wouldn't even know this place existed if it wasn't for me. It had been my special place, not his. I shook my head, relaxed my clenched fists and took a deep breath. I was surprised at how that memory could still make me so angry That was the most intense emotion the thought of him evoked since the day he left me.

I had decided I wasn't going to let him scare me away from making my dream a reality. At first, I was nervous I would see him, run into him at the grocery store or the post office. I never wanted to deal with him again on any level. It hadn't happened, fortunately, and eventually the daily worry about accidentally bumping into him faded away. Not once had I seen him, even from a distance, and I hoped he hadn't seen me. Soon, I wouldn't have to worry about it anymore.

I felt kind of sorry for his current girlfriend, Janice. They met when they worked together and became friends. Because of that, she had been a friend of mine too, until Jim and I separated. She was the second woman he lived with since he cheated on me with the first, but I knew he had lots of other casual relationships as well. I didn't hold anything against Janice, she was just another in his long line of conquests. I had no intention of befriending her again, but I hoped she would do all right once he was gone. She was a nice woman.

The sun was ready now, the bottom edge tickling the water. Once it started to set, it went fast. I marveled at that illusion every night. The timing was perfect as I arrived at the back walkway to my property when the last lick of the sun's flare slipped down into the envelope of the sea. Within seconds, the golds and mauves of the sky blended to dark blue and purple. I watched a bit longer and soaked in the residual energy. When dusk was on the verge of dark, I started up the short boardwalk that led to my house.

Gulfside provided the perfect setting for me in another way. I had a distinct spiritual identity here. As long as I could remember, even as a very young child, I knew I had a gift. I saw spirits that others could not. I talked with them and they told me their stories. I could touch an object and know where it came from and the history surrounding it.

I learned quickly, however, that this made people either very nervous or very angry. I had to hide my psychic gifts when I was married. Jim was afraid of "that craziness" so I kept it to myself, never divulging any of the spirit contact I experienced or the messages I received from beyond. Here in Gulfside, on my own without inhibitions caused by Jim's disdain, I was able to open myself to all the possibilities, and the more I practiced, the more fluent and open my ability became. I started reading Tarot cards and provided mediumship readings for a few select clients. It brought me peace and purpose. I knew in my soul this was exactly where and what I was supposed to be, and I would never turn back from that.

My house had gone on the market less than a week after I moved here and it was a great deal. I felt like it had been waiting for me and I bought it immediately. There was enough money from the sale of my house in Rhode Island to pay cash with some left over to put away for emergencies. It was perfect for me and exactly what I had always dreamed of—a small four-room cottage with a little back yard that snugged right up to the beach. From my back door I could look out and see sand, water, and sky in every direction. Once in a while, an adventurous tourist or two wandered this far north from the strip of public beach, but they never stayed long. Not one of them ever bothered me or came to my house. I felt safe and protected here.

Right away, I put in lots of native beach plants around the back yard. The low dunes already had several plants growing naturally over them, and I soon learned to identify them: beach elder, a low growing shrubby ground cover; bitter panicum in six-to-seven-foot tall grassy clumps with spikes of tiny purplish-gray flowers; wild sea oats with heavy seed-laden heads that waved in the breeze.

I supplemented these with some shorter palms—Sago with dark lush fern-like fronds and Pindo with feathery fronds. I planted several Sea Grape bushes whose wide paddle-shaped leaves formed a hedge that offered shade and protection. A few Lady Palms grew in big pots that accommodated their bunches of slender trunks and narrow-leaf fronds that looked like little umbrellas.

There were also two pots of beach roses I dug up and brought with me from up north. I loved these simple fuchsia-colored roses with their glossy green leaves, and they were a beautiful reminder of the rambling beaches of Rhode Island I had left behind. The practical side of me also added four tall urns with lemony-smelling citronella to keep the insects at bay. I arranged them all so they gave some shade and formed a garden grotto surrounding a pair of comfortable beach loungers and a small table and chairs. Here I could relax and do some meditation, read my cards or a book.

On the other side of the yard, there was a small patio table with an umbrella. This is where I ate most of my meals when I was home. There were lots of plants around there too, some native plants growing directly in the ground and large pots of tropical flowering bushes, hibiscus, bougainvillea and myrtle. When I moved in, there were some large boulder-sized pieces of fossilized coral around the perimeter with patches of sea grass and beach sunflower growing between them. I left those where they were. They formed a nice wall around the yard. A narrow shell-covered path wandered along the side of the house to the sidewalk at the street in front. It was all just perfect.

The light from the Himalayan salt lamp near the full-glass sliding doors in the back of the house threw a soft coral colored puddle onto the pavers and seeped into the garden. A faint aura reflected off the closest bushes. I walked into the house to use the bathroom and grabbed a bottle of Michelob from the refrigerator on my way back outside. My talk with Jimmy had left me on edge, to the point that I felt a bit unsettled. Without allowing my brain any chance for debate, I thought back to everything I'd been through that had led me to this moment. I knew I had to deal with my past, remind myself of why I left, and clear my mind of any more thoughts of Jim.

I nestled into the lounge chair and prepared myself for the memories that bristled to invade my mind. I rarely thought about my ex-husband. There was no need. I had dealt with all the nasty business and crippling emotions in the eighteen months between the separation and divorce. As a matter of fact, I hardly thought at all about my life before I moved here. It was as if I existed in two different lifetimes, like I had died and been reincarnated in this time and place.

But now these memories thrust their jagged little hooks into my brain. Even though I was loathe to acknowledge any part of them, I had to face them down or they would infest my whole being in their attempt to overwhelm my spirit. I could not and would not relive the heart-ache I had defeated so many years ago.

"Bring it on," I said out loud to the ghost of my memories. "I'm ready for you this time." I wriggled deeper into the chair cushion and took a big swig from the beer.

The first thing that came to mind was how often I fantasized that Jim was gone long before he actually left, probably over the last half of our thirty-year marriage. Fantasies about being single again, that he was killed in one of the blazes when he was on the volunteer fire department in town, that he died in a motorcycle crash or from some horrible disease. Sometimes I imagined he left me and other times that he just disappeared. There were a million different scenarios and I would play them out in my mind while I was driving, taking a shower, drifting off to sleep next to him or doing just about anything.

It took me a long time, years in fact, to understand that Jim was an abuser and I was his willing target. There were no physical scars or bruises, just a battered self-image and tattered confidence in the person I allowed myself to become because of his mental abuse and domineering control. Of course, in the beginning, he was sweet and considerate, lavishing me with gifts and compliments. After we were married, his behavior changed, subtly at first, and by the time I caught on, I was already immobilized by the choke hold he had on everything in my life. I was isolated from my friends and family, hadn't talked to my sister in years, had no money of my own apart from the "allowance" he gave me, and spent most of my time in the house. I refused to acknowledge his infidelities and prided myself on being a "good wife."

I still remember the day the light bulb flashed inside my brain like it was yesterday. It was our twentieth wedding anniversary. I had made dinner reservations at an upscale restaurant in downtown Providence, put on a flattering new dress, and styled my hair and makeup to perfection. He had come home in a foul mood, stomped around the house while getting ready, and driven like a crazy man to the restaurant. He complained about everything, including my folly in choosing that garbage dump for our dinner. Between the salad and the main course, his voice rose so that everyone in the place could hear him. He tore me to shreds, called me every name for a whore he could think of and told me I was nothing but a pig with lipstick. He stormed out of the restaurant and left me sobbing in my chair. I had been utterly decimated and humiliated. The manager took pity on me, helped me get myself together, and called me a cab after I paid the bill.

When I got home, the house was dark and empty. I learned later that Jim had a rendezvous with his latest female conquest. He didn't come home for four days and I went on a binge, trying to drink away the guilt he'd heaped on me. I drank straight through for twenty-four hours. Lucky for me, I worked from home at my editing job for a big publisher. Jim didn't want me working at all, another ploy to cut me off from the world, but I loved my job and refused to give it up. Finally, I passed out and woke in the middle of the night with a massive headache. As I sat there nursing my hangover, it struck me that I was to blame—not for being worthless as Jim claimed, but for letting him turn me into a person that felt worthless.

I spent the last ten years of our marriage recreating myself. It was hard, and he fought me every inch of the way. Jim handled the money, of course, but without his knowledge, I had a small amount of every pay direct deposited into a savings account. I began to stand up to his control, in small ways at first, but I grew bolder as my self-image and self-confidence returned. Fortunately, his abuse never took a physical turn. As I got better and he felt himself losing his dominance over me, he stayed away from home more frequently and for longer periods. I knew there were other women, but I didn't care. It suited my purpose. He always had a need for one-upmanship, and the week before I had an appointment with a lawyer, he told me he was leaving. He handed me the usual trite line: "I love you, but I'm not in love with you anymore." It was the first, last, and only time he moved out of our house, to leave me for another woman.

Her name was Maria, and she had been part of our circle of mutual friends for a couple of years. She was five years older than him, ten years older than me, and weighed about a hundred fifty pounds more than I did, with gray hair and glasses. Maria was married four times before she met Jim. I figured out very quickly that the overriding factor for him was that she had money, lots of money, and was more than willing to spend it for anything he wanted. There was no way I could compete with that nor did I want to by then. The two of them deserved everything that came with their dirty deed, and I'm quite sure she got far more than she bargained for.

She and Jim joined an outlaw motorcycle club together, which I had absolutely refused to do when he wanted me to. They made new friends, ones that were threatening, violent and vulgar. Finally, she bought him a brand-new top-of-the-line Harley Davidson, and apparently that sealed the deal. Little did the two of them know they did me a huge favor, setting me free from Jim and his abusive control.

So, I dried my tears, took back my maiden name and decided to strut my stuff. I had already lost twenty-two pounds from the stress and then deliberately lost thirty more. My slim five-foot-five figure looked as good as it did when I was in college. I changed my hair from straight to soft curls. My style of clothes went from housewife comfy to mature sexy. I looked damned good for fifty-one. I went to all the functions and events, especially those where I knew they would be, just to show off my new self. Maria was furious and her counter-attack was to demand that Jim get a divorce. This saved me the expense, and when Jim asked for half of everything, I threatened to expose all their escapades in court, which I knew wouldn't be good for Maria's academic career. I got everything I wanted in the settlement.

I had no qualms about taking everything I could from him in the divorce. She paid every penny of the court costs and his lawyer. The transformation from that sobbing, broken-hearted emotional wreck of an abused woman to a self-assured, positive, and fancy-free single lady was complete. The Universe made everything right in the end, and I vowed that I would never forgive or forget what he had done to me. Never again would I let anyone take control of me or my life.

I went to take a drink of my beer, and the bottle was empty. I had been in a vision-like trance while these memories replayed like old home movies in my mind. It was full night now but the soft light flowing out through the sliders was comforting and I felt no fear of the dark. I was safe and once my mind allowed that to sink in I was ready to go on with the show.

I made great plans, not the least of which was to move to Gulfside. That's when I found out Jim had left Maria. Out of the blue, I got an email from her. I didn't recognize the address or I would have deleted it. I couldn't help but laugh when I did read it.

"I know I'm probably the last person you expect to hear from," she wrote, "but I hope you'll consider this. I'd like to meet you for coffee. Jim left me for another woman and I decided to do a little digging. I hired a private investigator and what he found out blew me away. Jim is not what he says he is, all lies. I think you should know exactly what kind of person he is and the truth about him. Please let me know, I need to talk to you."

"I lived with him for thirty years," I said out loud, sitting at my desk looking at the computer screen. "You aren't going to tell me anything I don't already know after your piddly little stint with him." I deleted the email, still laughing.

I found out later from some mutual friends that he left her for our friend Janice. The word around town was that Maria felt I needed to know about Janice as well as the fact that Jim kept his own secret bank accounts and credit cards. What she failed to understand was that I really didn't care. It wasn't my concern anymore, and I certainly wasn't going to have any sympathy that she found herself in the same situation she put me in. She sent me three more emails, asking me to see her and talk. I had no intention of meeting with her for anything, much less to hear her whine about Jim.

The rest, as they say, is history. I'd lived here in Gulfside for three years now and not once had I spotted either Jim or Janice. I hadn't seen either of them in years and had no idea what they looked like. I might not have recognized them if they did pass me by. I didn't know if they had seen me but, if they had, they kept their distance. I didn't know their address or what part of town they lived in and that was fine with me.

Life was good in paradise. I went to bed and slept extremely well that night.

CHAPTER THREE

I was up before 7:00 A.M., drank a small glass of orange juice and headed out the door for my walk on the beach. The destination this morning was the jetty at Fisherman's Pass, about a mile away. I kept an eye out for suspicious pelicans, but there were none to be seen. The warning from yesterday's walk must have been an alert about Jim's death-bed request. That was done now, and there seemed to be nothing else to worry about.

I loved to walk the beach in the morning, especially early when the tourists weren't out yet. My route alternated each day, usually walking to the Pass one morning and heading south to the public beach the next. Either way I used the time to my advantage, collecting shells and pieces of wood or glass that washed up on the beach during the night, saying my morning ritual prayers and communicating with spirits. There was such powerful energy at the shore—in the water, the air, the sun and the sand beneath my feet. I always felt recharged and ready to face whatever the day held in store for me. No residual tension bothered me from yesterday morning's warnings or last night's marathon memory session. I was pleased with that and believed it confirmed that all those issues were truly resolved.

When I got back to the house about an hour later, I tossed a few shells into a basket near the door and headed inside. I showered and dressed before finally allowing myself to indulge in my morning coffee and bagel. I took my breakfast outside along with a novel and sat at the patio table across from the grotto. It was a lovely way to spend another hour before getting ready for the rest of the day.

I had an appointment at 11:00 for a psychic reading. Carol Lipton had done several previous sessions with me. She was a sad person, still grieving the loss of her mother and sister who died together in a car crash a few years ago. Carol always asked to contact them for answers to questions or to get advice from a Tarot reading. She was single and had few other supports in her life. Carol came to see me once a month for about an hour. She had been one of my first clients when I started practicing as a psychic here, and she always told me I was the best medium she had ever been to. I tried to give her some comfort with the readings, but even when they weren't exactly what she wanted to hear, she accepted them with grace. Sometimes I worried that she was becoming too dependent on the readings, and on me, but she denied it, saying only that she was at peace knowing that she could connect with her lost family at any time because of me.

There were a few other regular clients that I garnered over the past two years, and I did some occasional one-time readings for both tourists and locals. I wasn't looking to have a busy schedule or to make a lot of money, only to be able to practice my craft and use it to help people when I could. That was a considerable piece of why I was so happy here. The little money I made from these sessions went into what I called my vacation fund. Since it seemed like I was on vacation every day here, I wasn't sure where else I might want to go, but it was there if I ever got the urge.

Carol arrived five minutes ahead of her scheduled time and, surprisingly, was dressed in a bright tropical print dress of yellows and greens. Her usual outfits consisted of dark trousers or skirts and conservative pastel tops. At thirty-five, she boasted a slim build and her blond hair was styled in a straight bob. Her complexion was peachy and unblemished, though she never wore make-up. I always thought her natural beauty was stunning, but her sadness overrode any sparkle she might have had.

"You look great in that dress," I said after we greeted each other.

"Thanks." A faint blush rose in her cheeks. "I thought I'd try something a little different. You don't think it's too much?"

"Not at all," I said emphatically as I led her out to the grotto.

The garden was private and serene, a comfortable place to hold sessions for the clients. The day was calm with brilliant sunshine and a few puffy clouds in an azure sky. The sunlight through the leaves cast a dappled pattern over the table top but otherwise all was still. We chatted for a few minutes about the weather and happenings about town and then settled down for the session. She seemed a little edgy today, and I sensed she had something portentous on her mind.

"Sharon, I want you to do a quick card reading for me first, please," she said. "Then I need to ask my sister and mother a very important question. I won't tell you what it is now. Let's see if it comes out in the cards first, okay?"

"That sounds like a good approach. Let's get started." I was intrigued.

I believed in being honest and open in my readings, nothing spooky or surreal, and I always told my clients everything I saw, both the good and the not so good, though I was never overdramatic or insensitive. They seemed to appreciate that. I shuffled the Tarot deck and then asked Carol to shuffle and cut the deck into three piles face down on the table. She knew the routine well, but I always repeated the same instructions when we started the reading process. I stacked the piles and then placed the top five cards face up in a row.

"Okay, let's see what we have." I looked at the full spread of cards as a whole before focusing on each one in its place. From this first glance, it appeared she was about to make an important decision that could change her entire way of life, a very bold move for Carol. "First of all, the cards are all in the upright position, none reversed. That is very positive. You're considering decisions that could result in some significant changes in your life."

"That is correct, as usual." She grinned. "But there's a lot more to it than that."

"Yes, there definitely is a lot more. Let's go through each of the cards." I pointed to the card on the far left of the row. "The first is the Four of Pentacles in the Past position. What this tells me is that you've always been reluctant to let go of what you considered your safety net, where you're comfortable with the way things are. You've hesitated to change anything in your home or in your behavior for a long time." I placed another card face up overlaying the bottom of the first one. "This is the Four of Swords—the card of inaction, of letting things lie as they are without disturbance. For you, in this case, it reflects that you were afraid of changing anything from the way it was before your mother and sister died, that any change might make them think of you as disrespectful to their memory. You believed that if you kept everything as it was when they left you, it might mean they weren't really gone."

"Yes, I have to admit that's very true," she said with a slight quiver in her voice as she stared at the cards. She looked up at me with watery eyes. "What's next?"

"The next card is the Eight of Wands, the card of important news, rapid responses and travel. It's in the Present position. Have you received a message from someone important to you, an old friend perhaps, asking you to come to them or to travel with them? It's not some place anywhere near here and you'll have to travel some distance to get there but you need to let this individual know your answer quickly."

I turned the Two of Wands over. "It's across water, an ocean, so I would say Europe. A place you've always wanted to visit but never had the chance. Now that opportunity is literally being handed to you."

"You always amaze me. That's exactly right." Her smile widened. "I got a call yesterday from my best friend from college. She's been a pediatric nurse since she left nursing school twelve years ago and was just offered a position in Spain as the head of a new children's clinic. She intends to go but would rather not be alone in a foreign place, so she thought of me." Carol's gestured broadly with her hands as she spoke, far more animated than usual. "She asked me to travel with her and be her personal assistant at the clinic. She's leaving in a month and I have to let her know within the next few days so arrangements can be made. It's like a dream come true. I've wanted to go to Spain ever since I studied Spanish in junior high school."

Now it was my turn to smile. This was the first time I had seen Carol excited and happy about anything since she started coming to sessions with me.

"The Seven of Cups is in the Hidden Influence position. You are being indecisive, still afraid to give up the safety and protection of the life you've made for yourself, yet being drawn to your friend's offer." Carol nodded and began to fidget with her hands. "There are too many variables and you're having a hard time putting them all in perspective. This is why you want to make contact with your mother and sister today. You want to ask them what to do because you can't bring yourself to commit to a decision one way or the other."

"Yes, yes, yes. It's a great opportunity but it's also an enormous risk. I hate being in this kind of position. I haven't been able to call her back and give her my answer, but I have to do it today. It's my last chance." Her whole body was tense and she grasped the edge of the table so hard her knuckles were white. "Can you just tell me quickly what the last two cards say I should do? Then we can get to my mother and sister."

"Yes, definitely. The next two cards are incredible," I said. "They leave no room for doubt. The Advice card is The Fool, telling you to go ahead and begin that new adventure, and the Outcome card is Judgement, giving you a second chance at a positive new beginning. Those cards speak for themselves. I don't think we need any others for clarification."

"I knew it," she said, slouching back in her chair and releasing her grip on the table. "Let's get to Mom and Charlotte right now."

We'd been able to make contact with Carol's sister Charlotte and their mother Donna in previous sessions. Their spirits always seemed as eager to communicate with Carol as she was with them. Donna's husband, the girls' father, had died of cancer when the girls were only toddlers. They were a year apart and Donna had taken on the role of single mother with passion, according to Carol. Her daughters were everything to her. Likewise, she was the world to them. The three were inseparable for all their lives, none of them ever marrying. The accident that tore them apart left thirty-year-old Carol devastated with grief as she instantaneously became totally alone, something she had never experienced before in her whole life. She turned to mediums to help her find them again.

When she started coming to see me, she told me she had consulted with several other psychics and none of them had been able to help her. Then she came to me and we made contact with her family in the very first session. Even though they didn't come through every time we tried, Carol put a lot of faith and trust in me, and I never wanted to disappoint her. I also felt like I had a good rapport with Donna and Charlotte as spirits, and they seemed comfortable with me as their conduit to Carol.

I leaned back in my chair a bit, closed my eyes and went through the grounding and relaxation routine I always used when I wanted to make contact with a spirit. I mentally repeated a short invocation asking for access and protection as I relaxed the muscles throughout my body and cleared my mind, ready to receive the psychic messages. After a minute, I opened my eyes and reached out to Carol for her to put her hand in mine on the table.

"Donna and Charlotte, will you join us today? Carol wants to get your opinion on a very important matter. Please come to us."

I closed my eyes again and waited quietly for a response. After a few seconds an image of two women appeared in my mind's eye. This was the same image they sent to me each time we made contact. I had sketched it out after the third session and presented it to Carol the next time we met. She gasped but didn't utter a word as she opened her purse and drew a photo out of a clear plastic sleeve in her wallet. When she turned it over to show me a photo of the three of them together, I was the one who gasped. Although my artistic skills leave a lot to be desired, my rough sketch was clearly a match to the two women in the photograph, leaving no doubt to their spirit identity.

"Hello, Donna and Charlotte. Thank you so much for coming to us today. Carol has been eagerly waiting for you. She wants you to know how much she loves and misses you both. Today she wants to ask you a very important question."

A breeze suddenly stirred in the palm fronds overhead, causing a slight rattling noise. Carol looked up but wasn't put off by it. Rather, she seemed to welcome it as a sign that her family was there with her.

"Oh, Mom, I've gotten such a wonderful offer," she blurted out before I could say anything more. "I could go to Spain and work with Judy. You remember her, right? But I don't want to go away and leave you and Charlotte behind. Help me out here, Sis. What should I do?"

All in one blast I received a psychic message with very direct information. "Carol, do you have a cousin named Marley?"

"Yes... but I haven't heard from her in years. Why?"

"Your mother and sister want you to call Marley and tell her she can move into your house while you're gone. Her husband died a few weeks ago, she has to sell her house and she has nowhere to go."

"Does that mean...?"

"Carol, they're giving you their blessing to take advantage of this chance of a lifetime. Wait a minute, there's something else." I closed my eyes again and the image came through of the actual photograph of them being held by Carol as she sat in the seat of a plane looking out the window. "They said not to worry because they're going too. They'll be with you the whole time and watching out for you."

My eyes were still closed as I made this last comment to Carol. Suddenly everything changed. A dark cloud was cast over the vision but I could clearly see the image of the two women as I usually did. Their expressions changed, their foreheads furrowed and their mouths drawn down. Charlotte's eyes were wide and she looked ready to cry. I clearly heard in my mind the words, "Beware. Be warned. Beware. Be warned." I sat bolt upright in the chair, and my eyes flew open.

"What's the matter? I thought it was all going to be good." Carol looked alarmed.

I took some deep breaths to calm myself. "It's going to be fine for you. Don't worry. They want you to go and be happy. There was a lot of emotional energy in those messages, and I just reacted to that." In my heart I knew the last part of the message was not meant for her. It was intended for me. I would deal with it later. Right now, I had to finish up with Carol.

"Your mother and sister want you to go." I stuttered but reached for Carol's hand, hoping she wouldn't notice. "Now you have a few phone calls to make and then put together all your plans. Call your friend Judy and give her the good news right away, then call your cousin to work it all out. You're going to have a busy afternoon." I smiled at her, though my heart was pounding hard enough to break through my ribs.

"Oh, Sharon, I can't thank you enough. I'm so excited, especially to know that Mom and Charlotte agree and they'll come with me. You're right. I have a lot to do."

She stood up and got ready to leave. "I don't know if I'll have a chance to see you again before I go, but I'll definitely call you. I'm going to miss you so much. I don't know where I'd be if it wasn't for you."

"You have to give yourself some of that credit too, you know. You've come a long way since that first time we met. I'll miss you too, but we'll definitely stay in touch. I want to hear all about your adventures. Make sure you take lots of pictures." My voice wavered, and I hoped Carol would think it was from the emotion of the moment.

She smiled and handed me payment for the session along with a healthy fifty-dollar tip. I walked her to the car and gave her a big hug before she got in. We waved goodbye, and I went into the house through the front door. My stomach felt jittery, and I was sweating. The last part of the message from the spirit women had really thrown me, and I didn't know what to make of it. I needed to think about it clearly and calmly.

CHAPTER FOUR

I drummed my fingertips on the counter as water heated in the kettle for a cup of chamomile tea. The fact that the same message came from two completely different spirit sources confirmed that the warning warranted serious consideration. I took my tea out to the grotto and plopped down in the chair with a groan.

I had no idea why these spirits would give me such a clear and vehement warning. Nothing in my world should merit such a grave message. I drank my tea and reran the images of the spirit women and the bird with those sinister words through my mind over and over.

This got me nowhere. I had to be more proactive if I wanted any answers. Jimmy was the only new variable that had come into my life recently. I dialed his cell but my call went directly to his voice mail. I left a vague message asking him to call me back.

With a sigh, I decided that if I wanted answers about spirit messages I might as well go directly to the source. I adjusted my position in the chair to get comfortable, closed my eyes and began my preparation in the hopes of making contact with the spirits of Carol's mother and sister. I relaxed my body and cleared my mind.

"Donna and Charlotte, please come through, even though Carol isn't here with me. I'm in need of your wisdom and counsel. Help me to understand the meaning of the warning you brought to me earlier."

I inhaled with deep breaths and repeated this request twice more. Finally, on the third try, Donna's image appeared to me without Charlotte. She kept fading in and out, and it took a minute or two before the connection was strong enough to communicate with her. Her expression was brooding, her forehead furrowed and brows drawn together. Her mouth turned down in a frown. She hung her head, and her downcast eyes refused to meet mine.

"Donna, what's the matter?"

She lifted her head to look at me, and I saw a tear in her eye.

"I'm afraid." The message was faint, almost a whisper.

"Donna, please tell me what's going on. Are you afraid for me?"

She nodded.

"Then I really need you to tell me anything you know, so I can protect myself."

She opened her mouth, shut it and then opened it again. "There will be an evil spirit." She paused. "One who will do you significant harm."

"Who is this spirit? Where did it come from?"

"This spirit is from darkness and wants to possess you." She stopped and looked at me with wide eyes. Her lips parted and stretched in a tense line. "It is…"

The sound of a siren crashed through the meditation. Its blaring scream shattered the psychic connection with Donna before she could finish her message. The noise grew louder and closer, until it sounded like it was right outside my door. Abruptly, it ended without a blip or an echo, only utter silence where there had just been ear-splitting noise.

A staccato of red and blue lights flared over the top of the roof and reflected off the glass of the patio table. I usually had no interest in such incidents, but something drew me to this one. I walked around the side of the house to the curb and hugged my arms around me as I watched. An ambulance and a police cruiser were parked in front of the apartment building across the street. I was mesmerized by the flashing lights, my feet glued to the sidewalk. It made no sense that I felt so compelled to watch this scene, but I couldn't budge if I wanted to.

Suddenly, two paramedics barged through the front lobby doors and raced out of the building pulling a gurney toward the back of the ambulance. All I could see was the form of a body covered with a blue sheet. I couldn't make out the face or any features as they whisked the stretcher into the back of the vehicle. The ambulance bay doors slammed shut. The paramedics ran around to the front and climbed in. Their doors had barely closed when they raced away with the cruiser not far behind, and the cacophony of sirens blared again.

When they were finally out of sight, I looked back at the building. There was absolutely nothing out of the ordinary, not even a hint of what had just happened there. There were no on-lookers, no gawkers. Even the fronds on the palms in front were completely still. There was no sign of life at all. It was uncanny.

The street was empty in both directions, so I ran across and stood in front of the building. It was a non-descript concrete oblong, a two-story beige stucco with tiny patios in front of each apartment at ground level and balconies for those on the second floor. The parking lot was in the back, so I seldom had even a random glimpse of any of the people who lived there. The building was just there in the background and I never gave it a thought before that moment.

Now, though, the whole scene became eerie. Time and space were suspended, and if I reached out and touched the concrete of the walls, I was sure my hand would go right through them. My body shuddered from my toes to my scalp. I took one step forward. Nothing happened. My foot didn't sink through the concrete, and I didn't disappear into a vacuum. That broke the spell, and I was back in the middle of the sidewalk, facing an ordinary apartment building. A curtain fluttered at the patio door of the ground floor apartment to my left but stopped when I looked directly at it.

I shook my head and marched to the front door which was set back in a narrow vestibule. It was a typical metal and tinted glass security door. I knew it would be locked but I tugged on the handle anyway. A red light flashed on an electronic keypad to the right. To my left, built into the wall, was a bank of eight metal mailboxes, each a foot square, secured by individual doors with key locks. I read the names on the boxes, until I hit one in the bottom row for apartment seven. Latouche and Crawford. My mouth gaped open. That was Jim and Janice.

I blinked and sucked in my breath. Beneath the mailboxes was a row of buttons that buzzed into each apartment. I found theirs and pushed twice. No answer. Of course. Jim had to be in that ambulance and Janice must have gone with him. Jimmy said he was dying. That would explain the weird feelings. I pushed again anyway and waited until I noticed a button labeled "Office." A voice answered within a second after I buzzed.

"Can I help you?"

"Um. I'd like some information about an apartment?"

The keypad buzzed and a light flashed green. I pulled the heavy security door open and went inside. Across the lobby, just inside the office, a woman of about thirty sat at a desk staring at a computer screen.

"Hi. I'd like some information about one of your tenants." I stood in the office doorway waiting for her to acknowledge me.

"I thought you wanted rental information." She looked up and rolled her eyes, her mouth turning up at one corner. "We can't give out any information about our tenants." She went back to her computer with a snort.

"Listen. I think they just took my ex-husband out of here in an ambulance. I want to confirm if it was him or not."

"Sorry." This time she didn't even bother to look up. "I can't give you any information. Privacy laws, you know." She slid the mouse around and clicked it a few times.

"Listen, I'm not asking you to tell me if he pays his rent on time. I only want to know if he was the one that went out in the ambulance."

"I'm not telling you anything." She sat back in the chair and crossed her arms. "So you can leave now, or I'll call the police. Your choice."

I put my hands on my hips and stared right back at her. I opened my mouth but I knew an argument would do no good. "Fine."

I turned and huffed my way out into the lobby. When I reached the exit door, I looked back at the office. The desk was vacant, and the woman wasn't anywhere in sight. An open stairway to the right side led up to the second floor. I slipped off my flip-flops and ran on tiptoe to the stairs. The office door was out of sight from this spot, yet I had the distinct sense that I was being watched. I stepped on the first stair and looked up.

A flash of movement disappeared around the corner to the second floor. Somebody had been watching me, but they were gone before I saw who it was. All I could tell was that the person was short. I ran up the first set of stairs, pivoted on the landing and took the rest two at a time to the second floor. A door slammed as I reached the top, but I wasn't fast enough to see which one. It sounded like it was near the far end of the hall.

I stopped to catch my breath. Everything in front of me was painted a non-descript beige, and the floor was covered with beige tiles. On my right was the outside wall of the building, completely devoid of any decoration, with a long window that looked out over the parking lot. On the left were the doors to four apartments and a security door to the emergency exit stairs at the very end. I walked to the first door and noticed a peephole above a brass number five. A sign hung below the number that read "Welcome to our home—The Jacoby Family." The next door had a heart-shaped sign with welcome printed on it below the brass six and a ruffled wreath of artificial flowers hung on the last door.

By contrast, the third door, Jim and Janice's apartment according to the mailbox downstairs, had nothing on it besides the brass number seven. I was sure the person who was watching me went in there. No noise came from behind the door. I took a deep breath and knocked. After a minute, I knocked again but still got no response. The only thing I knew for sure from my brief glimpse, was that the person who spied on me didn't appear tall enough to be Jim or Janice, and certainly not Jimmy.

There was nothing more I could do here, and the woman in the office wasn't going to be of any help. I pushed through the emergency exit and trotted down the stairs. The back door opened onto a parking lot big enough for the tenants and a couple of guests. There were four cars and a pickup in the lot and I walked around to look at each one. The dusty and dented green Ford Ranger truck was parked in the spot closest to the street and it had Rhode Island plates. I grabbed my phone from my pocket and took a photo. I had no idea if I could find out who it belonged to, but I'd be sure to ask Jimmy what vehicle his father drove when I talked to him next.

I walked around the side of the building and then across the still empty street. When I reached the sidewalk, I turned and glared at the building, my eyes fixed on the balcony in front of Jim's apartment. From his windows, he had a direct view of the front of my house. He could have watched all my comings and goings, spied on me at any time of day or night. I'm sure he thought he had won, that he still controlled me without me even knowing it.

I felt the heat of anger rise to my head, but I wasn't going to allow him to get the best of me. I walked back around my house feeling even more out of sorts. I checked my phone but Jimmy hadn't called me back. I trotted over the wooden walkway to the beach and looked out to the horizon. Even the sunlight that glimmered over the waves couldn't soothe my nerves. To say the past two days were bizarre was a colossal understatement. The peaceful ambiance of my usual routine was in shambles, and I wasn't at all sure when or how it would right itself. My psychic sense was working overtime but there was only vague apprehension, absolutely nothing tangible I could identify to deal with. I didn't like it one bit.

CHAPTER FIVE

That evening I made a quick sandwich for dinner and ate outside at the patio table with a glass of lemonade. I was fidgety, and an unshakeable sense of foreboding filled my mind. My whole insides, every cell in my body, was vibrating and churning. I couldn't stop my hands trembling.

I sat there for a long time while I tried to make sense of everything that happened during the day. I wanted to dismiss the idea that Jim living across the street might be connected to the psychic warnings, but my intuition told me otherwise. I learned long ago not to second guess my intuitive sense. It was rarely wrong. It had taken me a long time and a lot of practice but I'd finally gotten to the point where I didn't question or over-think one bit of what my intuition held forth as true. I now just trusted that it must be so. Considering the events of the day, there was something extraordinary going on, even though I had no guess for what it might be at that point. The only thing I could be sure of was that there was more to come. I had to make sure I was ready for it.

I shook my head to try to clear it as I brought myself back to reality. It was now hours past sunset and I could see the moon high overhead. It was a waxing gibbous, and the full moon would be in six days. I wasn't sure why that fact popped into my head right then, but I didn't question it and stored it away in my memory. I stood and gathered the remains of my meager dinner. I had no idea what time it was, but I was definitely ready to end this strange day.

At least the beach was as it should be. The cadence of the tide coming in played softly on the air, a welcome counterpoint to the sound of sirens that still blared through my head when I let my guard down. I threw the trash in the barrel on the patio and walked down the boardwalk to the end where it gave way to sand. The warm salty air flooded deep into my lungs as I looked out over the water to the horizon. I needed it to flush out some of this unnatural energy vibrating in my body, but the waters of the Gulf couldn't help me right now. I had to figure this out some other way.

Back in the house, I got ready for bed. It was still early, a few minutes after ten according to the bedside clock, but I needed to sleep to relieve the now constant nagging of this puzzle I found myself in the middle of. I shut off the lights, leaving the salt lamp that was always on in the bedroom. Its soft light never bothered my sleep, and I believed it had some power to relieve whatever stress I accumulated during the day. When I crawled between the sheets and put my head down, I started to feel a little better, a little more secure. I was confident I would find out what I needed to know about all this in short order so it was useless to worry over it or try to figure it out. I must have dozed off pretty quickly after that into a deep dreamless sleep.

A crash and a thunderous *whooooosh* hurtled past me across the room. I jerked awake so violently that my head bounced off the pillow. My eyes shot open. It took several seconds to orient myself. The cold finally brought me to. It was absolutely freezing in the room and that didn't make sense. It had been a warm Spring night here on the Gulf coast of Florida. There should be nothing cold about it.

The Roman shade from the window lay in a heap on the floor but the window itself, about halfway open, seemed undisturbed. The room was suddenly warm again and quiet, nothing that might have caused the whooshing sound. There didn't seem to be any residual trace of what I had just experienced, yet I was sure it wasn't a dream. I glanced down at the shade. Yes, it did really happen. The digital clock on the nightstand read 3:52 A.M. I shivered despite the return of the night warmth in the room.

"What the hell was that?" I said out loud, more to test the reality of my presence than anything else. I got out of bed and stood up without any problem. I peered back at myself from the mirror, fully intact. I checked over the parts of my body I could see. Everything appeared to be okay.

"I'm all right," I said to my reflection. "That was crazy. I wish I knew what in the Universe is going on."

There was no going back to sleep. I wandered out into the kitchen and turned on the kettle. Another cup of chamomile might help, or at least calm the shivering. While I got the tea ready, I decided that I needed to write everything down as it happened so I could remember all the details. No matter how minute or inconsequential they might seem at the moment, they might be vital pieces of this mystery.

My journal was on the desk in the living room and I retrieved it while I waited for the kettle to boil. I kept a record of all my psychic and spiritual experiences since my separation from Jim. I was into the seventh volume now, each book of two hundred pages filled with descriptions of incidents and events related to my interactions with the spirit world. I chronicled my studies of Tarot and other methods of divination along with my personal psychic development over the years. I wrote down memories of what I considered significant dreams, my visions of spirits, all the circumstances that surrounded my interactions with them and just about any other extraordinary happenings and phenomena. I often re-read my journals and specific dates and entries were marked because I referred to them so often. I decided if I wrote down all the details of what was going on right now, I might be able to find a clue to what caused it.

I got my tea and sat at my desk with the journal. I dated the page for today and started to write. I scribbled down everything I could remember, starting with the previous morning on the beach and the warning from the pelican. When I re-read the paragraph, it sounded crazy, but, unfortunately, it was real.

Then I moved on to Carol arriving at the house for her appointment. It was funny but I could recollect every detail – all the Tarot cards in Carol's lay-out and what I told her about them, her reaction to them all, every one of her words as she excitedly told me about her friend's offer. I also remembered every word her mother and sister communicated in their message to Carol. The way the facial expressions changed on the images of Donna and Charlotte was seared into my brain from the happy one I always saw to that of extreme concern. Donna, at least, knew something about the evil spirit and was frightened by its intent to control me, but I didn't understand why she was so reluctant to tell me. At least she had told me that much.

I wrote about the strange scene with the ambulance across the street. Every detail of the building, the vehicles and the action was crystal clear in my memory, along with the eerie trance-like incident when I approached the door. I added my encounter at the office and the person upstairs I was sure had been watching me, as well as the unsettled feeling I was left with when it was all over and everything had returned to normal, as if nothing had happened.

I was about to close the journal when the memory of my discussion with Jimmy came to mind and I knew that had to be included as well. My ex-husband's impending death was related in some way to these eerie events, and I needed to figure out how. I chewed on the end of the pen and stared off into space. Finally, I gave up and wrote a couple of lines about what Jimmy had told me.

I finally finished writing everything I could remember. It filled a couple dozen pages and had taken me almost two hours. It was after six o'clock, and the sun would be coming up soon. There was no point in going back to bed and trying to sleep. I would take a nap later. A stroll down the beach was the best thing to do for now. Sunrise would be in about a half hour but already the sky was lightening. I threw on some shorts and a tank top and started out for a walk that I hoped would be peaceful and maybe even cathartic. I needed to try very hard to keep my thoughts from wandering to the unnerving events of the past two days and nights.

I walked toward Fisherman's Pass, since other early morning walkers would be less likely to go that far. It was quiet and peaceful and I was alone, just as I had hoped. When I got to the Pass, I climbed up on the rocks of the jetty and looked out over the Gulf. There was a slight breeze, and the water was calm with only a few ripples on the surface. Scattered puffy clouds in the sky were already starting to reflect the golden aura of sunrise. I said my morning ritual prayers and concentrated on watching the water, trying to keep my mind clear and thinking of absolutely nothing. It worked for a while.

CHAPTER SIX

offee was next on the agenda and I hummed while I spooned the grounds into the pot. The walk had cleared my head and calmed my nerves. It was probably a good day to do some housecleaning as I worked on the mystery of who or what was disrupting my peace and quiet. I didn't have to wait too long to find out what would come next. My cell phone rang as I took my empty mug over to the sink. Jimmy's photo looked back at me from the screen so I answered right away.

"Hi, sweetie. How're you doing?"

"Not too good. He's gone." There was a slight catch in his voice.

I knew something was wrong, but it took a few seconds for my brain to register what he was talking about. "I'm sorry for you," I said finally. "Are you all right?"

"Not really." His voice was unusually soft. "He was my father after all, even if he was a bastard."

"I know. It's hard for you. Do you want to come over for some coffee? You can talk about it if you want."

A brief pause as he considered. "Yes, I do. That would probably be a good thing. I'll be there in a few minutes, if that's all right."

"Of course. I'll put on a full pot. See you soon." I hung up and groaned. The last thing I wanted to talk about right now was my ex-husband, even if he had just died. Some things never changed. He always had to grab the center of attention. I felt sorry for my stepson, though. He needed me, and I would always be there for him no matter what. This was one of those times and I'd do what I could to help him work through this—and try not to compromise my own peace of mind while I was at it.

In the kitchen, I refilled the coffee pot with water and measured out the grounds. Just as I pushed the button to start the brewing, there was a knock on the door. I was about to call out for Jimmy to come in, but the warnings of the past two days made me stop. I walked over to the door and peeked around the curtain through the small window beside it. Yes, it was Jimmy.

"That was fast," I said as I opened the door and reached over to hug him.

"I was right here," he said, hugging me back. His eyes were bloodshot, and he looked like he had been crying for a while.

I bit my tongue and saved the questions for later. "Come on in. The coffee's on. Do you want something to eat?"

"No, I'm not hungry. I just need coffee. And to talk for a bit."

"Okay. Follow me. We can go out back on the patio." I walked into the kitchen. "Here, you take the mugs out, and I'll bring the coffee. Then we can talk." The coffee was in the last stages of brewing, making those gurgling, gasping sounds. "I'll be right out. Go ahead and make yourself comfortable," I said as I handed him the mugs. A minute later, when I went outside, he was standing on the boardwalk looking toward the beach.

"This is a nice place, really nice." He turned and walked back toward me. "It's cool that you're only a few steps from the water."

"Thanks. I do love it here. It's peaceful. Far enough away from the tourist hustle and bustle, but I can walk just about anywhere I want to go." I felt the smile slip into place at the mention of my oasis here, though I tried to be somber for his sake. I set everything down on the table.

"I think it really fits you well. I could tell you were happy here and now I know why."

I pulled out a chair and slid into it. "Have a seat and tell me what happened." I poured coffee into a mug and put it in front of him, then poured my own.

He dumped two spoonfuls of sugar into the dark steaming liquid and slowly stirred. "Dad died last night. I stayed in his hospital room, so I was there with him when it happened."

I reached over and placed my hand over his. He looked up at me and smiled, and I could see the glimmer of tears in his eyes.

"You can tell me about it if talking will help," I said. "Sometimes saying it out loud can be good for the soul."

"Thanks, I would like to if you're sure you don't mind. I need to talk about it. I've never been with anybody when they actually died before. One second he was there and the next you could tell it was over and nothing was left." He shuddered and took a long sip of coffee. "But it was more than that. I think he actually called out for you. I wasn't sure if I was going to tell you but you might as well know."

"What do you mean he called out for me?" I didn't know if I wanted to hear this.

"It was just so strange," he said, looking at me with a puzzled expression on his face, like he was still trying to figure it out. "Right near the end he was lying there in bed, all calm and quiet. The lights in the room were dim. He had oxygen tubes in his nose and an I.V. running. He was hooked up to a couple of monitors that beeped every now and then. I knew he had to be close. He hadn't opened his eyes or moved for almost an hour, and his skin was a funny gray color."

Jimmy stopped and I could tell he was in another place as he relived the moment his father passed. I waited until he was ready to go on. This was his time, and he had to deal with his feelings in his own way. He took a deep breath and continued.

"At one point, Janice went out to use the ladies' room. It happened a few seconds after she left. He was lying there peacefully and all of a sudden, he shot straight up in bed. He raised his arm and pointed across the room, but there was nothing there. A couple of the wires came undone when he sat up, and the alarms on the machines started going nuts. His eyes were closed. He opened his mouth and nothing came out at first. Then when he spoke his voice was a raspy whisper. I think he said, *Shar be warm*."

I didn't know what to say. An icy finger poked at my brain, telling me I needed to pay attention to this. *Shar be warm* could very easily be *Shar be warned*. I felt a chill run up my spine.

"That's what it sounded like, anyway. I know he used to call you Shar so I figured he was calling out to you. I don't know why he would tell you to be warm, though. He must have been hallucinating." He paused for a few seconds to take a drink from his coffee. "Right after he said it, Janice came back and two nurses rushed in. They laid him back down and fixed everything up again. He died while the nurses were still in the room. They reconnected him to the machines and within a minute they started beeping like mad and he was gone." He turned to look out toward the beach to hide the tears.

My mind was spinning but he was too upset. I waited a minute or two as he calmed himself. I at least had to be respectful of him and his loss.

"When did he go to the hospital?" I hoped it sounded like a normal question as I maneuvered the conversation in a different direction. "Didn't you say he was home when I talked to you Wednesday?"

"He was. I was at his apartment yesterday afternoon when he took a turn for the worse." He sniffed. "He asked me a few times when you were coming, and I kept putting him off. Finally, I told him what you said, or at least the part about you not wanting to see him. I didn't tell him the rest."

"Did he have anything to say?"

"He got really quiet and this weird expression came over his face. He kind of looked angry, but not really. It's hard to describe. It was more like willful, I think. Yeah, almost like he was working up some scheme in his head. It made me feel weird." He paused. "He never said a word for about forty-five minutes. Then he started gasping for air and grabbing at his chest. There was nothing we could do that gave him any relief. Janice asked him if he wanted to go to the hospital, and he shook his head yes immediately. I called 9-1-1, and an ambulance and the police came and took him away." He stopped to take the last swallow of his coffee, then poured himself another cup.

"What time was that?"

"I don't know, maybe about 1:30 or so."

"In the afternoon?" I had to be positive.

"Yeah. Why?"

"I saw him go out in the ambulance. I didn't know it was him at the time, until I went across the street and found out he lived there."

His face twisted into an odd expression. "I thought you already knew that. He lived in that tan apartment building across the street from here."

"I had no idea he lived there." My voice was almost a whisper. "I wish you would have told me."

"I really thought you knew." He sighed and shook his head. "He definitely knew you lived here. He told me the other day on the phone like it was no big deal. I had no idea where your address was until I got here two days ago to be with him."

"How long did he live there?"

"He moved there about a year ago. He used to live in an apartment at the other end of town but he said he didn't like some new neighbors and when his lease was up, he moved to that building across the street. His apartment looked out on the street in front. I guess he could look out his balcony and see your front door." He stopped abruptly as the impact of what he said hit him. "Wow, I'm so sorry. I really thought you knew."

I had no doubt he was telling the truth.

"It's not your fault. Knowing your father, he tracked me down and, as soon as he found out where I was, moved as close as he could." I put my hand over his. "You're not like him. You'd never do such a thing. But it's creepy. He could have spied on me for a whole year and I didn't know it." A shudder ran down my body.

"Why in hell would he do that?" Jimmy shook his head and shrugged. "Did he contact you?"

"No, and it's a good thing he didn't." I sighed. "Well, he won't be spying on me anymore." I realized how callous that sounded when he frowned. "Sorry. Is Janice still going to live there?" I really didn't want to see her either.

"Only temporarily. She's going back to Rhode Island to live with her daughter as soon as everything is taken care of and over with." He poured himself another cup of coffee and offered me some.

I didn't plan to tell him about my experiences of the past two days. He had enough to deal with already. I had a lot of thinking to do about all of it now, not least of which was how the details I had just learned from Jimmy of his father's death fit together with what had happened to me. I was convinced Jim and his spirit were at the center of all this. He was one of the worst narcissists I ever met. That wasn't going to disappear once he died. Once a bastard, always a bastard, even after death.

"There's going to be a service here for all his buddies from the American Legion and friends from the motorcycle club. After that his body's being shipped back to Rhode Island the next day for a funeral service. He'll be buried in the Veterans' Cemetery up there." He paused to take a drink, and I knew he was giving me a minute to think about what he'd said. "What are you going to do?" He looked at me expectantly.

I knew he wanted me to at least go to the service here in Gulfside and would like it even more if I said I would go back to Rhode Island with him for the services there.

"I'm not going to do anything, Jimmy. I'm sorry, but as far as I'm concerned my life with your father ended the day he left me. I'm not going to his funeral, either here or in Rhode Island."

"Are you sure? After all you were married for 30 years. Shouldn't there at least be a little respect for that? The guy's dead now, for chrissakes." There was an edge to his voice.

"No. I'm sorry, but I can't do this for you, Jimmy. I won't go." I had to stand my ground and, as much as I loved him, I could not and would not do this. I had no respect for the man that was his father and my ex-husband. I would not be hypocritical about it.

A deep sigh escaped from his lips. "Okay, I get it, I guess. I really hoped you would but I guess I understand how you feel. I hope no one ever treats me as badly as he treated you." There was a slight pause. "Though I guess he treated me that badly too, just in a different way. You shouldn't use people the way he used us. I'm glad I don't take after him."

"You couldn't act like him if you tried. There was some benefit to your father virtually abandoning you guys when you were little kids. None of you learned how to be as nasty as he was." I tried to lighten the situation at least a little. Then something else hit me hard, another jabbing finger poked my memory.

"Jimmy, what time did your father die?"

He tilted his head and wrinkled his forehead. "It was 3:52 this morning. I remember because I looked right at the clock beside his bed, though I don't know what made me do that. Why?"

"No reason." I stuttered, and I was sure all the color drained from my face. "Just curious."

He stared at me for a few seconds but didn't say anything else. "Well, I guess I need to go. I have a ton of things to take care of. Janice can't legally do anything since they weren't married. Besides, she's got a lot of things to do for herself. I told her I would take care of making the arrangements for the two funeral services and the burial."

We both got up from the table and walked toward the door, carrying the coffee and mugs. "Just put that down anywhere on the counter," I said.

"Thanks for the coffee and letting me talk. I know it really wasn't anything you wanted to hear but I really appreciate that you let me get it off my chest." He reached out and gathered me into his arms for a hug.

"Of course. You know I would always do that for you." I hugged him back. "The next visit will be better. We'll have much nicer things to talk about."

We walked to the door and he kissed my cheek. "I'll be back before you know it and all this will be behind us."

I watched him walk to the sidewalk and then run across the street at a break in the traffic, straight to the apartment building where his father had lived. He looked back and waved and then went inside the front door to the lobby. I closed my door and walked into the kitchen to take care of the coffee clutter. I was still reeling from what Jimmy told me, but I couldn't deal with it yet. I cleaned up the kitchen and poured myself another cup, though I probably didn't need more caffeine the way my mind and body were already buzzing.

CHAPTER SEVEN

I thought that maybe sitting for a while in the grotto would help me relax as I tried to process the information Jimmy had given me in the past hour. I took my coffee outside and nestled myself in the chair to begin sorting out all the bits and pieces. My stomach growled loudly, and I yawned so long my mouth hurt. That sandwich the previous evening was the last thing I'd eaten, and I'd been awake since before four this morning. It was now almost noon. I went back into the house to make myself something to eat. At least I could take care of that. The sleep could come later.

As much as I tried, I couldn't put my brain on pause while I washed and dried lettuce leaves. So, like I suspected, the warnings and manifestations of the past two days were connected to my ex-husband and his impending death, which was now done. I chided myself for being so cold about it as I got the container of chicken salad out of the refrigerator. It really didn't matter to me that he was dead, I reminded myself as I put the lettuce on the plate and scooped some chicken on top of it. He hadn't been a part of my life for almost twelve years, since we separated, and it wasn't going to be any different now. I grabbed a fork from the utensil tray as my thoughts pulled up short. At least I didn't see how it would be any different. I got some crackers out of the cabinet and headed outside.

Back in the grotto, the first bite of chicken salad tasted like wet cardboard. Now that the deluge of analysis and speculation had started, it was going to be impossible to keep it contained even for only a few minutes. The food had become a mechanical necessity as I dove head-first into the puzzle.

Before anything else, I had to acknowledge and accept that this whole ordeal revolved around Jim's death. As much as I didn't want to give him even that much credence, if I wasn't honest with myself right from the beginning, I wasn't going to make any headway in figuring the whole mess out.

I shivered. As weird as it might sound, I was glad I didn't know until after he died that he lived where he did. Now, at least, I wasn't going to worry that he watched every move I made. I was the only person who could fathom just what evil he was capable of. I was the only one who lived with his emotionally abusive and tortuous behavior for all those years, the primary victim of his conceited fantasies. A pained sigh bubbled up from deep inside my core.

It dawned on me that I might be using the bad marriage excuse to defend my own less than honorable behavior. Maybe I was afraid of what my reaction to Jim would be if I saw and talked with him. Or maybe it was my own fear of being near him again that led me to refuse his dying wish to visit him. I slapped my palm on the table to stop the direction of my self-blaming thoughts. I wasn't going to let him do this to me again—or let me do this to me. This was how he had controlled me in the past and I wasn't going to get sucked into it again. It was not my fault.

Over the next hour, I dissected all of it, every little detail of every incident that had happened over the past two days. At one point, I went back into the house to get my journal for an update. I had to be diligent about keeping track of everything going on. I had a feeling I was going to need those notes later on, or maybe someone else would.

Finally done, I put my pen down and closed the cover of the journal. Another huge yawn erupted without warning. I was exhausted and needed to sleep. After that I could put together a plan to protect myself.

Back in the house, I put the journal on my desk. I locked the doors, something I never did since moving to quiet and safe Gulfside. The town was a haven for me, but now I felt that sense of security was compromised. In the bedroom, I closed the shade to one window. The other shade was still on the floor from the previous night. I hung it back on its hooks and lowered it. I fluffed the pillows, kicked off my flip-flops and plopped down on the bed. I was out in seconds.

Three hours later, my eyes opened, and I lay there while reality seeped back in. I glanced over at the clock and was shocked fully awake—3:52 P.M. Exactly 12 hours since Jim died and his spirit rushed through this room, and here I was in the same physical position.

I sat up and looked around. Everything seemed to be all right, everything in its proper place. My feet slipped into flip-flops. I headed over to the windows and peeked out the side of one shade. I didn't know what I expected to see but the scene was perfectly normal. Traffic whizzed by on a busy late afternoon, the sun shone brightly, and a few clouds drifted in a light blue sky. All was well with the world.

"You're still a bastard." I looked up at the ceiling and pointed. After all these years, he was right back in the forefront of my life. I hated him for that. I put up with his monstrous behavior for years, and I deserved to have peace now. Yet here he was, back again and haunting me mentally, maybe even physically. I gritted my teeth and clenched my fists as I yelled at the ceiling. "Leave! Me! Alone!"

I took a deep breath and gathered myself back together. "I won't let him do this to me." Another deep breath. "Yeah. I'm okay now."

I wandered into the kitchen and grabbed a bottle of water from the refrigerator. Taking a swig, I considered what I needed to do next. I had to design a plan for protecting myself both physically and psychically. I wasn't going to take any chances, and I wanted to cover all the possibilities. I decided to take care of the physical aspects first. I manually checked the lock on both the front door and the back door, from the inside with the deadbolt and from the outside with the key. No problems there.

I wasn't sure what to do about the windows. I always kept them open so the breeze off the water could waft through the screens. I went from window to window, making sure the screens were locked in place. A person trying to get in would have to really work at it to get the screens out so they could climb through. They could always cut the screens if they really wanted in, but I wasn't going to make myself uncomfortable on the chance that somebody might try to break in. Besides, it wasn't really a person I was worried about. A mere window or screen wasn't going to stop Jim's ghost.

What I could do instead was make it as difficult as possible for a living person. I moved a few side tables and small chests around, placing them strategically in front of the windows, and then put lots of vases, picture frames and other odds and ends on top of them. If anybody tried to climb in, they would knock things over and make a racket. I was pretty satisfied with all those arrangements. It was the best I could do anyway.

I moved on to the psychic preparations to thwart the ghost. My crystal and stone collection was extensive, and there were quite a few I might be able to use. All stones emit vibrations at various frequencies and had healing or assistive properties based on those frequencies. I selected all the bloodstones I had, my black tourmaline tree and a few small pieces of hematite.

Bloodstone would provide powerful protection, especially against threatening entities, and a psychic barrier to keep the negative energy out. It would also bolster my courage to confront these energies and entities if necessary. Black tourmaline was used even in ancient times as a powerful protection shield to dispel and deflect all kinds of negative energy, both physical and psychic. My tree was a chunk of tourmaline that served as a base for a braided copper wire tree with dozens of small lapis lazuli chips woven into the branches. This was one of the prized pieces of my collection. The deep blue lapis lazuli was good for dealing with psychic attacks, and not only offered protection by blocking the negative energy, but had the added benefit of sending the negativity back to its source. Hematite was just as protective as the others, and it heightened psychic awareness and enhanced self-confidence, courage and willpower. It was used for its clearing and grounding properties as well.

That was a good start but I was going to need a lot more than the few crystals I had and there were others I wanted to add to them. I placed these around the house to get started. A bloodstone went over each of the five windows and on the floor at each side of both doors. I put the black tourmaline and lapis lazuli tree on the bedside table next to the clock. I had four smaller pieces of hematite. One went next to the tree on the table. I walked around the house to see where I could make the best use of the other three. I placed one on my desk, one on the kitchen counter beside the sink and one on a small table in the sitting area. That was all I could do for now. I'd make a list later of the other stones I might want to use.

Next, I wanted to make a mixture of protective herbs to place around the house. I had taken an intensive course for certification in herbalism a year after my divorce. It was one of the first classes I took after my separation. Since then I had studied on my own and taught myself their more esoteric uses. The knowledge I gained in that class could be used for all kinds of undertakings, from home remedies to enhancing my psychic ability and even cooking, of course. Herbs were potent and effective agents that could produce advantageous outcomes.

I had quite an extensive herb garden when I lived in Rhode Island and harvested, dried, and preserved most of what I grew. Those jars and containers had been carefully packed up and moved to Florida with me. Most of the plants wouldn't grow well in the southern heat but I had a good-sized container herb garden lining the patio out back with those I could grow here as well as some native to the area that I was just starting to learn about. As a result, I had a large assortment of herbs to choose from to put my mixture together.

Several reference books related to herb magic were in the bookcase. First on the agenda was to make up two small bowls with sea salt and bay leaves, one for each doorway. Bay leaves were used in ancient cultures to ward off evil. A very powerful but simple talisman was made with bay leaves placed in salt. I wrote bay leaf and sea salt at the top of the list and underlined it. Now to decide what herbs would be added to my protective blend.

I slowly flipped through the pages of the first book and, as the name of an herb caught my eye, I scanned the page for its properties described there. If it sounded right, I added it to the list. I finished scanning the pages in the first book and moved on to the second. It took a while but when I was done, I had a list of over a dozen different herbs to consider. I read the list and circled five I believed would be most effective for what I wanted. I didn't want to dilute the potency of any of the herbs by adding too many to the mix, and I wanted to be sure that each one I chose would work well in conjunction with the others. I reviewed the ones I had circled—rosemary, mugwort, ginger, clove, and basil. That should do it. I was pretty sure I had enough in my personal stock to cover what I needed.

I went over to the tall antique cabinet in the kitchen where I kept my jars and containers of herbs. I found this cabinet at a thrift shop and bought it for a very reasonable price when I first moved here. A good cleaning and a coat of white paint made it perfect for storing my herbs. The shelves were shallow, and I had the labeled jars alphabetized on each shelf so I could quickly find what I needed. First, I took out the tightly sealed container of sea salt that I kept on the bottom shelf with other supplies. I reached in for the jars of basil and bay leaf on the top shelf and mentally checked those off the list. Basil has many magical uses but through history has been used for protection as well as banishment, the removing of negative energy or spirits. I wanted both properties in this herb mixture.

Clove and ginger were on the second shelf. In psychic rituals, cloves were used to invoke protection and to exorcise unwanted spirits. Ginger has always been used as a booster to intensify and refine the properties of other herbs used with it. A piece of dried root will offer protection and ground ginger root will ward off trouble. Check to both of those.

Mugwort, on the next shelf, was utilized extensively by the Native Americans in the northeast where it grew wild but was also used by many cultures the world over. Its applications were numerous and diverse, most often as an aide to divination. Throughout history and in varied cultures, mugwort was hung in homes to ward off evil spirits and was purported to be most effective when picked by the user themselves. I had done just that in an area of my yard back in Rhode Island where I had allowed wild native plants to proliferate.

Finally, rosemary on the shelf next to the bottom of the cabinet was always an herb of choice in any of my protection blends. Besides the fact that it offered a strong barrier against negative and malevolent spirits, especially for women, it would also provide mental clarity and focus to the user, extremely valuable in times of crisis. I spied the jar of vervain nearby on the shelf when I took out the rosemary and decided to add that to the mixture as well. Vervain would add just a bit more oomph to what was going to be a very powerful protection mixture, another herb used to ward off negative energy and psychic attack.

I carried all my jars over to the counter near the sink. The coffee bean grinder I used for my herbs and the small clear custard cups I would put the herb mixture in were in the same cupboard over the counter. I got those out and set everything up. I poured sea salt into two of the cups so they were two-thirds full. I emptied the jar of bay leaves onto the counter and selected eighteen of similar size. I stuck the base of each leaf into the salt, so it would stand upright. Nine leaves were placed around the perimeter of each cup. Once I was done with these, I put one cup on the ground outside next to the front door and the other in the same position outside the back door.

Then I went back inside to work on the next task. I spooned the herbs out of their jars and added equal measures of each to the grinder. I filled each of six custard cups half full of the ground herb mixture. That should be enough. I put one cup on the kitchen window sill over the sink. I took two into the bedroom and placed one on the bedside table next to the tourmaline tree. The second one I placed on top of my bureau located between the two windows. Back to the kitchen, where I took two more cups, one for the living room and one for the spare bedroom. One went on top of my desk and the other on the small chest that I had put in front of one of the windows. I thought carefully about where I wanted the last cup to go. I suddenly realized I had not put anything in the bathroom, so this cup went on the counter of the vanity.

"There," I said out loud. "I think that does it." I had done as much as I could for now to protect myself from any negativity or harm. I hoped it was enough.

CHAPTER EIGHT

I needed some company after everything that went on, to slow down my brain from operating in hyper-speed, as it had for the past forty-eight hours. A little socializing in a neutral setting with people who had nothing to do with my ex-husband might be just the thing to soothe my stress. I decided to go to The Jolly Pelican for a light dinner and some conversation with whoever might be there. It was a Friday night, so I was sure I'd be able to find people I knew. I took my time with a shower and washed and fluffed my curls. I put on a nice pair of jeans and a lacy top. Make-up wasn't necessary now that I had a year-round tan but a little mascara and blush bolstered my ego. Getting ready gave me a little morale boost and I was feeling more normal by the time I left.

I pulled my car into the last spot at the far end of the shell-covered parking lot, next to a stand of trees separating the lot from the street. It was Friday night and the place was busy. I usually didn't do well in crowds because of all the discordant energy, but tonight I needed the distraction and a little socialization. I noticed a couple of familiar cars and that was good. I walked to the entrance and went inside.

"Hey, Sharon." Ann the server called out to me when she saw me come in. "How're you doing?"

"Great," I called back. "How are you?"

I glanced around the restaurant to see who was there. The place was close to full. Three women I was friends with were at a table over on one side of the room, and a few men I knew were at the bar along the other side. All but a couple of the tables scattered around the restaurant and out on the back deck were occupied. A three-piece band was setting up their equipment in the front of the room near the entrance. I was glad there'd be live music tonight to keep me distracted.

Mike, the owner, was working as bartender, as he did occasionally. Most often he could be found in the kitchen. He loved to cook and took great pride in the quality of the food at The Jolly Pelican. The restaurant had first opened twenty years ago and was still going strong. He was never going to make a fortune like some of the restaurants in the big beach resorts, but he didn't care. He always said his peace of mind and his independence were the best rewards he could have. His patrons were loyal customers, so he had no problems keeping the establishment thriving.

One of the women I knew called me over to join them. As I walked toward their table, I spotted another person in the bar that I hadn't noticed before. A woman sat by herself at the farthest table in the opposite corner up against the wall. It was pretty dark in that corner since the sun had set and the lights from the deck coming through the wide-open doorway didn't reach into that space. I could barely make her out and didn't know why I felt so compelled to take note of her.

From what I could see, she looked short and older than me, and her body was gaunt. Her long gray hair was pulled back in a ponytail but loose strands hung in straggly clumps around her face and frizzed out on top of her head. I couldn't tell what she was wearing in that low light but her overall appearance seemed disheveled. She looked down at a book in front of her. In the moment before I turned away from her, she raised her head and looked directly at me. I gasped and took a step backwards as her eyes met mine. They were completely white, almost luminescent. I envisioned her emitting a laser-like beam across the room, piercing my chest. I broke eye contact and hurried over to the table with my friends.

"Hi, Sharon," Karen greeted me. "What's up?" Her thin muscular build showed that she was the athletic one in the group. She worked out every morning at the gym in the next town and often invited me to join her.

"Yeah, what's up?" asked Deb, who had a sarcastic wit that always made everybody laugh. "You look like you've just seen a ghost?"

"Uh, nothing," I stuttered. "I was just trying to figure out who that woman was sitting over in the corner. I've never seen her before."

The three women looked over where I indicated. I turned to look with them and got a shock.

"What woman?" Deb asked. "There's nobody over there."

"I haven't noticed anybody there since I got here half an hour ago," said Elaine, whose long flowing ash blonde hair made everybody envious. She loved to laugh and kept everybody around her smiling.

Elaine was the newest member of our usual group who hung out here, having recently moved to Gulfside from a town in Connecticut not far from where I previously lived in Rhode Island. We connected right away. Karen lived here several years, moving from Michigan. Deb was a Gulfside native, living here all her life, one of a handful who could make that claim. We were all about the same age and all single.

"Oh." I tried to think of an explanation that would be convincing. "Uh, it must have been the way the shadows were playing out over there. I thought I saw somebody sitting at the table. No big deal." I gave a little giggle and pulled out a chair to sit down at the table with them. My eyes flicked over to the corner involuntarily.

"I think you need a drink," Karen said with a snicker. "What do you want? It's on me."

"Thanks." I smiled. "I'll have a Michelob draft. Can you bring me back a menu, too? I need something to eat."

"Anybody else?" Karen offered as she got up.

"All set," Deb and Elaine said in unison and then laughed together.

"So, what's new?" I asked the two of them.

"Nothing much," Elaine said. "More of the same, another day in paradise. It's tough, you know."

"That's the truth," Deb said as she smiled. "I heard this band tonight is supposed to be really good."

"What's good?" Karen asked as she returned with my beer, a menu, and a beer for herself. She placed her glass on the table and handed the rest to me.

"Thanks." I reached for the glass and the laminated ten-by-fourteen-inch placard. "The band is good," I said. "Maybe we can get some dancing in tonight." My eyes darted back to the corner, but the table was still empty.

My friends continued to chat as I looked over the menu and specials for the night. I hoped one of the items would strike my fancy as I scanned the list of available choices. "I'm going to the bar to order some food," I said to the group. "Anybody else want anything while I'm up there?" Ann was the only server and she looked very busy. I could save her a few steps.

"Yeah," said Elaine. "Put in an order of Buffalo wings for me. I'm kind of hungry too and we can all share."

"Will do," I said as I turned to walk to the bar. A few more customers had wandered in since I got there. All the tables were occupied now, including the one where I had seen the strange woman. I took two steps in that direction. A woman sat there, but as I got closer, she looked nothing like the figure of the woman I saw earlier.

A few more people occupied the bar. I got about halfway there when I stopped short. The strange woman sat on a stool at the other end, farthest away from me. As before, she looked down at a book with her head turned slightly toward the wall, so I couldn't get a good look at her. I headed for the service area to place my order with the bartender but kept my eye on her.

"Hey, Sharon." Mike was tall and good looking, slender but muscular. You could tell he could manage anything that came his way.

"Hi, Mike. Can I have fish tacos, please? And Elaine wants an order of Buffalo wings."

"Sure thing," Mike said as he scribbled the orders on two separate slips. "Anything else?"

"No, that's it for now."

"Okay, those'll be out in a few minutes. I'll have Ann bring them over to you." He turned away to enter the orders into the computer.

I turned slowly in the direction of the woman at the end of the bar but she was gone. The stool where she sat was empty. I looked toward the rest rooms and caught a quick glimpse of her unruly hair rounding the corner. Without a second thought, I ran after her. I almost knocked over an older man walking toward the bar and bumped into a few chairs on my way to the restroom entrance.

The men's and women's rooms were on opposite ends of a short hallway. The automatic closer on the women's room door squeaked shut two seconds before I reached it. I lunged and pushed it open hard enough to bang against the vanity behind it. I stopped short and stared into the mirror. The room was empty. Every door to the four stalls was ajar and nobody was in any of them. At each stall, I opened the door as far as it could go and peered around the small space. There was no place for anybody to hide. The space under the vanity was open except for a small cabinet at the far end. I pulled that open but found only cleaning supplies and rolls of toilet paper. Back in the hallway, I sighed when I saw the emergency exit that led to the parking lot.

Clearly this was another piece of the crazy puzzle which held me captive. Another incident with a person watching me. I wondered if the woman tonight might be the same person who spied on me in Jim's apartment building, but I hadn't seen either of them well enough to know. There wasn't anything I could do about it but continue to be extra vigilant. I took a deep breath and headed back to the table to join my friends. This was going to be an interesting night. So much for relaxing.

I got back to the table and took a drink of my beer. The band was starting to play its first set. The four of us just listened. They did sound good. I promised myself that I would make the best of the remainder of the night, despite the fact that my whole body seemed to be on edge. This wasn't the time or place to go into full blown analysis of what this latest apparition might mean and how it fit into the puzzle. The conversation buzzed around me but I couldn't concentrate to join in except for a few disjointed comments.

"Are you all right?" Elaine leaned over and whispered to me.

"Yes, I think so."

"You look like you're trying to solve the mysteries of the universe." She put her hand on my arm.

I nodded and gave her a half-hearted smile. "Something like that."

Ann brought over my tacos and Elaine's wings. My appetite was gone but I ate a few bites automatically. When Ann came back a little later to clear the dishes and clutter from the table, I asked her for a to-go box. We ordered another round of drinks and listened to the music.

"Anybody want to dance?" Deb asked us all as she pushed her chair back from the table.

The band was playing a fun dance tune from the 1980s. They all got up with a chorus of yeahs and cheers, and I decided to join them. There were a few other people up on the dance floor. The music and movements soothed my jitters, and I started to relax. All four of us danced every song after that, except the slow ones. One of the men from the bar came over and asked Karen to dance, which she did. Some of the other guys did the same for the slower ones after that, asking all of us in turn. It was a fun night, and I finally enjoyed it once I calmed down. I didn't see the mysterious woman again for the rest of the evening, and I was almost able to forget that she had ever appeared.

About midnight, the band played their last song. Many of the customers left before that and the few that remained got up, ready to go. The four of us were the last hold-outs.

"Mike, can we get one more round?" Deb called over to the bartender.

"Sure. You ladies drink up while I'm getting ready to close." He got four frosted glasses out of the cooler and started pouring the draft beers. Deb went over to the bar and brought two of the glasses back to the table. We had already paid our tabs.

"I'll get this round," I said cheerfully. "It's the least I can do in return for such a fun night." I walked back to the bar with some cash and handed it to Mike. "It's all set," I said as I picked up the remaining two glasses and carried them to the table.

The four of us raised our glasses and clinked them together to a round of "Cheers."

"You're right, Sharon," Elaine said. "It really was fun. I'm glad we all ended up here together."

Deb and Karen quickly agreed. We chatted a little more about the band, the music and the dances with the guys. Just girl talk.

"Okay, ladies," called Mike from the bar. "Lights out. You might not go home, but you can't stay here."

We all giggled as we took the last swig of beer and brought our glasses over to the bar. The four of us headed out to the parking lot. The other three had gotten spots closer to the door since they arrived earlier. My car was at the far end, near the tangle of trees and bushes that separated the lot from the street. We all said our good nights, they got in their cars, and I started the trek to mine. A minute later, most of the outside lights for the building shut off, leaving only two emergency lights and a street lamp near the end of the parking lot where I was headed. I wasn't concerned, as I was only a short walk from the car. I unlocked it, started it up, and put the shift in reverse. I looked up at the rearview mirror as I started to back out of the space.

"Damn!" I slammed on the brakes.

From behind the car, the woman from the bar stared at me through the back window. My eyes were riveted to her reflected image in the mirror as I looked into those glowing white orbs. As I watched, she raised her right arm and pointed at me with her index finger. I threw the shift into park and turned around at the same time. In the few seconds that move had taken, she disappeared.

"Damn. Damn. Damn." I yelled and banged on the steering wheel.

I knew I hadn't hit her. I would have felt it and heard the impact. I slung open the door and jumped out. I ran around to the back and scanned the parking lot for a glimpse of her but there was no sign of her at all. I bent down and looked under the car. Nothing but shells.

"Where the hell did she go?" I muttered out loud. My breathing was heavy from frustration and fear. I turned toward the street and glimpsed the shadow of a person weaving in and out among the tree trunks in the glow from the streetlight. It had to be the woman from the bar. I was about to follow her into the brush when a car drove around the side of the building. The headlights blinded me and shielding my eyes with my hand didn't help. The car stopped and a dark figure got out. I stood there immobile, unable to decide which direction to run.

"Sharon, is that you? Are you all right?" It was Mike.

I didn't realize I was holding my breath until it all rushed out at once.

"I'm fine," I yelled back. "I thought I ran over a big rock, but there's nothing. Everything's ok. Thanks." I waved at him, got in my car and closed the door quickly before he said anything else. He waved back and got in his car, but didn't move. He was waiting for me to pull out first. That meant no further search for the woman. I sighed as I put the car in drive and took one more look in the mirror. There was nothing behind me but the trees and bushes. I drove to the parking lot entrance at the street, gave the horn a quick honk for Mike and headed toward home. My heart stuttered as I drove slowly past the trees along the side of the road, but there was no sign of the woman.

It only took five minutes to reach my house. I pulled in the driveway and ran to the front door, locking it immediately when I got inside. The light of the salt lamps threw a dim but welcome radiance around the living room. I knew I might not be any safer here, but just the thought of being in my own house made me feel better. Regardless, I checked all the locks and my booby-traps. All the crystals and herbs were in place. Everything looked in order, nothing disturbed in any way that I could see.

Finally, I was satisfied that I was as safe as I could be. I would think about tonight's events tomorrow. I got into bed and, despite all the nervous energy whizzing through me, I was out in seconds.

CHAPTER NINE

The next morning, I woke to the lapping of the surf playing on the beach. Soft sunlight peeped under the window shades. I ran my eyes around the room, mentally taking inventory. Everything was there and where it should be. I had slept straight through without any interruptions. The clock on the bedside table gleamed a bright red 7:41. So far everything was good, which was a welcome relief. I slipped on a pair of shorts and a tank top and headed out for a morning walk on the beach, hoping to keep the past two days at bay for a little while longer.

It was a gorgeous morning. A thin haze covered the sun but there was little humidity. Even though the temperature was near eighty degrees, it was still quite comfortable. I decided to walk south toward the public beach this morning. The memory of birds with foreboding messages made me a little jittery and I wasn't eager to repeat that scene today when things were going so smoothly. There would be other people down that way, and their distant company would be welcome.

As I walked, I scanned the waterline for interesting bits that washed in with the tide. After three years of collecting, I literally had thousands of shells, sea glass and other prizes from the Gulf waters, so I was selective about what I chose to keep and deposited them in a plastic grocery bag I had tied to the belt loop on my shorts. There weren't many people on the beach, which surprised me until I remembered we were approaching the end of peak season. Now was the time when the snow-birds started heading to their homes back north, having avoided the cold and snowy winter weather. I didn't miss Rhode Island winters at all.

As I walked along, I noticed some kind of blob, odd-shaped and pretty large, on the beach maybe a hundred feet ahead of me, half in and half out of the waves. The water fell over it with each ebb and flow, but it didn't move even with the pull of the sand and tide. I wasn't sure why I was being so drawn to it but my curiosity was piqued. I had to see what it was, yet something about it repelled me. I picked up a stick near the sea grass. I wasn't going to touch that thing, whatever it was.

A woman a little older than myself approached from the opposite direction. I was more than a little relieved that I wouldn't be alone with the thing. She held a stick too. She got to the blob first and poked at it. It didn't move but just kind of squished and squirted out a small jet of water.

"It's a funny thing, isn't it?" she remarked with a slight accent. "Saturated for sure."

I looked at her and then back down at the black lump. I prodded it with my stick and found it was soft and pliable like a piece of cloth, but tough at the same time.

"Leather, I think, and yes, it is definitely saturated." I pushed my stick down under the mass and struggled to pull it farther up the beach away from the waves. It was heavy from being soaked with water. "Can you help me pull it up?" She watched what I was doing and then pushed the end of her stick under it too. Together we managed to drag it up higher on the sand and straighten it out a bit.

"What do you think it is?" she asked as she continued to push and pull at the water-logged leather.

It seemed familiar. Then it hit me and I knew exactly what it was. I had seen them often enough when I was married to Jim.

"It's a leather vest, the kind motorcyclists wear," I said to her and pointed with the stick. "See, here are the armholes and there are buttonholes along the edges here which would be the front."

"I think you've got it." She seemed rather excited that the black blob now had an identity.

"There are some patches on it but they're hard to read. The colors have all run together." I continued to poke and prod.

Jim used to wear his vest all the time, so I knew exactly what to look for. I straightened the leather to lie flat. Sure enough, there was a patch covering most of the back panel, very typical of a motorcycle club. The patch identified which club they belonged to. I could just make out the letters on this one, and I was sure it said Devil's Riders. This was one of the outlaw clubs that embraced their reputation as violent and criminal, always on the edge of lawlessness with a gang lifestyle. Jim belonged to a club in Rhode Island very similar to this one for a couple of months before we separated. My refusal to join with him as his biker chick was one of the reasons he left me. His girlfriend Maria had no such scruples.

The woman flipped the vest over again so the front was facing up. We both gasped at the same time and took a step back. I saw the biker's nickname embroidered over the front left pocket—Topper. She saw the dismembered finger that fell out on the sand from inside the vest.

"Oh my God!" The woman screeched.

I had no words. I saw the finger too but I wasn't sure which affected me more.

"Do you think we should call the authorities?" She looked at me hopefully.

"I don't have my phone with me. Do you?" I hoped she did. I didn't want to have to take the vest and finger anywhere.

"Yes, but can you do it? I don't think I have the nerve to talk about it." She held her phone out.

"Sure, I guess." There wasn't much choice. I considered for a few seconds and then decided this was appropriate for a 9-1-1 call. Besides, I didn't remember the police department non-emergency number off the top of my head. I tapped in the three digits.

"This is 9-1-1 dispatch. Your call is being recorded. What is your emergency?" The dispatcher answered on the first ring.

"I need to report that we have found a severed human finger at the edge of the water on the beach."

"Just a finger? Is there anyone nearby that could be having a medical emergency?" The dispatcher was all business. If he was surprised, his voice didn't show it.

"No, not that we can see. It seems to have been in the water for a while," I said.

"Who else is with you there, Ma'am?"

"Another woman. We were both just walking the beach and came upon this at the same time." I looked at her and she nodded.

"Can you tell me exactly where on the beach so we can send an officer?"

"Yes, we are at the north end of the public beach where it abuts the private beach property."

"All right, thank you. I'm not going to send an ambulance and there's no need for me to stay on this line, since there is no emergency," he said matter-of-factly. "You and the other woman will both need to stay there until the officer arrives so you can answer some questions. Please don't touch the object again. Do you understand?"

I looked at the woman and repeated his instructions. "He says we have to stay here until the police arrive so we can answer questions." She nodded her agreement. "Yes, we'll wait here," I said to the dispatcher.

"Good. I'm going to disconnect since there is no medical emergency. The officer has been dispatched and will be there shortly." A click indicated he hung up without waiting for any response from me.

"The police will be here soon," I said to the woman. She looked like she was going to faint. "My name is Sharon. What's yours?"

"I'm Louise. Sorry to be such a ninny. I'm going to go over there and sit down while we wait." She walked over to a large boulder that was at the edge of the grass, swiped the sand off the top, sat down and cradled her head down in her hands.

I probably should have gone over and tried to comfort her but I had other things to think about. I looked down again at the name sewn on the front of the vest. Topper had been Jim's nickname when he was a Master Sergeant in the Army. He was the NCOIC of his unit, Non-Commissioned Officer in Charge, and in that rank and job they were always called Topper, the top-ranking officer. I knew he used that biker name in the past and mutual friends told me he joined another motorcycle club when he moved here to Gulfside. What was weird was that this motorcycle vest was in the waters of the Gulf. I had no doubt this was Jim's vest with his club colors. He easily could have been a member of the Devil's Riders. It was his style. Most importantly, however, if it was his vest, it was probably his finger that was rolled up in it. How and why it got there was a much bigger mystery.

I had to call Jimmy and let him know about this. The police were probably going to want to talk to him and maybe to Janice. There was only the slightest chance, as far as I was concerned, that the finger and vest didn't belong to Jim. Deep down, I had no doubt they were his. I was sure I was going to have to hear the gruesome tale at some point, and I was also sure that I wasn't going to like it.

"Can I make one more call on your phone?" I asked Louise. She nodded.

I dialed Jimmy's number, but he didn't answer. I left a vague voice mail and asked him to call me.

I looked out over the turquoise waves of the Gulf and shook my head. So much for my peaceful morning.

CHAPTER TEN

"Hello, Ma'am?" A uniformed police officer stepped gingerly toward us along the beach as he tried to keep the sand out of his shoes. When he reached a spot a few feet away, he introduced himself. "I'm Officer Thomas with the Gulfside Police Department. I understand you found something in the water." He showed me his identification.

"Yes, it's right over there." I pointed to the black heap a few feet away. Louise didn't look up and was clearly going to leave this to me as much as she could. "We found it over there," I pointed again, this time toward the waterline. "At the edge, partially in the water. We didn't know what it was until we dragged it up onto the sand with some sticks."

"So, you never touched it with your hands?" The officer asked as he walked toward the vest.

"No, only with sticks."

He picked up one of the sticks we used and prodded at the soggy mass. As we had, he used the stick to turn the vest over. That's when he saw the finger on the sand underneath it.

"Okay, that's a finger all right." He poked at it with the stick. "I wasn't sure what to expect when dispatch said there was a vest and a finger, but that's exactly what we've got here." He walked several feet away and plucked his radio from the holster near his shoulder. He turned his back to us so we couldn't hear what he was saying. After a few minutes, he replaced the radio and turned back to face us.

"I just have to get some information from you both." He looked over at Louise and then back at me. "I'll start with her and then come back to you if you'll wait a few more minutes."

I couldn't pay any attention to what Officer Thomas asked Louise. All that registered in my brain was chatter. I had more serious matters to think about, and he would get to me soon enough. I had to decide how many of my suspicions to tell him. Jim wasn't the only Master Sergeant to be called Topper, and he probably wasn't the only Master Sergeant to belong to a motorcycle club either. What I couldn't get over was that these two unrelated details coincidentally occurred right here in Gulfside where Jim lived. I doubted many gang bikers who called themselves Topper actually lived in this town.

"Thank you, Mrs. Smith. If I need anything more, I have your number and I'll be in contact. You can go now." Louise got up and scampered away toward the public beach and the resort area. I was sure she couldn't wait to get out of there and once she calmed down, she would be telling this tale to every other tourist and bartender within earshot.

"Okay, Ma'am." Officer Thomas turned around to face me. "I just need a little information and then you can go too." He flipped the page in the small pad he had been writing notes on. "What is your full name and address?"

"My name is Sharon Coady, and my address is 3576 Gulfside Avenue here in town."

He wrote that down. "Now tell me what you were doing leading up to the discovery of the items and how you happened to find them."

"My house is on the beach about half a mile north of here, and I go for a walk almost every morning." I pointed behind me in that direction and then toward a pile of coral boulders. "I got about where those rocks are and saw this black thing half in the water with the waves washing over it. The other woman walked toward it from the other direction. I picked up a stick and started poking at it. It was obviously not alive so the two of us used our sticks to pull it up higher on the sand out of the water. We pushed it around in different directions and turned it over trying to see what it was. That's what we were doing when the finger fell out." I took a breath, still uncertain if I should say more.

"Are you sure the finger actually fell out of the vest and wasn't on the beach before you moved the vest?"

"Yes, I am positive. It fell out when we turned the vest over."

"Fine, then. Is there anything else you want to tell me?" He squinted at me, waiting for my answer.

I took another breath and then, before I could change my mind, blurted it all out. "I'm not really certain at all but I might have an idea who the vest belonged to. Not the finger, really. I don't recognize that, but the vest..."

He sighed. "All right. Just take a minute and tell me what you think."

I took a deep breath and paused a few seconds. It was out now, and there was no way to avoid telling the rest.

"When I was looking at the vest, I saw the patch for Devil's Riders on the back and sewn on the front over the pocket was the biker nickname Topper." I hesitated.

"Go on," he said.

"My ex-husband belonged to a motorcycle biker gang and his nickname in the past was Topper. I haven't seen him or talked to him in about twelve years, so I don't know any details about his life since then. I just know that he lived here in Gulfside. He died yesterday."

"I see. And that makes you think the vest and the finger belonged to your ex-husband?" he asked, holding pen to paper, ready to write down my response.

I should have known he wasn't going to make this easy for me. "I really don't have any way of knowing if it did or it didn't. I'm just trying to tell you that these things are a coincidence and I just happened to think of them when I saw the patches on the vest." I gave him my best take-it-or-leave-it look.

"I understand. Can you tell me your husband's name and address?" He held the pen poised over the pad.

"My *ex-husband*," I corrected. "We were divorced ten years ago." I gave him the get-it-right look. "His name was James Latouche. I don't actually know the address but he lived in an apartment in the building across the street from me. His girlfriend lives there now, and his son is there until the funeral service."

"Across the street from you?" he asked with a slight tinge of disbelief in his voice.

"Yes, I didn't know that until yesterday either when I found out he died."

"All right." He paused and made more notes on the pad. "That's it for now. I appreciate you sharing the information, and I'll follow up. If you'll just give me your phone number in case we have any more questions, that will be it."

I recited the phone number, and he wrote it in the notebook. I would have loved to see the notes he wrote about our conversation. He thanked me and turned back to the mound of vest and the finger. He took vinyl gloves out of a pouch on his belt and put them on and then plucked and poked at the vest a few times. He pulled a cell phone from a holster on his belt and began taking photos from different angles. He turned and seemed surprised that I was still standing there.

"You can go now," he said. "I'm all set here."

I turned and started walking back toward my house.

"I'm sorry," he said.

I stopped and looked back at him without understanding his comment, which must have shown on my face.

"About your husband, or your ex-husband. You said he died yesterday."

"He did but you don't have to be sorry. I'm not. He was nothing to me anymore." This time I turned and hurried away before he could say anything else. I'd had enough for one day, and the morning wasn't even half over yet.

I got home and put on some coffee and a bagel in the toaster. My stomach grumbled as I got my cell phone from my desk and pulled up Jimmy's number in my contact list. He answered on the second ring.

"Hi, Sharon," he said. "I got your message. What's up?"

"I'm really sorry to bother you when I know you have so much to do, but I really need to tell you something."

"That's no problem. What is it?"

"I went for a walk on the beach this morning, and I found something. I think it might have belonged to your father but I don't really know for sure. Anyway, I had to call the police and I told the officer that I thought it was your father's, so they might be getting in touch with you or with Janice."

"Wait. What? What did you find?" He sounded confused.

"It was a leather biker vest. The nickname on it was Topper. I think it was his. And... and... something else."

"Okay, hold on. Let me check." I could hear him put the phone down and walk into the other room. Then I heard him ask Janice where Jim kept his biker vest. That was all. About a minute later, he picked up the phone again. "His vest isn't here where Janice said it's supposed to be. You found it on the beach?" he sounded puzzled.

"Yes. It was lying there on the sand half in the water. It was saturated so I think it had been there for at least a few hours. It had a Devil's Riders patch on the back."

"Yeah, that's the club he belonged to down here. But why did you call the police for a vest? You could have just called me to check it out." It was time to tell him the rest.

"There was something else." I hesitated.

"What was it?"

"There was a finger wrapped up in the vest. A human finger, but I don't know whose it was, cut off somebody's hand. There was another woman there on the beach who saw it too, so I had to call the police. I couldn't just walk away and leave it there."

"Damn. A finger? That's crazy. Yeah, you had to call, no question. I don't think it was Dad's. How could it be? He had all his fingers when I left him at the hospital and then the funeral home came to pick him up." He paused, and I knew he was trying to think what to do about this. He sighed and said, "I'm going to have to talk to the police and make a couple of other phone calls. I'll call you back later."

"All right. I'm sorry." I truly was sorry that he was going to have to deal with this mess. I felt bad but relieved to hand it off to him. I didn't want to be a part of any of it.

"Don't be, it's not your fault. At least it was you who found it. I'll talk to you soon. Bye." He sounded harried as he ended the call.

I put the phone on mute and placed it on my desk. I didn't want to talk to anybody else for a while, not even Jimmy if it had to be more about his father.

"So much for that peaceful morning." I shuffled back to the kitchen for my coffee and bagel. I was beginning to sound repetitious.

CHAPTER ELEVEN

I sat on the end of the boardwalk and looked out over the water. I believed everything happened for a reason, so there had to be some purpose why I was the one to find the vest and severed finger on the beach. In combination with the warnings I received, this morning's misadventure seemed like the next step in a series of incidents intended for me personally. That they belonged to my ex-husband was without doubt. What I couldn't begin to fathom was why. With all that commotion on the beach this morning, I hadn't had a moment to consider who or what the woman was at the bar last night. She had to be a part of this tangle too.

No matter how I tried now, my thoughts swung back to Jim. Even after he was dead , I couldn't be free of him. I was beginning to believe this was a deliberate trick. During our marriage, he always rejected any thoughts of a spirit afterlife, abhorred the idea, and would not tolerate any discussion of ghosts or the paranormal at all. It wasn't worth stressing over an argument that I'd never win, so I just kept it to myself.

Whether he wanted to believe or not, our soul doesn't rush to some imaginary heaven above or hell below. It's a scientific fact that our bodies are made of energy and can't function without it, intake and output, positive and negative. We're all taught that energy is never destroyed but can change form, so with death our physical bodies are terminated but the energy, our soul, continues on. Jim was certainly haunting my thoughts, but I needed to figure out why his spirit was physically haunting me as well.

The one good thing, if there was anything good, about this morning's events was that the incident occurred away from my house. Hopefully, the barriers I set up yesterday with the herbs and stones kept the negativity away and gave me and my home the protection we needed. That protection had to be bolstered, though, and I wanted to go to the crystal shop to find more stones to reinforce and enhance what I had already done. I had a few in mind but I wanted to check my reference books first.

Back inside, I went to my desk and turned on the computer. While it was booting up, I swiveled in the chair to face the bookcase and took out the reference book on crystals, one that I had for years, with lots of my handwritten notes jotted in the margins. A Google search for the phrase "crystals for protection" produced a list of 10,000 websites. The one I wanted was on the first page and I clicked the link.

I spent about forty minutes reading the online pages for different crystals and stones and then comparing that information with what was in my own reference. In the end I came up with a list of about six more stones to buy. I also added hematite and black tourmaline to the list so I could get more of each of those. I clicked the X up in the corner to close out the internet, expecting to return to my desktop screen. Nothing happened. I tried again and still the page wouldn't close.

"Hmmm," I said out loud. "It wasn't slow while I was checking out the crystals." I waited a few seconds and tried clicking the X again.

This time something did happen but not what I expected. Simultaneously with the click, the whole screen turned a brilliant white and then within two seconds turned bright crimson. I hit the enter button, the backspace, the delete, clicked both sides of the mouse, every trick I could think of but nothing changed. There wasn't even a flicker. Just as I was about to push down the power button to turn it off so I could reboot it, a voice came through the speakers. I jumped and rolled backwards in my desk chair.

"Be warned."

I sat where I was, frozen. The voice sounded gravelly and had that electronic monotone to it, though with a slightly familiar pitch. It sounded like Jim. I waited for more as I sat there with my head back and looked at the ceiling.

"Hello?" I called out after a couple of minutes. The voice had been real, not a figment of my imagination. I sat forward, looked back at the screen and gasped. The computer was still on, but now there was a picture filling the display—a photograph of my ex-husband.

"Be warned. Beware." It was the same voice, but this time a sarcastic tone mocked me. "Hello."

The chair flew backwards and slammed into the wall as I jumped up. Ghosts didn't scare me. I dealt with them all the time in my psychic world. It was that face on the computer screen. This new computer was only a year old. I knew there were no photographs of Jim on it. At the time of the divorce, I had gone through each file and deleted every single picture of him I could find from the old computer I used at the time. I cropped him out of the ones I wanted to keep of my stepsons. The photo on the screen was not one I had ever seen before. There was something strange going on with my computer, and I didn't like it one bit.

"Don't you dare threaten me," I said to the photo on the screen. "I won't tolerate this treatment from you ever again."

The more I stared at the photo on the computer, the angrier I became. With myself as much as at Jim. He got to me again, but I wasn't going to let him, or whatever it was, get away with these antics that made me lose control. I relaxed my clenched fists and tight jaw, took a deep breath and rolled the chair back to its place at the desk. As I stood and watched, the computer shut off and the screen went blank. Maybe there really was something malfunctioning with the electronics. I pushed the power button to see what would happen and it started to boot up right away.

When the computer finished its start-up, the display on the screen was my usual wallpaper, a beach scene that I photographed and up-loaded when I bought the computer. Nothing seemed amiss. I clicked on the internet icon, and my home screen loaded right away. When it finished, I clicked on a few links to my favorite websites. Everything worked perfectly.

I closed out the internet and went to my pictures folder. I opened each folder and scanned every file for the photo of Jim that appeared on my screen earlier. I almost gave up when I found it. It was in a folder of photos labeled *MiscOld*. I clicked the thumbnail of the photo to display it full size, then shook my head. I still didn't recognize it as a picture I'd ever taken or saved. I opened the photo properties drop-down box but that didn't tell me anything useful except that the photo file was created today.

I clicked on the photo again to select it and hit delete. When the "are you sure" prompt popped up, I clicked yes without one bit of hesitation. I went to the recycle bin and deleted it from there. Done and gone. At this point I wasn't sure if it was my own oversight, or that Jim tried to get to me from beyond, but I made sure I wasn't going to be ambushed by that face again. I shut down the computer and headed for the shower.

The water felt refreshing and my whole body relaxed as I let the soothing coolness sluice over my head for quite a while. When I finished, I got myself together and dressed. I went to the desk to get the crystal reference book so I could bring it with me to the shop and pulled up short. The same picture of Jim that I just deleted from my computer files was now printed out and framed, a full five-by-seven portrait of Jim sat on my desk next to the computer. I ran over and checked both doors but they were locked. All the windows and their booby-traps looked undisturbed. I snatched up that frame and heaved it with all my strength in the trash basket next to the desk.

"You are not going to win this." I snarled between clenched teeth as I pointed to the frame in the trash. "I broke free from you once in this life already and I have no intention of letting you gain control over me ever again. So let go and move on. I don't belong to you."

I grabbed the book, got my purse and slammed out the front door. I had enough presence of mind to lock it behind me. My breath was coming in angry spurts as I stomped down the walk to the car in the driveway. If Jim's spirit thought he could scare me into submission, he had another thing coming. Ghost or no ghost, I was not afraid. Like I always said, once a bastard, always a bastard, even after death. I would become super-vigilant and protect myself with whatever means I could. Sooner or later, I would send him away and he would be gone for good. I didn't care how or where he went or if his soul ever found peace. It wasn't my job to take care of him anymore, but I certainly intended to take care of myself.

CHAPTER TWELVE

Traffic was extra heavy, even for a Saturday afternoon. It was a perfect day, weather-wise. All these tourists should be at the beach, not driving around town. One thing I still had to deal with was the big difference in tempo between Rhode Island and Florida. Nothing much happened quickly here, especially not traffic. The number of pedestrian crosswalks and traffic lights gave you no choice but to follow the low speed limit. In Rhode Island, we did everything as fast as we could. I worked on altering my life-long pattern every day, trying to be more patient. My mission today wasn't critical, but I was anxious to get to the crystal shop and get the stones I needed.

There was an empty parking space only a few feet away from the door of the shop. At least something was going my way. I hoped there wouldn't be too many customers in the shop. I never felt good among a lot of people in a confined space. All the incongruent energy they sent off bounced every which way and ricocheted off every available surface.

Inevitably, it would find me on the rebound. It felt like a million tiny prickers piercing my skin. That's why I always carried protection stones with me in my purse. They shielded me from most energy attacks but the barricade was never truly strong enough to repel every major crowd onslaught, especially from those who were energy vampires, who sucked every particle from an unwary and unprotected victim. Even when the barrier was able to keep these attacks at bay, I always knew they were there.

A trill of tiny chimes greeted me as I opened the door to the shop. I didn't see anybody but I could hear soft voices coming from the back of the store. Lynn, the owner of the shop, must be with another customer. While I waited, I browsed around to find the stones I was looking for. I wandered among the shelves and cases, scanned the various stones while detecting their distinct and diverse vibrations and energies as I strolled along. It was important to be well-grounded if a person sensitive to energy vibrations wanted to spend some time in a shop like this. Otherwise, all these crystals and stones could make you giddy and light-headed, almost to the point of feeling high or nauseous. Personally, I just loved to draw in all the vibrations and experience what they had to offer. I supposed I had used them so long and in so many ways that I could deflect the energy I didn't want and absorb what I needed. That's what grounding was all about.

A display on one of the shelves caught my eye. I picked one up to look it over. These were obviously man-made and not natural configurations. "ORGONITE" was printed in large letters at the top center of the display sign. Under it I read,

"An invaluable spiritual healing tool, Orgonite can provide protection against the potentially harmful effects of EMF, Electro Magnetic Frequencies. Orgone is the Universal life force present in all things, both animate and inanimate. Made from layers of crystals, resin, and metals, its non-organic metals both deflect and attract energy, while its organic resin materials attract and hold energy. These elements in orgonite are continuously attracting and deflecting energy while the crystals give off a charge, causing a cleaning action to occur that clears negative and stagnant energy, bringing you back to a healthy and peaceful state. Orgonite does not actually reduce EMF, but it does protect your body from the damaging effects of electromagnetic radiation coming from your cell phone, TV, computer, laptop, tablet, microwave oven, fridge, power outlets, or other household appliances."

I decided I definitely needed some of this. The display contained a number of Orgonite pieces in various sizes and geometric shapes. I put down the first one and picked up a number of them, holding one of them at a time in my hand to sense the energy of each of them. I felt particularly drawn to a pyramid, about four inches tall with layers of silvery metal and blue-green crystals. That was the one I wanted, so I carried it with me as I continued to browse around the other displays.

Two women appeared around a corner from the back of the shop and walked toward the display case and sales counter along the far wall near the door.

"Thank you so much," the customer said to Lynn. "That was such great advice." She fished in her purse and handed Lynn a credit card.

"You're welcome," Lynn replied as she registered the sale on the counter-top computer. "Now you just have to decide what to do with it." She smiled as she handed the woman her card and a receipt.

"That's always the hardest part for me." She giggled as she signed the receipt and handed it back to Lynn. "See you again soon." She left to the sprightly tune of the chimes.

"Hey, Sharon, how are you?" Lynn turned to me after the door closed behind the customer.

"I'm okay." My voice was flat with a tinge of the frustration I felt.

"Well, sounds like something's going on. Not like you to be stressed out." She looked right at me. "What do you need?"

"First of all, I need some protection stones. I had some hematite and black tourmaline at home, but I want to get more and a few others."

"Wow, sounds like a major energy crisis. I have both of those, of course." She moved from behind the sales counter to join me near another counter where dozens of types of stones were displayed in clear acrylic boxes. The different stones were sorted and labeled in each box and a small card identifying the properties of each stone was attached to the back of the box for easy reference. These boxes filled nearly every counter and shelf in the store.

"I see you found the Orgonite. I just got that in the other day." She nodded toward the pyramid I was holding.

"I like it," I said as I held the bluish-green pyramid up to the light. "I was impressed by the write-up. Do you think it works?"

"I don't know but it sure sounds good. I have a piece over near the computer. It can't hurt." She shrugged and smiled. "What else did you have in mind?"

"I was thinking of getting black obsidian and black kyanite." I sifted through the stones in a box of black tourmaline. "I need to put up a strong shield and deflect negative vibes back to the source. I have some labradorite at home, but I've been using it for psychic connections when I do a reading so I need a good piece to designate as a protection stone."

"Wow, you mean business. Those certainly should do the trick. How about some pyrite too?" she said. "It will send negative energy back to the sender, right along with the obsidian. The kyanite will clean it up before sending it back. It depends on your intention which you want to use."

"I had pyrite on my list, along with fire agate and kunzite for shield-ing." She handed me a few bright silverish stones, Fool's Gold as they were commonly called, and I enclosed them in my fist for a few seconds. I opened my hand and picked two out of the bunch. "I'll take these two,"

I said and held the selected pieces of pyrite out to her. I put the rest back into the box she had taken them from.

She reached for a small white ceramic bowl from the top of a short stack on the side of the counter. "I'll put these in here while you check out the others," she said to me as another customer strolled through the door of the shop. "Take your time. You're not going anywhere until we've had a chance to talk. Do you want to hold onto the pyramid, or should I put it on the counter until you are done?"

I placed the base of the piece in one hand and covered the top point with the other. "I think I'll hold on to it for now."

Lynn and I had become good friends over the many enjoyable hours I spent here at her shop. Besides the beach, it was one of the places I most liked to visit. We occasionally had dinner or a drink together, but not often, because of the hours she put in at the store. She was the owner and sole employee. Most of her business was from amateur and professional designers and crafters who purchased the crystals and stones for jewelry and other artistic pieces. Some of them incorporated the stones into their designs based on their energy properties but most used them based on color and sales appeal alone. She also sold jewelry-making supplies and other similar items.

There were only a few people like me who came in solely for the stones themselves to make use of their healing or spiritual properties. Lynn occasionally read Tarot as part of her business too, but she always insisted she was not a psychic and claimed she never had any interaction with ghosts or spirits. There were a few clients she referred to me when they wanted more than what a simple Tarot reading could offer, and I fully appreciated her confidence in me, since any referral she made would reflect on her own business.

I continued to wander around the cases of stones and crystals as she waited on her customer, picking up a stone here and there and testing out the vibration I felt from each one. I added a few pieces to the bowl with the pyrite—three black tourmaline, four black obsidian, and three kunzite, along with one large and one small piece of labradorite. There were so many I could choose, but I didn't want to go overboard. Sometimes, too many could be just as bad as too few. If the vibrational frequencies were discordant, it could cause more harm than good or cancel each other out and defeat the whole purpose for using them.

Finally, the customer left, and Lynn was able to resume our conversation. I took my bowl filled with stones over to the sales counter and handed it to her, putting the Orgonite pyramid down next to it.

"Did you find all the ones you were looking for? You've got some nice ones here." She emptied the stones from the bowl onto a woven fiber mat on the glass countertop.

"I think the only one I couldn't find was fire agate," I said as I watched her separate the stones into groups according to their price. "That was one I really wanted."

She gave me a baffled look. "Oh really? There were some over there. Let me check." She slipped out from behind the counter and made her way directly to one of the acrylic boxes on a shelf against the opposite wall.

"I didn't see any but I wouldn't be surprised if somebody bought them all before I got here. That's exactly how it's been going for me the past few days." I followed her over to the set of shelves where I saw an empty box with the label for the fire agate I wanted.

She shook her head. "Hmm, that's strange. I could have sworn there were at least five or six in there but now the box is empty. I know I didn't sell any. I hate to think somebody came in and stole them. It's not like they're that rare or expensive," she said as she made her way back to the sales counter. "Do you want to tell me what's going on?"

I hesitated before I replied. "It probably would be helpful to talk to somebody about it, I suppose." I wasn't sure I was ready to recite the whole tale out loud, but Lynn was certainly one of only a very few people I could comfortably do that with.

She was entering the prices into the computer and then separating the stones by type into small zip-lock bags. "The total is thirty-two fifty. Is it about a who or a what?" She asked as she took the debit card I was holding out to her and slid it through the card reader.

"Both," I said with a sigh. "At least I think it's both."

Just then the door chimes tinkled as another customer came into the shop. Lynn handed me back my card and exhaled loudly. "Look, can you meet me for dinner later, say about six thirty? We can talk then and not be interrupted. I just happen to be free tonight, and I think you need a supportive ear." She handed me the small paper bag that she had put all my stones and the pyramid in.

I nodded in agreement. "That sounds good. Want to meet at the Pelican?"

"Great idea," she said. "Then we can take our time and have a couple drinks. I'll meet you there."

The new customer walked toward the sales counter, so I waved and headed for the door. It probably was a good idea to run all of this by Lynn. At least she would have some understanding of what I was talking about and wouldn't sit there rolling her eyes while I talked about ghosts and spirits. She could be objective about it and rein me in if I was over-reacting or even imagining things. Always an optimist, I felt better once again as I got back in my car for the drive home.

CHAPTER THIRTEEN

The traffic had eased, and the trip home was quicker. After a stop at the market, I headed home. Five minutes later, I pulled in my driveway, grabbed the mail from the mailbox, put the small bag of stones in my purse, and gathered my groceries from the car. My key was halfway in the lock when I noticed a box leaning against the bottom of the door. With my other hand full of bags, I opened the door first and nudged the box over the threshold with my foot. I put the bags down on the kitchen counter and went back to retrieve it.

The box was just plain brown cardboard, about two feet square, with nothing written or printed on it, no company logos or shipping address. It wasn't a delivery, so somebody must have brought it to my door in person. That's strange, I thought as I carried the box over to the counter. It wasn't very heavy, and nothing rattled around when I shook it. My heart was pounding as I placed it on the kitchen counter.

I got a pair of scissors out of the drawer but just as I was about to slice open the tape that held the box closed my phone rang. I put the scissors down next to the box and fished in my purse for the phone. Jimmy's photo was on the screen.

"Hi, Jimmy. Just got home and was going to call you. Are you all right?"

"I'm okay, I guess. I wanted to tell you before you saw it on TV or something. They always put this stuff on the news." He sounded tired and a little upset.

"What is it? What's the matter?" I didn't like the ominous undertone.

"I got a call from a police detective, about the vest and the finger. They were definitely both Dad's." He coughed, not completely covering the catch in his voice. "I asked for more info, but they're not telling me anything else about what happened. The detective only said it was under investigation. I have to call them tomorrow to set up a time so they can come to the apartment and look around. I'm sure he'll have questions for me, too."

"I knew they were his when I found them on the beach." My mind was already racing to come up with possible explanations. "I just don't understand why anybody would do that. It's too weird."

"I know. I can't figure it out either. Janice is beside herself. She bought an emergency ticket and she's leaving early tomorrow morning for Rhode Island. The apartment is paid through the end of the month so I'm going to stay here and get everything packed up and shipped off."

"You could stay over here, you know," I said.

"I appreciate that. There's still a ton to do over here, though. Packing things up and cleaning the place out. If I stay here, I can work early and late and not disturb you. I will take you up on an offer of meals though. I'd really rather not eat alone, or I probably wouldn't eat at all."

"Sounds good to me," I said. "I have plans for tonight with a friend but otherwise I'm yours. I'd offer to help with the apartment, but I don't really want to get involved with that. I hope you understand."

"Of course, I do. I didn't even expect you to offer it." He paused for a moment. "The funeral service is tomorrow morning and then there's the collation at the American Legion afterward."

"You know I'm not going to either one," I said quickly.

"Yes, I know. I know. I wasn't asking you again," he said. "I'll manage by myself. I don't think there will be too many people there. Janice is taking a shuttle to the airport at four in the morning so I don't have to worry about her."

"Okay, well if you want to do dinner or anything tomorrow night, call me. I'm open."

"I will. I'd better go now. I just wanted to make sure you knew about the... uh, finger. I don't know if the police will want to talk to you again."

"I appreciate the head's up. I hope they don't need anything else from me. I don't know anything more than what I've already told them," I said. "Anyway, bye. Call me tomorrow."

"I will. Bye."

I hit the disconnect on the phone. As much as I hated that Jim was still dominating what seemed like my entire world these days, I was curious how the finger was severed and ended up on the beach. The photograph suddenly popped into my head, and I slowly turned to look at my desk, half expecting to see it back there watching me. It wasn't. I had to stop this. I was creeping myself out, and I hated being constantly on guard. Yet, at the same time, I had that threatening sense deep inside. Something was going to happen, and I was sure it would to be nasty. After all, I had already received two warnings from the Universe. I wasn't one to take those kinds of signals lightly.

I went over to the desk and peeked into the trash basket. The frame was still there. I gingerly plucked it out, holding it between two fingers, like some kind of rotten vegetable. It was face down and I hated to do it, but I turned the frame over to make sure the photo was still in it. Nothing would surprise me at this point. The whole situation was surreal. It was still there, and I flipped the frame back over so I didn't have to look at that face. I grabbed one of the plastic grocery bags, emptied the contents on the counter and shoved the frame in it, tying the handles of the bag in a knot. Then I took it outside and threw it into the big trash barrel. The city trash pick-up was Monday and off it would go.

Back in the kitchen, I put away the groceries but kept eyeing the box. You would think that I would be eager to see what was in it, but for some reason, I wasn't. Jimmy's call unnerved me even though the news wasn't unexpected. My brain was in crazy imagination mode, and the last thing I wanted to see in this box was another body part.

"Don't be silly." I scolded myself out loud. "It's probably something I forgot I ordered." My mind didn't believe that for one second, however. There should be some sender information if it was a normal delivery. I snatched up the scissors before I could change my mind and sliced through the tape. I drew open the flaps one at a time. Inside, the box was filled with Styrofoam peanuts, and as I dug through them, I came upon bubble wrap protecting whatever was inside. I lifted it out but I couldn't see through the plastic. Reaching for the scissors again, I snipped through the layers of tape that held it in place.

"What!" I gasped as the wrapping fell away and almost dropped the snow globe that was inside.

My grandmother had given it to me when I was eight, an antique that originally belonged to her grandmother, a glass ball fixed to a gold metal stand. As a child, I spent hours shaking that heavy globe and watching the snow fall on tiny figures skating on a mirrored pond next to a star-topped Christmas tree. It always held a place of honor when the holiday decorations came out of the closet on Thanksgiving weekend.

I ran to the spare bedroom and gaped at the empty spot on top of the dresser where the globe usually sat. My whole body trembled from head to toe with the realization that someone had sneaked in my house and taken something so important to me. I had no idea who would have done this or why. As unrealistic as it was, my thoughts immediately turned to Jim. It was just the kind of trick he'd pull, just to let me know he was still in charge.

"This is ridiculous." I looked up at the ceiling and yelled. "How dare you violate my space this way." I continued with teeth clenched and every bit of my fury in my voice. "You will never win this battle—or me—so you'd better just quit. Right now. Leave. Me. Alone. Or I swear I will kick your ghostly ass all the way into the biggest, baddest black hole I can find, and you'll never find your way out. Don't push me because you know I can do it, and I will."

I pointed my finger at the ceiling and glared. I stood there panting and shaking, my hands balled into fists and my eyes squeezed shut, refusing to let myself cry.

At last, my anger and fear spent, I raised my head and glanced at the snow globe on the bed beside me. I ran my hand over the smooth, cool glass as I cradled it in my palm and walked it over to my desk to put it in the top drawer. It would be safe there for now.

I still had plenty of time to get ready to meet Lynn at the restaurant. I needed to talk to her more now than ever. I finished getting ready and looked at the clock—five before six. I picked up my phone and punched in Jimmy's number.

"Hey, what's up?"

"I'm sorry to bother you but I have a quick question."

He didn't seem to notice the quiver in my voice.

"Okay, shoot."

I paused for a moment, not sure I wanted to know the answer. There were just too many ways this could go.

"Did you leave a package on my doorstep this afternoon while I was out, before I talked to you?"

"No, if you got one, it wasn't from me," he said. "I would have asked you about it when I talked to you."

"That's what I thought." That was one possibility ruled out as I ticked it off my mental checklist. "Could you do me a favor and ask Janice if she packed up anything of mine she might have happened to find in the apartment and have it sent over here?"

"I doubt it but hold on and I'll ask her." He sounded baffled. I heard him put the phone down but I couldn't hear any conversation with Janice. Within a minute, he was back. "She said no, she hasn't found anything of yours. She said to tell you that if there's something you think might be here, she'll keep an eye out for it and send it over if she comes across it."

"No, there's nothing in particular but tell her thank you. I was just curious. There was a box at my front door when I got home and there was no return address so I didn't know where it came from." I tried to explain it away without saying too much, but he persisted.

"What was in it? Was it yours?"

"Yes, it was something of mine, but I'm just not sure where it came from or who would have had it. It's not a big deal, just wondering. Listen, I have to go. I have just enough time to get to the restaurant to meet my friend."

"Okay. Have fun. I'll talk to you soon."

"Thanks," I said, relieved that he asked no more questions. "I hope tomorrow's not too hard for you. Let me know if you want to get together tomorrow night when it's all over."

"I probably will. I'll call you. Bye."

I leaned back against the kitchen counter and sighed. The two simplest and least distressing possibilities for the source of the box were just ruled out

CHAPTER FOURTEEN

I pulled into the parking lot of The Jolly Pelican just as Lynn was getting out of her car. I gave the horn a short beep as I pulled into a parking space one car away from hers. She waved and waited for me to get out and join her.

"Hi," she said as I got out of the car. "Perfect timing."

"I know," I said as I caught up to her. We started walking toward the entrance together.

"I haven't been here in ages," Lynn said as we entered into the cool interior of the building. "I do love it here, though. I'm glad you suggested it."

"It's my favorite place in Gulfside, I think. I was just here last night, too. Do you want to sit at that booth back there on the deck?" I pointed to a booth in the back of the room that was technically inside the restaurant, but the back side was a low quarter-wall and the space above it was open to the deck. Both seats of the booth offered an unobstructed view of the beach and the sunset, which would be in about fifteen minutes.

"That looks great. Let's grab it." She was already making her way to the booth in the back. I followed her and we both slid onto the opposite bench seats. "Oh, that breeze off the Gulf is amazing." She looked out over the sand to the water as she settled in.

"It'll be sunset pretty soon. We'll be able to watch it from here."

A server I knew named Jeannie appeared at the booth just then. "What would you ladies like to drink this evening?" She had a pad and pen out, ready to take our orders. "We have half-price house margaritas for two fifty all night and Corona or Corona Light draft for two dollars."

"I think I'll have a margarita," I said. "That sounds good."

"Me too," said Lynn.

"Great." She scribbled on her pad. "Do you want menus?"

"Yes," Lynn said. "I'm starving."

Jeannie smiled. "I'll be right back with your drinks."

We both turned and looked at the horizon simultaneously. I sighed. It was such a peaceful scene I could almost forget how bizarre my life was right now. There were a few high clouds, but the sky was clear for a picture-perfect view of the sunset that was coming soon. I sighed again involuntarily. Lynn was quiet too, apparently caught up in her own musings. Life here really was paradise.

Our reverie was broken by Jeannie arriving with our drinks. She set down two cardboard coasters and placed a pale green colored cocktail garnished with a slice of lime in the center of each one. "Here's the menu. The specials tonight are the Load-it-up Jolly Burger and a mahi mahi sandwich. I'll give you a few minutes and come back to take your order." She placed a menu down in front of each of us before she turned and moved on to another booth on the other side of the room.

There weren't too many patrons in the place tonight. That was good for me. I didn't really want anybody eavesdropping on the conversation I was about to have with Lynn. From across the room, somebody waved at me and called out, "Hey, Sharon. How are you?" I answered with a quick wave, recognizing Tom who was one of the regulars. I quickly looked down at my menu. I didn't want to appear unfriendly, but Tom was a talker and I wasn't in the mood for any extended conversation about town gossip tonight. He must have taken the hint because he didn't wander over to our booth.

"What are you going to have?" Lynn asked me, thinking I had been studying the menu.

"I can't decide. What about you?"

"I was going to have a salad, but I think I should live it up a little. I'm going to have the chicken-bacon-ranch wrap. With fries." She giggled.

"Good for you. I think I'll have the mahi mahi sandwich. With fries." We looked at each other and laughed. I raised my margarita and said "Cheers!" We clinked our glasses together as she said, "Cheers back at you!"

We both took a sip of our drinks. "Mmm... that's good," Lynn said. "Oops, here comes the waitress."

"Are you ladies ready to order?" Jeannie asked as she arrived at the table. We each gave her our selections, surrendered the menus and went back to our cocktails as she went to punch the orders into the computer.

"It must be almost sunset now," I said as I pivoted to look toward the beach again. I was right. The sun was almost to the horizon.

"I'm glad we didn't miss it." Lynn shifted her position sideways on the bench seat so she was facing the water. "It's going to be a nice one."

For the next few minutes, we both sat captivated by the glorious scene before us. Because of the brightness of its aura against the azure sky, the sun appeared gigantic as it inched closer to the earth's rim. The water of the Gulf shimmered and sparkled as the reflection created a gleaming path from the horizon all the way to the beach. It looked like you could walk to the end of the world on a path strewn with golden crystals. We both sat quietly, enthralled with Mother Nature's performance. Finally, the last sliver of orange halo melted below the dark blue line of the sea, and the show was finished, leaving its shadow behind in a mauve and indigo sky.

"That was amazing." Lynn cleared her throat. She had clearly been moved by the spectacle. "That had to be one of the best sunsets I've ever watched."

"It was stunning," I said, sipping my margarita. "I never get tired of watching sunsets, no matter where or how I see them. Gulfside beach has to have some of the best, though."

"Uh huh." She nodded. "So, you need to tell me what's going on. I could tell from the way you were acting in the shop that whatever it is, it's definitely not pretty. It's not like you to be so stressed out. I envy you, how you always have everything under control. You know exactly what path you're on and where it's heading. My life is always such a jumble."

Lynn looked at me expectantly, but I didn't know where to begin.

"It's really weird, what's going on. I think the reason I feel so stressed is exactly because I have no control over what's happened, and I know it's not over yet. I'm stressed mostly because I'm angry." I admitted this to myself as much as to my friend.

I glanced away and saw the waitress on her way to the table with our food. It was a brief reprieve before I would have to resume my story. I needed a few seconds to decide which direction I was going to go with it and whether or not to tell Lynn everything. If that was the case, I was going to have to give her an abridged version. Otherwise, we could be here all night.

"Do you need anything else?" Jeannie asked as she put the plates down in front of us. "Can I get you each another drink?"

"That's probably a good idea," I answered looking at the level of liquid in my glass. "I think we're going to need it."

Lynn gave me a knowing look. "Yes, I'll have one too."

The waitress smiled. "Coming right up, ladies," she said with a sympathetic grin.

I spread some tartar sauce on the inside of the roll and laid it down over the fish. I cut the sandwich in half to make it more manageable to eat. "I'm just going to dive in with this," I said as I was cutting, "but you're going to get the Reader's Digest version. Otherwise, it will take forever. Besides, it has to do with my ex-husband, and I don't really want to rehash all that crap." I took a bite of my sandwich to give her a minute to react.

She held up a half of her sandwich, ready to bite. "Your ex-husband? I thought you hadn't seen him in years. You didn't finally run into him in town, did you?" She started to eat as she waited for me to explain. Shortly after we became friends, I shared with Lynn my experiences with Jim and all about our marriage. She shared her similar marriage horror story with me. Since we were both divorced, we could complain about our exes to each other to our heart's content.

"No, I didn't see him. Well, not really. OK, let me start by giving you the headlines, and then you can ask me questions and we can talk about it." I took a sip of margarita. "My ex died yesterday." I could see the look of astonishment on her face as she stopped mid-chew. "In the wee hours of the morning. My step-son had been here for a couple of days staying with him and his girlfriend. I guess they all knew the end was near. My step-son filled me in on Wednesday night about what was going on, two days before he died. And Jim wanted me to go see him on his deathbed."

"Oh my God." Lynn gasped and almost choked on her food. "What did you say? Did you go?"

"I said no, and I didn't go." I took a bite and chewed for a few seconds. "The last thing I wanted was to see him. He wanted to have me back in his good graces, I suppose. I wanted nothing to do with it. He died overnight on Friday, early in the morning. I received two psychic warnings two days in a row, one before he died and one after, though I didn't know at the time he was already dead. I think his spirit came through my house when it left his body. It was like a whirlwind freight train smashed through the room." I let Lynn absorb all that before I went on.

"That's incredible. What were the warnings?"

"The first was a talking pelican and the second was during a Tarot reading for a client, from the spirits of her two dead relatives." Her nose scrunched up and I could tell she was skeptical. "I know it sounds ridiculous but I'm telling you that's what it was. Both gave me the same message—beware and be warned. Both of them used those exact same words in exactly the same way."

"That's crazy. No wonder you've been upset. I'm guessing that's not all."

"Right, there's plenty more." I pushed my plate away, even though I had only eaten half of my dinner. I lost my appetite as I recounted what was happening around me.

Lynn followed suit, pushing her plate to the end of the table. She had eaten a little more than I had but not much. I saw Jeannie, ever alert to her customers, headed over our way.

"Are you finished? Was everything all right?" She asked a little nervously, maybe expecting the unhappy customer routine.

"It was fine," Lynn said quickly to the waitress's obvious relief. "Just not as hungry as we thought."

"Do you want take-away boxes? I can wrap those up for you," she offered.

"Sure," Lynn said. "But we're going to stay here for a while. Probably have another round of margaritas later, if that's ok."

"No problem," she said with a smile as she scooped up the two plates. "Stay as long as you want. Wave me over when you want your drinks refilled." With that she wandered away to check on another table.

"Keep going," Lynn prompted. "I've got all night and you need to get this all out."

CHAPTER FIFTEEN

Lynn settled deeper into her seat. "I want to hear everything."

"So, after that, my step-son came over to tell me Jim had died." I started in again, grateful for her support and understanding, not to mention that she accepted what I was talking about as fact, "That was at the exact time during the night that I felt the spirit barge through my room, I found out that he lived across the street from me for the past year and had deliberately chosen that location. I'm sure it was so he could spy on me."

"What?" Lynn looked like she was getting angry now. "What a bastard. Why would he do that?"

"I have absolutely no idea." I shrugged. "I had no contact with him for over ten years, never tried to find him even though I knew he was living in town. He got no encouragement from me at all. Now you know part of why I was so upset." I took a long drink from my margarita glass. "Wait, though, there's more."

"More? Isn't that enough?" She took another drink too.

"I wish it was. First thing this morning, I was taking my usual walk on the beach and found a leather motorcycle vest. When I turned it over, there was a severed finger inside." It was hard to believe that happened only this morning.

She let out another gasp. "Are you kidding me? Don't tell me they belonged to your ex."

"Yes, they did. I called the police and they came to get them. They called my step-son this afternoon to confirm they both were his."

"How did you end up being the one to find them?" She looked like she was getting a bit overwhelmed. "I can't believe you've been going through all this."

"I know, right? And it's only been since Wednesday. Four days," I said as I held up four fingers to emphasize the point. I paused to take a deep breath. "Besides all that, my ex-husband's photo somehow got loaded onto my computer and showed up on the screen and I got the same exact words of warning. I deleted it but it wasn't a photo I had ever seen before. Then a half hour after I deleted it, it showed up printed and in a frame on my desk. I threw it away in the trash. This happened before I came to your shop this afternoon. That's why I was looking for protection stones, as powerful as I could get." I took another deep breath.

"Well, now I understand why," she said as she nodded. "No wonder you're so stressed."

"Oh, it's not done yet." I sighed. "When I got home, there was another incident. Somehow, somebody stole my grandmother's antique snow globe from my spare bedroom. It was wrapped up in bubble-wrap, put in a plain brown cardboard box and was sitting on my doorstep when I got home this afternoon. I called my step-son but neither he nor my ex's girlfriend knew anything about it. I really believe his spirit was messing around with my stuff, but there's no way a spirit can physically do some of those things. I think somebody's been in my house.

"How could they get in your house? Was it unlocked?"

"Yeah, I never lock my doors here in Gulfside. Well, at least until all this started happening. I didn't think I needed to. Now I feel like a prisoner in my own house!"

Lynn's eyes were bugging out and her lip quivered. Obviously she'd heard enough. I decided not to tell her about the woman I'd seen three times last night at this very place, since I didn't know if she was real or an apparition. I caught Jeannie's attention and signaled that we needed another round of cocktails. This was definitely a three-margarita night. While we waited, I excused myself to use the ladies' room. I needed to stretch and physically move in a different direction. When I returned, our fresh drinks and carry-out boxes were on the table, and Lynn looked like she had recovered from the shock of my story.

"Okay, this is what I think," she said as we both took a sip of our drinks. "First of all, I definitely think the spirit of your dead ex-husband may be around you. After all, the two of you were married for thirty years, right? That significant meshing of energy will dissipate over time when you're separated but it doesn't happen overnight. Besides, there was a ton of negative emotional energy between the two of you. There's probably a lot of residual left that you haven't gotten rid of yet. So at the time of his death, his spirit was attracted to the next nearest place that had a high concentration of his own energy. That was with you."

"Hmmm. I hadn't considered it that way." I thought for a few seconds. "So, you're saying that the initial rush of energy through my room when he died wasn't so much that he was trying to threaten me as it was that he was trying to find the remainder of his energy to take with him."

"Yes, that's exactly what I think," she said and leaned in toward me. "However, that's not to say that once he found out where the remainder of his energy was—with you, unfortunately—he didn't decide to stay rather than move on. You said he was trying to get you to physically come see him before he died. Well, you wouldn't, so he decided to ethereally come to you instead. Either way, he got what he wanted."

"I know. He always had to have his own way no matter how he got it." I let out a long hard exasperated breath.

"So that could explain how he got to you and decided to stick around. I think there might be more though." She gave me a long hard glare. "Are you ready to hear this?"

"I guess so," I said, though inside I wasn't so sure. "How much worse can it get? You heard what I've had to deal with for the past few days."

"Well, this doesn't explain everything but I think it takes care of some of these incidents." She paused to take a drink of her margarita, then looked straight at me. "I think you might be responsible for causing some of these things yourself."

"Are you kidding? What do you mean?" I gasped and scrunched up my face, annoyed and hurt at the same time.

"Don't be upset with me," she said gently. "Let me explain what I mean and why I'm saying it."

"Okay." I sighed. "Let me hear it." I folded my arms across my chest.

"Just think about how many intense emotions have been whirling around inside you since all this began on Wednesday. Let me see..." Lynn held up her hand and counted off on each finger as she spoke. "Definitely relief that you didn't have to deal with him anymore. Indignation as you learned about his maneuvering to spy on you. Aggravation that you were dragged into the whole death and dying scene. Maybe some fear as you tried to figure out what was going on around you. Anger as you realized you couldn't control it. That's a lot of incongruent energy rushing about and building to a frenzy."

"I guess you're right about all that," I said as I tried to digest all she had just listed. "It was a lot of stressful energy I was both putting out and keeping inside."

"Then added to all this turmoil were even more emotions that were more intense than all of the others together." She gave me a look that had compassion and empathy written all over it. "Regret. Self-reproach. Guilt."

"I'm not sure what you're talking about," I said defensively, but even at that point what she hinted at was beginning to take form in my brain. "Wait, are you saying I might be manifesting some of these things myself? Because I feel guilty that I didn't see him and let him apologize."

"That's exactly what I'm saying," she said with a nod of her head.

"I don't feel one bit guilty, and I have no regret that I didn't allow him to apologize." I pointed at her as I talked, not a good thing, but a definite indicator that I was irritated. "I wasn't trying to get revenge for all he put me through. I really felt that I didn't owe him anything. Maybe I was guilty of being indifferent but that's it." I truly believed what I said.

"Okay, okay." She put her hands up palms toward me. "Think about it though. You know undirected energy and intentions can bring about physical results. You might not even be aware of what you're doing. Take the photo on the computer, for example. It was probably there all along, and you didn't remember it. As you were hitting keys and pushing buttons to get the computer to work, you could have subconsciously gone to that file and clicked open the picture."

"Okay, maybe I can give you that, but explain to me how it got printed out and framed and then put on my desk. And what about the vest and the finger? How did I bring that about?" I sounded like a prosecutor badgering a witness. I hated to admit she could be right about some of this. Emotion was extremely powerful energy and the human subconscious could do incredible things.

"I'm not saying you're doing everything," she said calmly. "All I'm trying to propose is that you should try to sort through all the events, figure out which ones you might be causing and be more aware of what your emotional energy is doing. Once you take care of your own stuff, then you can concentrate on the rest and figure out where that's coming from."

"Alright." I conceded with a begrudging smile. "That makes sense. I can do that, and I will. Sorry I got so defensive. But what about the rest of it? Do you agree Jim's spirit is trying to haunt me?"

"Yes, I think he definitely could be." Now it was she who acquiesced. "I'm not going to discount that one bit. I guess the question to be answered there is why he would do it and what would the purpose be."

"I don't have a clue," I said. "Other than anger and control. If that's true then I need to be extremely careful. Maybe that's what my two spirit warnings were trying to tell me."

"Maybe so." She pointed her index finger at me. "Have you tried to do a reading or make contact with his spirit at all?"

"No. I think I was in denial about all this. I really didn't want anything to do with him alive or dead. I guess I'm going to have to go forward on the premise that I'm partly responsible but he, or his spirit, owns the rest. Trying to make contact might ultimately be a good idea so I can find out for sure if it is him and what he wants of me." I let out another long breath and smiled at her. "Thanks, I knew I could count on you to help me put it all in perspective—even if I don't like it."

"You're welcome," she said softly. "It might not be what you wanted to hear, but I think it was what you needed to know."

We both reached a hand across the table and held on tightly to each other for a full minute.

"You're right." I glanced out toward the beach. It was fully dark now with a faint glow from the almost full moon that was still rising in the east. "I really appreciate you listening to all this. You are a good friend, and I know you understand what I'm talking about."

"I'm really glad I could help. I know you would do the same for me if I needed it. You never know, I might someday." She chuckled.

I grinned. "It's getting late." I glanced around the room and then up at the clock behind the bar. "Wow, it's after eleven. We're the only ones left. They probably want us out of here so they can close up and go home."

"Yes, we should go. I have to open the store tomorrow, but at least not until noon."

We both got up from the booth and walked over to the bar. It looked like the waitress was gone for the night but the bartender was still there. I asked for our check and handed him my credit card. While he was punching keys at the cash register, I said to Lynn, "Tonight is on me, for all your help. I meant it when I said I appreciated it."

"Thank you," she said without any argument. "I'll take care of it next time. By then, I'll probably need some psychic counseling from you." She laughed as I scribbled my name on the bill, took the receipt and my card, and shoved them in my purse.

In the parking lot, we hugged before getting in our cars. I let mine idle for a minute as I watched her drive away, giving me a short beep with her horn. I had a lot to consider after our conversation. "Tomorrow's going to be quite a day," I said to myself as I drove out of the parking lot and headed for home.

CHAPTER SIXTEEN

M uted sunlight streamed through the shades and a breeze that smelled of sea air teased my eyes open. I had slept through the night without any interruptions, psychic or physical, and woke feeling rested. If I had any dreams, I couldn't remember them. I did remember, however, the discussion I had with Lynn the previous evening. There was a lot to think about today. Normally, I would jump up, throw on some clothes and head out to the beach for a morning walk, but my walks over the past few days hadn't worked out so well. I was determined not to let apprehension get the best of me.

"I'm not going to stop doing what I love to do or change my life for any spirit, especially if that spirit happens to be my damned ex-husband," I said out loud as I sat up in bed. The days of letting him control me were long over. I was not ever letting that happen again, no matter what. With that, I tossed off the covers and marched over to the bureau. "I am going for a lovely long walk." I grabbed my clothes, put them on and practically ran to the back door. I didn't look at anything on the way, not wanting to see what might be out of place.

The beach was peaceful, and the morning sparkled with the sunshine that reflected off water and sand. The walk to Fisherman's Pass and back went along without a single incident. I spent the time considering all the issues and possibilities that Lynn and I talked about. What she said about Jim's attraction to residual energy and how it kept him hanging around made sense to me. However, I didn't want to believe that I might be the one who generated what seemed like spirit activity because of guilt, or to acknowledge that I regretted my refusal to forgive him for all the hurt he put me through. I tried to be objective and consider every angle. By the time I got back to the house, I'd decided on two tasks. First, a search for the names and addresses of Gulfside residents to see if I could find the owner of the Rhode Island pickup and see if it belonged to Jim or somebody else. Second, I would read the tarot for myself and then maybe a psychic session to contact any other spirit that might be involved.

The day was my own to do with as I wanted, so I took my time with every part of my morning routine. I wasn't mindlessly dawdling but I did go slowly, carefully monitoring my every action and maneuver as I worked through each task. I wanted to evaluate every move I made to be sure I wasn't calling in any negativity or manifesting any unwanted intentions. If I was going to have to deal with a spirit, I wanted to make sure I wasn't feeding it any of my own energy.

By half past nine I had taken care of all the household chores. The dishes were done, a load of laundry was in the dryer, and my bed linen was changed. I sorted through the week's mail, pulled out the bills and made the payments online, checked my emails, answered the ones I needed to and deleted the junk mail. There was nothing left to do and the rest of the morning remained to take care of the two tasks I'd decided to tackle earlier.

It was easy enough to find an alphabetical directory of residents on the Gulfside town website. Although I didn't know the address of the apartment building across the street, I quickly found both Jim and Janice on the list. The address was 3573 Gulfside Avenue. I only had to browse through the directory to find the names of nine other occupants. It looked like there were two other couples besides Jim and Janice, and both shared the same last name so they were likely married. That left five single tenants. I didn't recognize any of the names. Once I wrote them all down, I searched Google for anything about each individual but came up empty-handed as far as useful information.

Luckily, there was a website with a free look-up of owner and vehicle information based on license plate number. The pickup was registered to M. Isabella Santos with a Providence address. That meant somebody else from Rhode Island was living in the same building as Jim and Janice. The name wasn't one I recognized, and it could be a coincidence. I searched again for that name, but nothing useful came up.

When I searched the Providence address, it returned an apartment building with twenty names but nobody named Santos was among them. One of the tenants, M. Benevides, caught my attention. That was the name of Jim's former girlfriend, Maria Benevides, but it was such a common name in Rhode Island, I really couldn't be sure if it was her or not. Either way, it wasn't the name on the pickup's registration. Still, something didn't jive, so I printed out the page and then went back and printed out the truck's registration page too.

I leaned back in my chair and gazed at the two pieces of paper. My intuitive sense poked at my brain. The Isabella Santos that owned the pickup was not on the list of tenants in Jim's building, but neither was she listed as an occupant of the apartment building at the address in Providence she used for the truck's registration. I took another look at the people in Jim's building. Three of them, one couple and two singles, had primary addresses in another state up north. It was possible they rented out their apartments, and the renter wasn't on the official city directory.

One other notion dawned on me. Maria had been married four times before she dated Jim. I had to wonder if she ever used one of her previous names. She probably still had identification with one of those names on it. It was certainly something to consider, but I couldn't understand why she might want to live in the same building as Jim and Janice. From what I'd heard, their separation wasn't on the best of terms. Even if they had sorted out their differences and she did live there, I didn't know what impact that might have on my situation. I probably wouldn't get back into the building any time soon with that woman in the office. I'd definitely have to pay more attention to the people coming and going from Jim's building.

A knock at the front door made me jump. I tiptoed to the window at the side of the door and peeked out from behind the curtain. I breathed a sigh of relief when I saw Lynn there.

"Hi, come on in," I said as I opened the door. "When I heard the knock, I couldn't imagine who it might be. What's up?"

"I know I probably should have called first but I just had this premonition when I woke up that I should come see you before I went to work. I don't have to open until noon today, so here I am." She walked in and handed me a tiny pouch tied with a ribbon. "Here this is for you. I had a couple at home."

"Oh, wow." I grinned and held the small stone from the pouch up to the light from the window. "This is a beautiful piece of fire agate with a very strong vibration. But I don't want to take it if it's yours to work with."

"No worries." She waved her hand at me. "I can always get another. You definitely need it more than I do right now. My gift to you. I've already cleared and charged it for you."

"Thank you so much. I really do appreciate it." I put the pouch with the stone in the pocket of my shorts.

"And I'm going to do something else for you. Another piece of my premonition," she said. "I'm going to read your tarot. It needs to be done and you should have an unbiased reading. I can do that for you. Actually I was thinking we could read the cards together. That should help target in on what you already know and what you need to know."

"I planned to do a reading for myself this morning, but I'd love for you to do it. You know, reading together sounds like an awesome plan. That would definitely work, with your objectivity and my knowledge of the details of what's going on." I gave her a big smile. "I really am very lucky to have you for a friend."

"We should use one of your decks," Lynn said. "That way the cards are already in tune with your own energy."

"Good idea." I turned to the bookcase. "Let's do this right now so you aren't late to open the shop."

I scanned the shelf where all my tarot decks were arranged and selected the Celtic Tarot. Its artwork seemed to resonate with me, and I always used it when I did a reading for myself. It was charged and synchronized to my own energy pattern. The deck was worn, and I needed to replace it soon, as much as I hated to do that. These cards were like old friends, comfortable to hold and always ready to give me the appropriate messages at the proper time. Lynn's plan of doing the reading together as a team was fitting, and this was the best deck to use for that. The two of us reading together would give me the messages I needed to receive, not just what I wanted to hear.

A bowl of crystals sat on the back corner of the desk, and I selected three to share my pocket with the fire agate. Sodalite and clear quartz to enhance the psychic connection and hematite for grounding and protection. I grabbed my journal and a pen and turned back to Lynn.

"All set," I said. "Let's go out back."

She followed me outside to the grotto. I put everything down on the table and sat back in the chair while she sat opposite me. We both closed our eyes and began our personal rituals to prepare for the reading. I needed to be relaxed and open to any messages as well as to make sure I was fully grounded against unwanted psychic energy attacks. Opposites are drawn together, and negative energy in the universe seeks sources of positive. The last thing I needed was a negative entity attaching itself to me, especially now. When I was done, I opened my eyes and took several deep breaths. I felt good. Lynn opened hers a second later.

"Ready," she said.

"Ready," I repeated.

CHAPTER SEVENTEEN

Lynn shuffled the tarot deck and then handed it to me to do the same. She and the cards would guide the process as I followed along. After I finished shuffling enough to infuse my energy into the cards, I cut the deck in three piles, holding my purpose for this reading in my mind. Any spirit that had been around me for the past few days needed to be identified, and we had to determine what the spirit wanted of me. From that perspective, I didn't want to direct anything we were doing. I had to let the reading go on spontaneously, doing what was correct without any consideration or deliberation on my part. Lynn picked up each of the three piles in turn and put them back together as one deck.

She placed five cards face up on the table to form a star when the points were connected, one card at each point starting at the top. I scanned them quickly. Then she took the next card from the top of the deck.

"This card represents the force and character of the spirit we want to identify, the active agent in this reading." She didn't turn it over until the moment before laying it on the table in the center of the star.

It was the Emperor reversed, not a card I wanted to see in that position. The Emperor generally represented a father figure with all the traits of a good leader, including power, authority, structure, and stability. When the Emperor appeared reversed in a reading, however, it indicated the opposite of those traits.

Lynn began the reading. "This is the character of the spirit we are trying to identify. It represents someone who would abuse their power and authority. This spirit would be overly controlling, critical and deceitful, as well as rigid and uncompromising in his thinking. He would put himself and his wishes first before considering those of anyone else he dealt with, disregarding rules and structure, with the potential for harm and chaos. Do you have anything to add, Sharon?"

"No, I think that sums it up pretty much." Although I tried to be open-minded, this certainly described the personality of my ex-husband. Whether the spirit was Jim or not, dealing with a spirit of this character would be difficult and possibly even dangerous. I had to consider the spirit within the context of the other cards that would provide the answers I needed.

"The next card is at the top point of the star," Lynn continued as she pointed to the position. "The Two of Cups reversed."

The card glared up at me from the top point position. I had, of course, seen the card as I quickly scanned the layout before she turned the center spirit card over, but the meaning was ambiguous without context.

"This card is the indicator of your relationship to the spirit represented by the Emperor reversed," Lynn said matter-of-factly.

"That's not good," I said.

Lynn looked up at me but didn't reveal anything with her expression. "The Two of Cups is the card of union, the coming together of two to create a new identity as one, and often refers to marriage or romantic relationships."

I knew this was the meaning, of course, but Lynn was being a professional rather than my friend at this point. This was exactly what she should do to maintain objectivity in her interpretation of the cards. I accepted her method and would have done the same if I was leading the session.

"As with the Emperor, when the Two of Cups is reversed, its meaning is dramatically changed, becoming a card of disharmony and disunity. In a marriage situation, it generally refers to a dysfunctional relationship, most often leading to separation and divorce. One or both of the partners might be manipulative, selfish, controlling or abusive, or a combination of any or all of those. It represents an imbalance of power and control."

For me, the Two of Cups reversed only reinforced that the spirit I was dealing with was Jim and I said so. "With both the Emperor and the Two of Cups in these positions, I have to believe that the spirit is my ex-husband. These cards describe his behavior when he was alive, during our marriage and, as I've now learned, even after we were divorced."

"I agree," Lynn said, nodding her head as she looked at me. "I don't see how it could be anything else."

At least we confirmed what I had guessed during this whole ordeal. "Well, looking on the positive side, if I have to deal with a negative entity, at least I'm familiar with this one. I know his personality as well as his strengths and weaknesses. I can use that to my advantage." I picked up my journal and pen. "I'm going to write this down as we're going along. I don't want to forget anything later."

"Good idea," she said. She gave me a few minutes to jot down my notes.

I planned to record the positions of the cards within the layout as well as their meanings and interconnections, noting the specific card in each position and both of our interpretations. Later, I would be able to refer back to my notes and know exactly what this reading told me without relying on my memory alone. I didn't want to enhance the meanings with each successive recollection. When I was done, I turned back to the cards, and Lynn continued.

"Turning to the card at the left bottom point next, this should tell us the overt expression of the spirit's purpose." Lynn pointed to the card. "Here we have the Seven of Swords, upright this time, and I think it presents an interesting situation. This card is about self-serving interests and that the ends justify the means, with the traits of the active agent of the Emperor reversed being deception, manipulation and subversion. That goes along with the other cards so far, as it would have impacted on the dysfunction of the marriage but I sense there is more, perhaps a double meaning here. This card can also appear when the agent is plagued by guilt over what has already been done. Maybe now, after death, he feels sorry for what he did."

"That's interesting. I never experienced that from Jim when he was alive. I'm not sure how I feel about it now but I understand why you're reading it that way. Are you saying that he's acknowledged he was wrong and wants to make up for it somehow?" I asked, jotting it down in my journal for more consideration later.

"Yes, that's the sense I'm getting. Let's see what's next." She tapped the card on the right bottom point of the star. "This shows the underlying covert purpose, that which is to remain hidden, the secret agenda. Here we have the Eight of Swords, representing a victim mentality, making excuses for bad behavior, while being stuck in a situation and imprisoned by the person's own flawed thinking."

"That sounds more like him." I snickered. "He would have an ulterior motive to any apology." We were definitely still headed downhill, and as far as I was concerned, there was nothing redeeming about this reading at all. "Maybe another interpretation is that he presents as repentant when, in fact, he's using deceit to further his own ends."

"That could be true. I'm also getting a distinct feeling there are two different personalities here, one at each point. But, that doesn't make any sense in this layout. The left should be the expressed outward purpose, and the right should be the underlying motivation, sometimes one that the agent might not even be aware of. I feel some very negative energy from that right point. What do you think?" she asked as she looked up at me from the cards. She wrinkled her forehead and squinted at the cards.

When I looked at the two cards, at each side of the bottom of the layout, there was the feeling something was not quite meshing. Lynn was right. The cards should apply to the same agent, but it did feel like there were two different forces at work here. I wasn't ready to accept that my ex-husband could be truly repentant as the Seven of Swords on the left might indicate, and so the Eight of Swords on the right made sense with what I knew of his behavior. If there was a second agent at work here, I had no idea who it could be. But then, that was the whole point of this reading—to identify who the spirit was. Even though, in my opinion, my ex-husband fit the description provided by the cards, it was completely possible there was another spirit at work here besides Jim. I had to be careful not to read my own feelings into the cards. That's why I was glad Lynn was involved.

"I can sense the two different forces. I believe one is definitely Jim, but I have no idea about the second one. I'm trying to be objective, but I'm not sure I can be for this situation. Why don't we go on to the last two cards and maybe they can help explain this," I said.

"Okay, let's see," she said. "The last two points, at the sides of the star are the proposed action on the left side and the probable outcome on the right. On the left is the Six of Swords reversed, which means the agent is unable to move forward and is stuck in the current situation with no way to get beyond it. That seems to make sense for a spirit that can't or won't let go. There's no movement since the spirit refuses to act."

"No argument from me there," I said. "Spot on."

Lynn smiled. "On the right, we have the card for the outcome of this non-action. This is the Tower, indicating swift and immediate destruction, total loss. That's pretty severe."

"Wow, I guess so." I shook my head. "I knew this whole situation was bad but from the looks of things, it's going to get far worse than I could have imagined."

This was probably the most foreboding reading I had ever seen, which made it more alarming as far as I was concerned. There was not one thing positive that I could see when all the cards were interpreted together as a whole. If we were correct, and the spirit here was my ex-husband, then the outcome could be catastrophic. I still didn't understand what his purpose was, though. Nor could I fathom the twisted reasoning behind his spirit stalking me and perhaps even intending to harm me. Could he really be so vengeful just because I didn't want to be part of his life after we divorced?

"I know," Lynn said, shaking her head again. "So, to sum it up... The spirit is likely your ex-husband, who seems to fit the description to a tee with the validation of the reversed Two of Cups. I'm not completely satisfied with the interpretation of the two purpose cards, though. He or another spirit, or both of them together, are seemingly determined on some kind of vengeful act against you, because you wouldn't yield to his wishes. His spirit can't move on until the issue is resolved. You need to be extremely careful because whatever means the spirit is contemplating to achieve this conclusion could be vicious and destructive for you." She exhaled slowly. "I'm sorry, Sharon. This is horrible."

"It's not your fault. You're just doing the reading. You're not responsible for the action. Besides, I agree with everything you said." I tried to sound calm but my insides were in turmoil, my stomach twisted in knots, and my heart beat in staccato. "At least I know what to expect. Forewarned is forearmed, as they say. It's better than being taken by surprise, especially when you're dealing with spirit entities."

I picked up my journal to write notes on the rest of the reading. At the exact same moment, a gust of wind blew through the grotto so hard it rifled the pages in the journal and blew the cards around the table. The layout was a jumbled mess now and totally out of order. Several cards flew off the top of the deck on the table and scattered all around. We both looked down at the table at the same time and, at just that instant, one more single card catapulted from the top of the deck and landed dead-center on the jumble of cards. I blinked twice to make sure I had actually seen it. Lynn gasped. The Queen of Wands reversed had landed as perfectly as if Lynn had placed it there.

"Oh no!" Lynn cried out.

There was no mistaking the meaning of that card in the position of the lay-out—misdirected anger, meanness and selfishness, hurting others to put herself in a better position, unpredictable and unreasonable. I shivered. Who was the wicked Queen the card referred to? This dreadful reading just became a nightmare.

CHAPTER EIGHTEEN

I walked Lynn to the front door. She had no more time to discuss the strange tarot reading. It was 11:25 and she had to get to her shop in order to open on time at noon. We promised to talk later and waved goodbye. My phone rang as I closed the door behind her. The number on the screen wasn't in my contacts, and it wasn't one I recognized, but it was a local Gulfside number, ending in three zeroes. I usually didn't usually respond to calls with a number I didn't know but all those zeroes looked official.

"Hello?"

"Hello, ma'am." The voice on the other end sounded stern and serious. "This is Detective John Brandon from the Gulfside Police Department. Is this Ms. Sharon Coady?"

"Yes, I'm Sharon." I supposed I expected this call. It was the timing that threw me off. I didn't have a chance to catch a breath.

"Ms. Coady, I'm investigating the incident related to the items that were found on the beach yesterday morning. I understand you were one of the persons that found the items," he said, still sounding very gruff.

"Yes, I came upon them while I was walking. Another woman came from the other direction, and we saw them at the same time." I wasn't taking the whole responsibility for it. "I gave my statement to the officer that arrived there after it happened."

"I'm aware of that, Ms. Coady." Now there was an edge of sarcasm. "However, I need to ask you a few questions to complete the investigation. I'd like to come to your house, if that's all right with you. Otherwise, you'll have to come to the station." It almost sounded like a threat.

"Yes, of course. When would this be?" I asked as politely as I could, though I was irritated with his attitude.

"I'm at the station only a few minutes away from you. I'd like to come by now."

"Yes, that would be fine." There wasn't really an option to refuse.

"Good. I'll see you in a few minutes. Goodbye." He hung up before I had any chance to respond.

I went to my desk to put the stones and tarot deck away when a knock sounded on the door. I expected it was the detective, but when I pulled the curtain back slightly and looked out, nobody was there. I opened the door, leaned forward and looked in each direction. Nothing. The step in front of me was empty.

I drew up short as I turned around to go back inside. A small shopping bag leaned up against the house. The logo on the front of the bag was from Lynn's crystal shop. Confused, I picked it up and brought it inside. Lynn left here only a few minutes ago and would have handed me anything she had for me. She knew I was here and wouldn't have left a package on the step without letting me know. I opened the handles and looked inside. A smaller packet of bubble wrap lay at the bottom of the bag. I reached in cautiously, mindful of a possible booby-trap. I didn't like that I even thought of that.

"You're being absolutely ridiculous now," I said out loud as I carried the bag inside. "Just stop it and see what it is."

I snipped the tape that held the wrapping in place and opened it up. Inside was a sandwich-sized clear zip-lock bag about a third full of reddish-orange powder with some small shiny pieces mixed in. The powder felt gritty as I rubbed a pinch between my fingers. I pulled the little pouch with the fire agate that Lynn gave me out of my pocket. When I compared the two, they were the same color. This powder had to be the smashed and pulverized remains of the fire agate crystals missing from Lynn's shop. There was probably enough in the bag for five or six crystals—exactly how many Lynn said she had. My mouth hung open, and I stared at the bag in my hand.

A knock on the door right then startled me and I dropped the bag and my stone on the floor. I scrambled to pick them up and put them both in the shopping bag on the kitchen counter. This time it had to be the detective. I hoped.

Gathering my wits, I hurried to the door and pulled it open. "You must be Detective Brandon," I said with a sigh of relief when I saw the man standing there.

"Yes." He showed me his identification and badge in a leather wallet. "You're Sharon Coady?"

"I am. Come in." I moved aside and waved him into the living room. "Have a seat." He was about my age, tall and of medium build with a full head of neatly combed thick gray and white hair which sported a wave over his forehead. His clothes were neat and pressed, a short-sleeved button up shirt, light blue, open at the collar and a gray pair of trousers with a perfect crease. He had a police radio clipped to his belt next to a leather holster which I presumed held a gun. He stood straight with perfect posture. His manner was steeped with understated confidence and experience.

"Thanks." He stared at me for a moment, reached to turn the volume down on the radio and then sat down. "You look a little flustered. Is everything all right?"

"Oh. Oh, yes. I just had a phone call with some surprising news is all." I hoped he would be satisfied with that explanation. I sat down in the chair opposite him. "You have some questions for me?"

"Just a few routine questions. We can get through these very quickly and then I'll be out of your way." He pulled a small notebook and pen out of his pants pocket. He flipped a few pages and read something. "You're a resident here in Gulfside?"

"Yes." I knew he had already checked that out before he got here.

"How long have you lived in town?" He flipped another page.

"About three years."

"At this address?" he asked as he looked up from his notes.

"Just about. I bought this house within a few weeks of moving here, so I've lived here almost the whole three years."

"And what do you do here? Are you employed?" He looked back down at the pad.

"I don't work. I'm retired." Nothing to be anxious about. It was common enough among Gulfside's residents.

"Now, let's start with why you were on the beach at that time. You found the items at approximately 8:10 yesterday, Saturday morning."

"I was taking a walk on the beach." I remembered what every lawyer in every television show always told their client—never give them more information than they ask for.

"Is that something you do often?" Just a routine question as he briefly glanced up from his notebook at me.

"Yes, almost every morning." His energy was strong, in a positive way, yet my palms were sweaty and my mouth was dry. I didn't understand why I was having this reaction.

"I see. So, this was just a routine morning walk on the beach," he said as he looked down again.

"Yes." It felt like I was waiting for something to happen.

"Thank you. Would you tell me what transpired leading up to your finding the items?" Now he looked up and stared me right in the eye.

"Well, I was walking from my house here down toward the public beach."

"You were alone?" He interrupted.

"Yes, I always walk by myself." I hesitated to see if he was going to say anything more but he didn't so I continued. "I was just about to the point where the public beach starts when I spotted what looked like a black heap at the waterline, half in and half out of the water. The waves flowed in and out of it, but it didn't move, so I figured it must be something kind of heavy." I stopped to take a breath.

"Go on."

"I couldn't tell what it was. Then I noticed another woman walking toward me and the black thing."

"Did you recognize this woman?"

"No, I didn't know her," I said. "I picked up a stick as I approached the thing. Even when I got right up close, I couldn't tell what it was. The other woman got there right about the same time I did. She had a stick too. We both poked at it and then with the two of us using the sticks, we managed to pull it farther up on the sand out of the water."

"Could you recognize what it was at that point?" he asked as he wrote some notes.

"No. Only that it was something like fabric but very tough. I guessed it was leather. The two of us poked and pulled at it with the sticks and finally managed to turn it over and get it opened up a bit. That's when I saw the patches on it." I waited for the question I knew was coming.

"What kind of patches?" He didn't disappoint.

"They were motorcycle related, and there was a large one on the back. They were faded and the colors had run together, so they were hard to read. I finally figured out that the name patch on the front said Topper and the large patch on the back said Devil's Riders." I took a deep breath to prepare me for the next sentence I knew I had to say. The detective just watched me and waited. "Then we turned the vest over again, and the finger fell out on the sand."

"I see," he said. "Just a few more questions."

He looked at me, and I nodded. There wasn't anything else I could do but wait for him to launch them at me.

"Did you recognize the item as a finger right away?" he asked.

"Yes, it was all in one piece and recognizable."

"So, it was intact." He nodded and wrote something in the notebook. "Did you touch it or move it? With your hand or with the stick?"

"Oh, no."

"What about the other woman?"

"No, I didn't see her touch it either. She seemed pretty frightened of it."

"Were you frightened of it?" He looked right at me.

"No, I wasn't afraid of it," I said truthfully. "I knew what it was. It was very strange and rather gruesome to find it there but I didn't think it was going to hurt me in any way."

"All right. Now about the vest. You could tell it was leather. You saw the patches on it and recognized it as a motorcycle vest. How did you know that?"

"Well," I said slowly while I decided how to best phrase my answer. "My ex-husband belonged to a motorcycle club for many years, so I knew what a biker's leather vest looked like."

"Can you confirm for me your ex-husband's name?"

That was an odd thing to ask. Of course, he knew what Jim's name was. Maybe he wanted to make sure I had been married only once and we were talking about the same man. "His name was James Latouche," I said. "I was only married once." Just in case he was going to ask.

"Thank you. And did you belong to that motorcycle club with him?"

"No, I did not."

"I see." He scribbled some more notes. "You told the officer on the scene that you thought the vest might belong to your ex-husband. Is that right?"

"Yes." I figured I might as well get it over with and put it all out there, since I knew he was going to ask anyway. "As I said, my ex-husband belonged to a motorcycle club, one of the one percent clubs, when we were still married back in Rhode Island. That was one of the reasons we split up. I refused to join the club with him." I had been looking down at my hands but I raised my head and met his gaze. "His biker name was Topper, which was the name on the vest. I've heard of the Devil's Riders here in the Gulf area, and I know they're the same kind of club. I'd had no contact with my ex since the divorce, so I had no idea if it was really his or not. But it seemed like too much of a coincidence, so I thought I should mention it to the officer." I let out a long breath, glad that I gotten through that part. Now I waited for him to probe deeper.

He was writing copiously in that little notebook of his. I stopped my foot from its nervous tapping on the floor.

"Ms. Coady, you say you had no contact with your ex-husband. Didn't you know he was living right across the street from you? You must have run into him at some point. This is a small town." No more writing, he stared directly at me, daring me to contradict him.

"No, really, I had no idea. I only found out Friday when his son told me he died. Detective, you can believe me when I say he had no part in my life for twelve years. I didn't pay any attention to what he did or care where he lived. I knew he moved to Gulfside only a few months before I did but that was all. If our paths did cross, I never recognized him because I swear, I never saw him here in town." Now I stared straight back at him, daring him to call me a liar. This was the absolute truth and I wouldn't back down.

"All right." He wrote a few more notes in the notebook and then snapped it shut. "I think that's all I need to ask you. If there is anything else, I'll give you a call. Do you have any questions?"

As a matter of fact, I did. "My stepson told me it was confirmed that the vest and finger belonged to my ex-husband. Is that right?"

"Well," he said slowly, "only because you have already been informed by your stepson, I will tell you that it has been verified. Normally, I wouldn't be able to tell you that kind of information."

"I understand. Thank you. Is there any theory about how or why the finger was severed and inside the vest?" I tried to sound like I deserved and expected an answer.

"Now, that I can't tell you," he said with a slight smirk. "Nice try, though." He got up from the chair and took a few steps. "Oh, just one more thing, Ms. Coady. Do you have a boyfriend?"

That really caught me off guard. "No, I don't. Is there a reason you're asking?"

"Just need to make sure I have all the bases covered," he said with that same smirk.

I walked him to the door and opened it to let him out.

"Here's my card." He handed me an official business card with his name and phone number. "Give me a call if you think of anything else I should know. Thanks for your time, Ms. Coady."

"Your welcome," I said as he turned and walked toward his car in the driveway.

I closed the door and leaned my back against it, exhaling loudly. I don't know why that interview unsettled me so much. If anything, I was a victim in all this mess. All these incidents taken by themselves seemed totally ridiculous. My psychic intuition told me something different. There was some larger scene playing out here, but I simply could not put it all together. Not yet. I knew without a doubt, however, that it wasn't over.

CHAPTER NINETEEN

W hen the phone rang again, I sighed and looked at the screen. This time it was Jimmy. I wanted to tell him about the police detective but decided we could talk about that later.

"Hi. How are you? Don't you have the funeral going on?"

"Yeah. I just left the funeral home, and I'm on the way to the Legion Hall. But I had to tell you this. I just got a call from Janice's daughter in Providence. Janice never arrived at the airport. She was supposed to fly out at 6:30 and get to Providence at 9:45, but she wasn't on the plane when it landed. Her daughter called the airline, and they said she never checked in for her flight in Tampa."

"Maybe she missed the flight."

He was upset. As much as I didn't need another problem to worry about, I wanted to be a support for him.

"They searched the airport, and she wasn't there. I know she left in the shuttle this morning. I saw her get in the van and the driver load her bags in the back. That was at 4:15 and she hasn't been seen or heard from since. I called the shuttle service. They said they had no record of sending a driver to get her or even that they had any booking for her ride."

"Wow, that doesn't sound good. I wonder who picked her up." Janice's disappearance might be connected to all the other strange occurrences around here after all. It didn't make any sense.

"I don't have any idea," he said. "I have to get through this collation with Dad's buddies that's probably going to last a couple of hours. I wondered if you could do me a big favor though."

"Sure, what do you need?"

"Would you mind going over to Dad's and staying there in case Janice shows up or somebody needs to get in the apartment?"

"Umm..." My first impulse was to say no. I really wanted no part of Janice's disappearance or to be responsible for anything related to her and Jim. But, it might be my only opportunity to get back into the apartment building and figure out the mystery of the Rhode Island truck owner. "Okay, I can do that. But how am I going to get in?"

"Thanks." He sounded relieved. "I'll call the office and tell them you're coming over. They'll let you in."

"Anything you want me to do while I'm there? I don't mind, and it'll give me something to do."

"Actually it would be a lot of help if you would go through Dad's desk and separate out anything that might be of value from the junk."

"I guess I can do that."

"Awesome. Thanks. There are some boxes in the kitchen. Take what you need." He exhaled. "Look, I'm pulling into the parking lot right now. I'll meet you at the apartment when this is over. We can get some dinner and talk later."

"Sounds good," I said. "No matter what time, whenever you're done is fine."

"Thanks. I've got to go now, but text me if anything comes up."

"I will. No problem. Love you. Hang in there."

"Love you, too. Bye." He clicked off.

I packed my journal, a bottle of water, and an apple in a tote bag along with my phone and wallet. As an afterthought, I grabbed a spray vial of sage-infused water from my herb cabinet and tucked that in the tote too. A few squirts of that would clear away any residual negative energy in the immediate environment, and I was sure I'd need that in Jim's apartment. Within minutes, I locked the door behind me and headed across the street. It seemed ironic that the nondescript building, barely noticed before, now loomed large in my life. When I reached the bank of mailboxes near the entrance door, I took photos with my phone, first of the top row and then the bottom so I'd have the names and apartment numbers to work on later.

I pushed the buzzer for the office and peeked through the glass while I waited. The office door was open but I didn't see anybody inside. After a minute with no response, I pushed the buzzer again. Still nothing. The lobby was empty. I tapped my foot and glanced around the vestibule. A security camera, that I hadn't spotted before, was mounted high up in the corner above the mailboxes. As I reached to push the buzzer for the third time, a movement inside caught my attention. A young man in his early twenties strolled around the back corner behind the stairs and walked toward the office. I banged on the door with my fist, and his head whipped around in my direction. He turned toward the door, and I waved.

"Sorry, I was out back," he said as he opened the door. "Can I help you?"

The smell of cigarette smoke drifted toward me and my nose wrinkled involuntarily. At least it wasn't the same woman I ran into the other day

"I need to get into the Latouche apartment. My stepson was supposed to call to ask you to let me in."

"Yeah, he called just before I went outside." He held the door open wide. "Wait at the stairs and I'll get the key."

The other day, I was distracted by the woman spying on me and hadn't stopped to look around the lobby. There was a hallway behind the office that led to the ground floor apartments. A back entrance door like the one in the front lobby was visible opposite the opening to the hall and looked out over the parking lot. Two security cameras were mounted against the ceiling over the door, one aimed down the hall and the other pointed at the lobby.

"Here we are. Follow me." The man jiggled the keys and started up the stairs.

I plodded along behind him, glancing around for anything else I might have missed. We walked down the second-floor hall to the third door, Apartment 7, where that woman had gone in. I hoped a little sleuthing today might answer who she was and what her connection to Jim might be.

"Thanks a lot." I walked through the opened door as the young man saluted from the hallway.

"Anything else you need, just call down to the office. I'm there until five."

"I will, thanks." I waved and closed the door.

It was a small apartment with one bedroom and one bathroom. Clearly, Jim hadn't spent much on furnishings. A worn wooden table with two chairs sat half-way between the open kitchen and living room. Janice had clearly tried to make it look nice, with teal vinyl place mats and a ceramic dolphin napkin holder in the middle flanked by jumping dolphin salt and pepper shakers. A number of boxes secured with packing tape were stacked in the corner next to several large black trash bags. Empty boxes were piled on the floor against the wall beside the dining table and an open package of trash bags was on the table.

The living room walls were bare except for a television mounted on one side of the room and a framed print of a beach sunset on the opposite wall hung over a cheap faux wood and chrome desk. Except for a metal folding chair in front of the desk, two leather recliners arranged to face the television were the only other furniture in the room. Plain teal sheers hung on each side of the slider that led out to the balcony. A camera was set up on a tripod in front of the glass. I shivered when I saw that it was pointed in the direction of my front door. I sprayed around the door with the sage.

I wandered into the bedroom and looked around. The sheets were rumpled, and a suitcase rested on top of the one dresser in the room. The drawers were partially open and empty. A half-full box of men's clothes sat in front of the closet where more clothes waited on hangers. A walker and cane leaned against a commode in the corner near the window where odds and ends of medical supplies were piled. Nothing provided a clue to any of the information I wanted.

"Very cozy." I snorted and shook my head as I sprayed the sage toward the center of the room.

In contrast to the sparse accommodations of the rest of the apartment, the desk was a jumble of paper, files, and books. Every drawer was packed to the point where nothing else would fit, and they jammed when I tried to open or close them. A Disney souvenir beer mug stuffed with pens and pencils of every description sat on the left corner hidden behind a stack of overflowing file folders. The other corner had a framed photo of Jim in his Army uniform when he made Master Sergeant. In front of that was pile of photo albums that I recognized from when we were married. I flipped through them. They held mostly shots from when the kids were young at various family functions. A lot of the sleeves were empty, in no particular pattern that I could figure out. A pocket calendar, stapler and other small office supplies were strewn haphazardly across the desk top. I remembered Jim being fanatical about neatness so the condition of his desk surprised me, but I wasn't surprised about why Jimmy asked me to deal with the mess.

I grabbed two boxes and a bag and sat on the folding chair to start to work. Supplies like the pens and stapler I placed in one box. I figured they could be donated somewhere, maybe a senior center. Bills and receipts, personal items, and important papers went in the other box, while trash and unnecessary odds and ends went in the bag. I tackled the top of the desk first and then worked my way through the drawers. The files and piles of papers were the worse since I had to review each piece of paper before tossing it or putting it back in a folder for safe keeping.

It took an hour and a half to clear the top and the two drawers on the left side. The trash bag was almost full. There were just the two more drawers on the right side of the desk left to go through. I stood and stretched my stiff muscles. My water bottle was empty, but I grabbed one from the otherwise empty refrigerator and munched on my apple. I wandered over to the slider and stepped out on the balcony.

The traffic was light, and I watched a few vehicles pass by. Suddenly the old pickup with the Rhode Island plates rumbled by the front of the building and turned the corner to head toward the parking lot in back. I ran to the door and used my water bottle as a prop to stop it from closing and locking behind me. From the window that looked out over the back, I could see the truck pull into the same space it was in the other day. As I watched, the door opened and the driver climbed out. I gasped and stared at the woman from the Jolly Pelican on Friday night. She had changed her shirt but her hair was unkempt and it looked like she had on the same jeans.

I was paralyzed as I watched her walk to the back entrance. I shook myself out of the trance and sprinted to the top of the lobby stairs. The door below me slammed shut, and her footsteps headed away from me down the tiled floor of the hallway. I skipped down to the bottom of the stairs just in time to see her go through the door of the apartment below

Jim's. I still didn't get a good look at her face though. I slapped my hand on the railing and trudged back up the stairs.

All I could think was that this woman had to have some connection to Jim. She didn't look like his girlfriend Maria as I remembered her, and there seemed to be no logical reason Maria would live in the same building as Jim and his new girlfriend. I picked up my water bottle and let the door slam behind me.

The final desk drawers waited for me. Jimmy should be back soon, and I'd at least have this job done for him. The top drawer was easy, filled with boxes of paper clips and staples along with a myriad of other little office gadgets. Most of these went into the donation box. Some social service agency with a tight budget would be happy to get these.

I pulled on the handle of the bottom drawer but it was jammed. Something inside was wedged tight, and the drawer would only open two inches. I tugged on it with one hand and stuck my other hand in through the gap as far as it would go. A thick package blocked it from opening. I pushed it down as hard as I could with my fingers and yanked the drawer at the same time. I heard paper rip, and the drawer burst open.

The package turned out to be a large manila envelope about two inches thick. The corner of the flap had torn when I pulled the drawer. I flipped it over and sucked in my breath. My name was scrawled across the front in black marker. The flap was sealed but, through the torn corner, it looked like the envelope was filled with photographs.

I heard a key jiggle in the lock and looked up toward the apartment door.

"Hey," Jimmy said as he walked in.

"Hi. How'd it go?" I placed the envelope on top of the desk.

"All right, I guess." He threw his suit jacket over the back of a kitchen chair and loosened his tie. "I'm glad it's over." He leaned over and kissed my cheek. "How'd you do with the desk?"

"Good. It's all done, actually." I picked up the envelope and turned the front toward him. "I found this in the bottom drawer."

"It's got your name on it."

"Yes, and it's filled with photos." I stood and put it back on the desk. "I don't know why but it looks like your father pulled them from the albums and put them in here specifically for me. I'll take the envelope home and go through them. Any I don't want, I'll give back to you."

"That sounds good." He unbuttoned his shirt. "I really appreciate you cleaning out the desk."

"No problem."

"I'm really beat. I'd like to go lie down for an hour or so, if you don't mind."

"I'm sure you're exhausted." I put the envelope of photos in my tote bag. "Call me when you're ready and we'll figure out something for dinner. How's that?"

"Sounds good. Give me a couple of hours, okay?"

"Of course. We can talk over dinner. I've got a few things to tell you about."

I walked toward the door and he followed me.

"Thanks for being the best step-mom ever." He said as he leaned over and gave me a hug. "See you in a bit."

He shut the door behind me, and I walked over to the window. The pickup was still there. At the bottom of the stairs I turned toward the back hallway and looked toward the apartment the woman had gone in. The hall was empty so I walked to the door. There was no decoration or name plate, just the number 3 below the peep hole. I shrugged and walked back to the lobby on the way out.

CHAPTER TWENTY

I had some time before Jimmy would be ready for dinner. It was only 3:30, and I had a few things to take care of. I wanted to call Lynn to tell her about the pulverized fire agates left on my step. There was no doubt they were from her shop since they were in one of her little customized shopping bags. I didn't think she had a surveillance camera in her store since that would be a significant investment for the type of merchandise she sold. She at least needed to know, though, that there potentially had been a shoplifter there since she didn't remember selling the stones.

That reminded me that I still had the bag of crystals I bought at Lynn's shop yesterday in my purse. These were all protective stones, and they needed to be placed around the house. I put the bag on the kitchen counter and took the Orgonite pyramid out first. With no hesitation, I walked over to my desk and placed it to the left side of my computer monitor, next to the CPU. That should take care of any more electronic spirit shenanigans, or at least I hoped so.

I put a dish towel down on the kitchen counter and spilled the remainder of the bag's contents on top of it. The plastic baggie that contained the crushed fire agates, along with the one Lynn had given me, was still on the counter, and I added the intact stone to the pile. I picked out some smaller stones and put them aside. The rest I took with me as I began a tour of the house. Each stone would be placed strategically to act as a barrier to any negative energy or a booster to the stones that were already in place.

First, at the back door, one of the pyrite stones went on top of the sea salt in the center of the cup with the bay leaves. In combination with the bay leaves, the pyrite would not only prevent any negative energy from entering but would return it directly where it came from. Back in the house, the bathroom was next. There was only one cup of herbs in there, and it needed some reinforcement, so I dropped a black tourmaline on top. In the living room, I glanced at my desk. That should be covered with the Orgonite along with the herbs and hematite I had put there previously. I put a kunzite in the cup of herbs on the small chest in front of one window. A black obsidian went on the small table at the other window along with the hematite that was already there. Outside the front door, I dropped the other piece of pyrite on the sea salt in the cup with the bay leaves that was to the side. Both doors were now taken care of.

On to the bedroom where I looked around at what was already in place. The bedside table held my tourmaline tree, as well as hematite and a cup of herbs, so that was fine. I decided to put one of the two remaining black obsidian on the side table in front of the window. Then the last tourmaline went into the cup of herbs on the bureau. Two kunzite stones were left in my hand, along with one obsidian. I chose one kunzite carefully based on the energy vibrations I felt from it and put that one under my pillow as a buffer. It would act as a shield yet be gentle in repelling any negative energy that tried to come at me while during my sleep. I didn't need any violent energy struggle going on around my head. The kunzite would also help me sleep by soothing and reducing stress.

Back in the kitchen, I looked at what was left: the fire agate Lynn had given me, one kunzite, and one black obsidian. After the episode with the mystery woman at The Jolly Pelican, one should probably go in my car. I decide that the kunzite would be best there as it was often used as a travel crystal to guard against road rage and the stress of driving. Besides, its shielding properties would be beneficial in case of negative energy attacks while I drove. I headed out the front door to the car. There was a recessed storage tray in the center of the dashboard for holding sunglasses, and I dropped the kunzite in there. Suddenly I remembered I hadn't placed any stones in the spare room. Although I spent little time there, I couldn't leave any gaps in my protection for negative energy to enter through. The obsidian went on the window sill, and I put the fire agate on the back of the sofa. Now, I had everywhere in the house well covered.

The stones left on the kitchen counter were mostly the small ones I had pulled out from the pile earlier. From my desk drawer, I dug out a small silver-colored metal cage and a spool of black silk cord. The cage was made from one long strand of wire wound into a spiral, wider in the center and closed at each end, creating a spring. The circles of wire could be pulled apart and then snapped back into place when released. I took the small stones—tourmaline, obsidian, kunzite, and a small labradorite—and inserted them through the strands of wire into the cage. Once I let go, the wire sprung back into place to hold the bundle of stones inside. I threaded a long length of cord through a small loop on one end of the cage and knotted the two ends together. I now had a protection amulet with the bundle of stones that I could wear around my neck, stick in my pocket or purse or hang anywhere handy. For now, I slipped it over my head.

The large labradorite was the last stone left on the counter. This was a special stone for me. I'd always felt a strong connection to it and kept it nearby whenever I did any kind of reading or worked a psychic connection. This piece was a beauty, shimmering and iridescent in all shades of blue, green, and goldish-brown. I knew exactly where it was supposed to go.

I headed out the back door to the grotto and sat in one of the chairs. Cupping the stone in my two hands, I held it up in front of my face. With my eyes closed, I conjured a vision in my mind of rays of light emanating from the stone in all directions that expanded with my every breath until they encompassed me in a protective bubble and filled me with a positive energy shield. I sat this way, with the protective bubble around me, for several minutes. When I finally let the image fade, I opened my eyes and brought my hands down to my lap. A sense of peace and security filled my spirit and I placed the labradorite in the center of the table.

After a few more seconds, I went to get my cell phone. Now should be a good time to call Lynn. I glanced at the clock in the kitchen as I grabbed the phone from my purse on the counter. It was twenty minutes after four, and the store should be relatively quiet. I tapped her icon on my frequent call list and waited for the ring.

"Hi, Sharon. How are you doing? I hope you're not calling to tell me something else happened. I only left you a few hours ago."

"Oh, a lot has happened. You're not going to believe this one," I said. "Besides being questioned by the police, I got another package. Do you have a couple of minutes to talk or do you have customers?"

"The police?" Her voice confirmed her utter astonishment. "There's nobody here right now. Go ahead and tell me what happened."

"Well, first the police were here because of the vest and the finger I found on the beach," I said. "It was the detective who's handling the investigation."

"Oh, right," she said, remembering what I had told her. "Of course, they would want to talk to you about that. Did it go all right?"

"I guess so." I shrugged my shoulders. "I only told him what happened on the beach and why I thought it belonged to my ex. That was all he asked about, and that's all I talked about."

"Good," she said with an exhale. "What else?"

"You know the fire agates that were missing from your shop?" I asked.

"Yes, of course." She hesitated. "Why?"

"I think I found them on my front doorstep this afternoon." I glanced over at the baggie on the counter.

"What do you mean? How could they be there?" Her voice was filled with disbelief.

"It's really weird." I had to warn her.

"Of course it is. Go ahead."

"The police detective called me right after you left this morning," I said. "He said he wanted to come over in a few minutes. So, when there was a knock on the door, I expected it to be him. I opened the door and there was nobody there, but one of your little shopping bags with the logo on it was on the front step." I heard Lynn give a small gasp over the phone. "When I opened it, there was a plastic baggie with an orangey crushed powder inside. I compared the color with the fire agate you gave me this morning and they were the same. I think somebody took the bag and the stones from your shop, crushed them up and left them for me to find."

"That's incredible. Are you sure? How could that happen? Who would do that?" She was almost babbling.

"I have no idea how or who but I am as sure as I can be," I said quietly, mostly to calm her down.

"Wait a minute," she said. "Ghosts don't shoplift stones and then deliver them to your door. There has to be a real person involved in this."

"That thought crossed my mind too." I nodded. "I don't know what to think. Except that somebody was trying to send me a message."

"What kind of message?" She sounded unsure.

"That no matter what I do, they can beat me." I hated to consider it but I had to keep in mind what I had been thinking all along, especially when my ex-husband might be involved. "Somebody or something wants to let me know that they are in control and I'm not."

"This is crazy," she muttered, sounding as baffled as I felt. "What are you going to do?"

"I don't know," I said truthfully. "I've done everything I can think of to keep myself safe. The problem is I just don't know where this is headed."

She paused a few seconds. "Maybe you should call that detective back and tell him what's going on around you. It all has to be connected somehow."

"I don't know," I repeated. I was beginning to hate that phrase. "There are too many pieces of this, and I can't think of any other link except supernatural. I doubt the police are going to take kindly to somebody who reports threats from a ghost."

"But you might be in some kind of danger."

"There hasn't been any attempt to harm me physically." I was trying to be logical about this. I definitely didn't want to report this to the police. "I really don't feel threatened in that way. It's all just tricks to taunt me so far, to scare me but not hurt me."

"Damn. Somebody just walked in." She sounded annoyed. "Just be careful. I'm worried about you. I'll talk to you later. Got to go. Bye."

I put the phone down on the counter and stood still. It was bad enough I believed I was being haunted by my ex-husband's ghost and maybe even my own feelings of guilt about his death. To think there was some real living person out there who was behind the rest of this harassment made me queasy. There wasn't anyone I could think of who wished me such ill-will. I always tried to be as nice as I could to everyone. I was a helper in most situations, never asked for anything in return. I just didn't understand it. I bit my lip and wiped water from my eyes before it spilled down my cheek.

There was one positive thing about having a living stalker. It meant I really wasn't doing these things to myself as Lynn had suggested when we talked last night. If there was another person who was harassing me, whatever their reason, that person could be caught and stopped. I would make sure that happened.

There was the ghostly woman in The Jolly Pelican who turned out to live across the street. She was definitely real and not some figment of my imagination, as I originally thought. I needed to find out who she was and her connection to Jim. Maybe she was the one who threw the vest in the water, but that would mean she had probably severed his finger, too. It was just too strange, and I hated to think she had been in my house and put that photo up as the background on my computer screen and then printed it out. I shivered. The thought that she, or anyone else for that matter, had invaded my home that way gave me the creeps.

Then there was the snow globe and the smashed fire agates. If the same person was responsible for all of this, I had to admit I must be a target. The reason behind it remained a total mystery. There was nothing at all to point to that woman or anybody else, and I couldn't jump to conclusions. The only thing that woman had done was disappear when I chased her and show up in back of my car in the parking lot. I shook my head as the phone rang. It was Jimmy.

"Hi," I said as cheerily as I could. "Did you get your nap?"

"Yes. I just woke up and I feel much better." He exhaled loudly. "I'm going to take a quick shower, and then I'll be over. Okay?"

"Sounds good," I said. "I'll be here."

CHAPTER TWENTY-ONE

About an hour later, the phone rang. It was Jimmy again. "I'm on my way," he announced. "I'm going to get us some beer first. I really don't feel like going out anywhere else, so why don't you order a pizza and have it delivered."

"That sounds good to me," I said. "There's a great pizza place in town that I order from all the time. You still like pepperoni and onion?"

"You bet." He almost sounded like his usual self. "Get an extra-large. I didn't have much of anything to eat today, even at the collation, and I'm starved."

"Okay, will do." I laughed. "See you soon. Bye."

I hung up and scrolled through my saved numbers until I found the one for the pizza parlor. They answered on the first ring, and I gave them the order and the address. They had my debit card number already on file, so I paid over the phone. Pizza was my favorite food, and I was a frequent flyer with them. The clerk said the pizza would be delivered in about a half hour. The timing would be perfect.

Twenty minutes later Jimmy knocked and opened the front door. "I'm here," he called out.

"Hi." I called from outside the back door where I was watering some of my plants. "Be there in a second." When I came in, he was standing in the kitchen and I greeted him with a hug. "How're you doing?"

"Not too bad." He shrugged. "I put some beer in the fridge and these are for us." He held up two bottles of Michelob and carried them into the living room. He twisted off the cap and handed me one. "It went off better than I figured it would." He walked to the couch and sat down. "There were a lot of people there. I'd say Dad had a lot of friends, but I think most of them were there for the free food." He laughed, which was nice to hear. "I guess that motorcycle club is a big one. There were a lot of bikers there and they all arrived in formation on their bikes wearing their colors. They couldn't fit them all in the parking lot and the bikes were parked all over the side streets. No complaints from the neighbors though. You never want to complain about bikers."

"That's for sure." My own experience with Jim had taught me that.

"Oh, and they still haven't found Janice." He said with some concern in his voice. "Nobody knows what happened to her after she left the apartment building but they did see surveillance video from the parking lot security cameras. She definitely got into a shuttle van and somebody put her luggage in the back. The van looked like one of those blue ones that she said she booked but all the records of that company have been checked and there was no record of her booking a ride. They couldn't see what the driver looked like on the tape though, so they don't have a suspect. The police are treating it as a missing person for now, thinking she could have booked a different company. Her daughter is a wreck. I don't know Janice very well, only from visiting Dad a couple of times and these last few days. Still, it's a terrible thing to happen."

"It certainly is," I said to him as a knock came at the door. "Must be the pizza."

"I'll get it," he said and stood up before I could contradict him.

"It's already paid for." I headed for the kitchen to get some plates and napkins.

"Okay." He pulled a few dollar bills out of his pocket. "I'll give him the tip."

He opened the door, and I noticed the delivery person was a woman, not the college kid who usually delivered. I didn't recognize this person from the pizza place, but I didn't really give it much thought or pay much attention. The guy probably needed the night off and somebody was filling in. Jimmy took the pizza, handed the woman the cash and shut the door. "Smells good," he said with a smile as he put the box down on the coffee table.

I sat down next to him on the couch and handed him a plate and a couple of napkins. Almost simultaneously there was another knock on the door. Jimmy and I looked at each other. I had no idea who it could be.

"I'll get it," I said, getting up and walking over to the door. I opened it to see the regular delivery kid from the pizza place standing there.

"Hi, Sharon," he said, holding out a large pizza box that looked exactly like the one sitting on the coffee table. "How ya doin'?"

"Uh, fine, Joey." I glanced at Jimmy, and he had the same baffled look on his face that I was sure I had on mine. "Umm... We already got the pizza. What's this one?"

"No, this is the one you ordered from us." Now it was Joey who looked confused. "It wasn't busy so I stood there and chatted while it was in the oven. I brought it right over when it was done. There wasn't another one."

"Ok, sorry." I shook my head. "Hold on a sec while I get you a tip."

Jimmy was way ahead of me. He was beside me before I could move and handed Joey some ones. I took the pizza box.

"Thanks," Joey called. "See ya."

Jimmy closed the door. "What just happened? Why do we have two pizzas?"

"I don't know," I muttered. "But there's a lot you don't know that's been going on and I'm afraid this might be part of it." We both walked over to the couch. He sat down but I just stood there holding the second pizza box, thinking the worst. "Can you open the cover of that first box? Slowly."

"Why? What's going on?" He reached for the tab on the lid of the box and tugged it open. "Damn!" He jumped up from the couch as I screeched.

A big black snake coiled around the middle of the pizza.

"Holy crap!" Jimmy blurted out from where he was standing behind the couch.

We both gaped at the snake on the pizza, frozen in place. I held the other pizza box so tightly I crushed the sides.

"Wait a minute," said Jimmy as he started to walk around the couch toward the box on the coffee table. "That thing hasn't moved at all since we opened the cover." He grabbed a pencil off the table, reached toward the pizza and poked the snake. There was no response. "I thought so," he said as he grabbed the snake in the middle and pulled it off the pizza. He held it up in the air and shook it around. "It's fake," he said. "A rubber snake."

I let out the breath I had been holding with one big blow. I wasn't sure which was greater, my sense of relief or feelings of anger. "This is ridiculous." I yelped and clenched my fists.

"What's this all about?" Jimmy asked as he stood there still holding the snake.

"It's a very long story, and it's going to sound like I'm crazy, so get ready."

"I guess I'm ready," he said, looking at me expectantly. "Hold on a minute. Sit down and I'll be right back." He closed the cover on the snake's pizza and went into the kitchen taking the snake and its box with him. "Do you have any bags handy?" he asked.

"In a tote bag on the bottom shelf in the pantry cupboard."

I watched as he dug a couple of plastic bags out of the cupboard. He placed the rubber snake in one, tying the two top handles together in a knot. He dumped the slices of pizza into another bag and knotted that one. Then he placed the two bags in the box and put that on top of my antique cabinet.

He came back to sit on the couch next to me. "First things first," he said as he opened the cover on the pizza that Joey had delivered. "Perfect," he announced. "No problem with this one and I'm starved." I appreciated that he was trying to lighten the mood as he dug out a slice of pizza and took a huge bite.

I had to laugh. "Okay," I said and removed a slice of my own. "I'm pretty hungry myself, and pepperoni looks better than reptile." We both giggled with mouths full.

"Now," he said after putting the rest of the slice on a plate and taking a sip of his beer. "Tell me your story. I need to hear everything."

"First, I need to ask you something."

"Okay, go ahead."

"Do you know another woman from Rhode Island who lives in that building?"

"No, why?"

"I saw her when I was over there. She lives in the apartment right below your father's and drives an old pickup with Rhode Island plates. It's parked out back in the lot."

No, but I really haven't spent much time there. Dad never had anybody else in his apartment when I was there. Does she have something to do with all this?"

"I don't know, but she was at the Jolly Pelican the other night when I was there too, and I felt like she was watching me."

"How did you know it was her?"

"I didn't get a good look at her face today, but I'm sure it was the same woman."

"All right, why don't you tell me the whole story, and then we can talk about it."

"Okay, here goes. You know some of it already," I said. "Most of it has to do with your father."

I took a deep breath and let him have it—all of it. Between bites of pizza and sips of beer, it all came out. I went over every detail, both physical and supernatural, and left nothing out. He asked questions, and I answered as best I could. Sometimes he snorted, and other times he scoffed. Through it all, though, he was intent, and I could tell he listened closely and considered every word I said.

"Well, that's it." I finished and leaned back on the couch. I could feel my muscles relax. I hadn't realized how tense I was as I told the story.

"Okay then," he said in a soft voice. "I had no idea about all of this."

"I know you didn't." I waited for him to say whether he believed it all or not.

Several minutes of silence went by as he thought everything over carefully. I didn't want to interrupt his train of thought. I felt like I was on trial, that he was a jury of one about to pass judgment on my life for the past few days.

"There is definitely something going on, I'll give you that for sure." He stood up and paced around the room. "Have you told anybody else about all of this?"

"Only my friend Lynn. There isn't anybody else who would believe it."

"That's the point." He rubbed his chin as he spoke. "Here's the thing. As a skeptic, or whatever you want to call it, it's hard for me to accept that a ghost might be involved in some of these incidents. I understand what you believe and to you, that kind of thing is possible. Even if I grant you that, I still can't buy it. I mean, I know my father was a bastard most of the time but I don't think he could be that vindictive, especially to somebody he cared about." He looked over at me. "And he did still care about you, you know. No matter what he did, he still loved you. He told me that, and he was completely sincere when he said it."

"Okay, so maybe he did care in some weird, perverted way, but that didn't stop him from being a jerk when he was alive. I doubt that would change after he died." I could not give Jim any measure of sympathy.

"All right. I understand how you feel." He continued pacing, silent and thinking for a few more minutes.

He stopped abruptly in front of me and put his hands on his hips. "I think you have to report this to the police."

"I can't do that." I moaned. "Look how hard a time you're having with all this. Do you think it will be any easier to get them to believe it?"

"I know, I know. You're right. I just hate the thought of you being alone and in any kind of danger." He sat down on the couch. "Maybe you could just report some of the incidents as harassment, like the packages you got and maybe the photograph. Maybe that woman at the restaurant the other night has something to do with it. You could give the police a description of her."

"I don't really think I'm in any danger," I said. "If it's not from the spirit world, then it's somebody's twisted idea of a practical joke. Except, I'm not finding it very funny. If that's what it is, I don't want to give them any credence or acknowledge that they're getting under my skin.

That would be just what they're after. I only want to find out who or what is doing this and make them stop."

"Okay, how about this?" He suggested after thinking for another minute. "I have to fly back to Rhode Island early in the morning to take care of Dad's service and a few other issues there. The funeral and burial are Tuesday morning, and I'm flying back down here Tuesday afternoon so I can finish cleaning out the apartment. I'll check in with you while I'm gone and as soon as I get back. If anything else happens between now and then, we will go to the police on Wednesday morning together. If there are no other incidents until then, we'll let it be." He looked me straight in the eye. "Deal?"

I hesitated and then acquiesced. "Okay, it's a deal." I didn't have a better plan, and he wasn't going to let it drop. I don't know what I was expecting, but this discussion hadn't exactly turned out the way I wanted. Maybe I wanted him to tell me not to worry, that it would all go away soon. Realistically, I knew that was unlikely. "It's a deal on one condition."

"What's that?" he asked suspiciously.

"Once this is over you have to promise to come and stay for a few days so we can enjoy the visit and have fun without any crazy stuff going on to sidetrack us."

"Now that's a deal." He agreed quickly and with a smile. "You've got it." He looked at his watch. "Wow, it's late, after ten. I still have to pack and get ready to fly out in the morning. I wish I could stay here tonight, but I have too much to do. Will you be all right?"

"I'll be fine," I insisted. "I've been here alone all this time. I can handle it. You go ahead and do what you have to. Don't worry about me."

"I do worry, and you can't stop me," he said with a grin. "I know you're a strong woman and can manage just about anything. It's one of the things I've always admired about you. You were a great role model when I was growing up, whether you know it or not."

"Thank you, that's very sweet." My face grew warm as the blush rose on my cheeks. "You go ahead now. I'll clean up and then I'm going to bed. It's been a long day."

"Okay. Good night, sleep tight. I'll see you in a couple of days." He leaned over and kissed my cheek. "Love you. Take care and be safe."

"Not to worry," I said as I gave him a hug. "Love you too. Have a safe trip."

"Thanks," he said as he gave me a quick hug back. He headed out the door, but called over his shoulder as he left, "Make sure all the doors are locked."

"I will," I called back as he walked toward the street. I closed the door and locked it behind him. I might be stubborn about it, but I wasn't foolish enough to take chances.

I picked up the trash from the pizza and the two empty beer bottles from the coffee table and carried them to the kitchen where I tossed them all in the trash. I considered throwing out the snake and its box too. No, I decided, if I ever do have to talk to the police, I might need that. I did take out the bag of pizza and threw that away. As I was moving the snake box over to the other side of the counter, I noticed the manila envelope from Jim's desk on the counter and sighed. I wasn't looking forward to sorting through old family photos especially since Jim would be in most of them. That's how he was.

"Well, I'm not doing it now," I said to the envelope. "I'm going to bed." I shut off the light and headed to the bathroom to get ready. Within minutes I was snuggled under the sheets.

CHAPTER TWENTY-TWO

The ringing of the phone startled me awake. I grabbed it to check the caller ID and noticed the time.

"Yikes!" I cried. "It's after nine." I never sleep that late, ever. The phone didn't care, it just kept ringing. The number was familiar but I couldn't place it in my sleepy daze.

"Hello," I said automatically.

"Good morning," said the voice on the other end. "This is Detective John Brandon from the Gulfside Police Department. Is this Ms. Coady?"

"Yes." I was instantly alert. "This is Sharon. Can I help you with something, Detective?"

"As a matter of fact, you can." He said with that same no-nonsense manner that I remembered from our interview yesterday. "I was wondering if I could come by later this morning, maybe about eleven-thirty. I need to speak with you about another incident. Do you know Ms. Janice Crawford?"

"Well, I used to know her." My guard went up immediately. "I haven't seen her in years, though I am aware she was in a relationship with my ex-husband."

"Are you aware that she's missing?"

"My stepson told me that yesterday," I said, not sure where this was going.

"All right. Because of the incident with the items on the beach, I have to be sure that there is no connection. I'm sure you understand. Will you be available at home at eleven-thirty?"

"Yes, I'll be here." I didn't have much of a choice. If I had to talk to him again, I might as well get it over with.

"Fine. I'll see you then," he said. "Goodbye, Ms. Coady." He sounded very formal as he hung up.

I threw off the sheet and trudged toward the bathroom. I didn't even feel like taking my walk on the beach this morning. I had two hours before the detective arrived. While I was brushing my teeth, I decided that maybe after I had some coffee and something to eat, I would feel better. Somehow, I didn't think that was going to work either.

Sitting on the patio after breakfast, I tried to calm my brain down. Despite being so lethargic when I woke up, my insides raced in circles. I watered my plants, pulled off dead leaves, and removed spent blooms. That usually was a task I enjoyed and could get lost in. Not today. I decided to sit in the grotto for a while and try a relaxation meditation. The sun reflected off the labradorite crystal I put there yesterday and showed off its brilliant colors. I picked the stone up and cupped it between my two palms, resting them in my lap, then leaned back, closed my eyes and began the ritual to clear my mind and ease the tension in my muscles. I envisioned myself sitting on the beach, empty of other people, with just the waves rolling in and a slight breeze ruffling my hair. The only sound was the lulling cadence of the waves and the occasional call of a gull. Within a few minutes, I was feeling more at peace. I allowed these tranquil sensations to roll over me and I absorbed them like a sponge.

Suddenly the calm serenity of my image was interrupted by the emergence of a black cloud coming in over the water on a direct course toward me, bringing with it a sense of ominous and threatening peril. This was not supposed to be part of my meditation. I tried to rouse myself and open my eyes, but I was held captive. Something had hold of me, and I couldn't break loose from its grasp, couldn't rise from my sitting position on the sand in my vision. I was trapped and all I could do was wait, at the mercy of whatever was headed my way.

The black cloud cast a shadow over the water as it came closer. Crawling slowly forward, the darkness filled me with a sense of dread. The shade reached the sand and crept nearer to where I was seated, until I was completely sheathed in its gloom. It swallowed the light whole but I had no strength to struggle against its grip. Foul tentacles snaked their way through my entire being. My soul was almost ready to give in to the negative energy when I noticed a sliver of almost imperceptibly brighter dark seeping under the edge of the shadow, an ever so slightly lighter shade of charcoal than the blackness that enveloped me. The sliver grew to a slice and at last to a wedge, cutting into the blackness despite the darkness of its own. I had no choice but to watch as a war was waged between the malignant and the malicious. I didn't know how or why but I was certain that I was the reason for this battle, the prize for which both sides fought so vehemently.

Without any warning, there was an ear-splitting thunderclap directly overhead. The violence of the crash jolted me from my trance, and my eyes popped wide open. I was never so relieved to find myself sitting in the grotto unharmed and bathed in sunshine. As I came back to reality, the labradorite felt ice cold in my hands but burned my fingertips. My hands released it on the table top and I gasped. The crystal was singed around the edges as if it had been in a searing fire, and a jagged crack ran along one side that had not been there before. Wisps of icy vapor rose from the stone and ascended in curlicues into the air.

I had no idea what had occurred while I was trapped in the vision, but there was no doubt in my mind that its impact had overflowed into the physical world. The proof of that was the labradorite in front of me. I was convinced that distinct outside forces at least influenced, if not actually caused, some or maybe all of the events of the past few days. I was sure a combination of supernatural and spiritual forces were at work, and somehow I had to determine their nature and purpose. There was no doubt in my mind that the spirit of my ex-husband was somehow involved, and I had to banish that if I was going to regain any peace and serenity.

"Hello, Ms. Coady?" The voice roused me from my dark musings.

"Detective Brandon, I'm sorry." I apologized when I realized who it was. "I got involved in a... uh... project and I lost track of time." I jogged over to the patio. In light of what had just happened there, I didn't want him in the grotto. "Have a seat," I said as I gestured to the table and chairs on the patio.

"I didn't mean to intrude," he said without any note of apology in his voice as he sat down. "But there was no answer when I knocked and you did say you would be here."

"That's all right," I said and waved it off. "Now, what can I do for you? You said you had more questions for me."

"Yes, just a few." He took out his notepad and flipped through a few pages. "On the phone, you said you knew Janice Crawford. Please tell me how you became acquainted with her."

"She used to work with my ex-husband at a day care program for the elderly," I said. "She was the nurse and he worked there as the administrator. They became friends because they both rode motorcycles, so I knew her from some of the biker functions we all went to."

"And how long ago was that?" He wrote something in his notepad.

I thought back, trying to do the math. "Oh, probably about fourteen or fifteen years ago."

"When was the last time you saw her?" Still writing.

"I would say it was probably the summer of the year Jim and I separated, so twelve years ago."

"Did you know that she and your ex-husband had a romantic relationship?" He looked up at me.

"Yes, I heard about it from some mutual friends." I answered the next question before he asked. "That was about four years ago."

"Did that upset you, Ms. Coady?" He made direct eye contact, holding my gaze as he waited for his answer.

"Not at all," I said with a shrug. "I was completely done with my ex by that time, and I didn't care what he did. When I heard of it, I kind of felt bad for her, knowing what she had to put up with. I always thought she was a nice person."

"I see," he said as he went back to scribbling in his notes. "I think I asked you this before, but when did you become aware that the two of them lived across the street from you?"

"I only found out a few days ago, when my stepson told me."

"Yes, right." He flipped a few pages back, looked at his notes for a few seconds and then flipped them forward again. "What did you know about her life here in Gulfside?"

"Nothing really. The only things I knew were what people who knew us both told me. She lived in Gulfside and the two of them still rode motorcycles. That was it. I never asked about her or my ex or encouraged any conversation about them."

"I see." He jotted a few more notes. "Were any of these mutual friends here in Gulfside?"

"No. They were all back in Rhode Island."

"Have you met anyone here in the Gulfside area who also knew Ms. Crawford or your ex-husband?" He asked without looking up.

"No, I haven't."

"Do you know of any reason why she might want to disappear?"

"If my ex-husband was still alive, there might be a reason." I felt a smirk take over my face. "Otherwise, I have no idea."

"Do you know of anyone who might want to harm her in any way?" He raised his head and made eye contact with a stern expression that dared me to give him a wrong answer.

"No, not at all."

"Are you sure you didn't feel a little animosity toward her, knowing that she was living with your husband?" His stare never wavered.

There was the zinger, and I almost laughed out loud. "Detective, I could be insulted by that question," I said, looking directly at him. "The thought of feeling vengeful toward Janice is almost comical. I wanted nothing to do with my ex-husband, not then or at any time since my divorce. If she wanted him, she could have him as far as I was concerned. I would have offered her pity, not revenge."

Surprisingly, he smiled. Maybe my answer surprised him. I didn't recall that I had seen him smile like that in our previous interview.

"Thank you, Ms. Coady. I think that will be all." He got up to leave.

I stood up, ready to walk him to the front of the house. He extended his hand for me to shake. As soon as our hands touched, a surge of energy, strong and positive, ran through my fingers and into my palm. Reflexively, I started to pull my hand away, but he held it tight for two seconds longer while the spark of a smile crossed his face. I resisted so hard that when he did let go, I stumbled a step backward and nearly lost my balance.

"If you think of anything else, please give me a call," he said, that hint of grin still playing at the corner of his mouth. "Or if there's anything I can do for you."

"Uh, thanks. Thank you." I stuttered. "I will."

"I can find my way back out front," he said as he stuck his notepad and pen in his pocket, He turned and walked up the path around the side of the house to the street. I just stared. I felt confused and unsure of what just passed between us. I knew my mouth hung open, and I must have looked like ridiculous. I shook myself to physically break whatever spell I was under.

"Great," I mumbled aloud. "One more crazy thing to try and figure out."

I plopped back in the chair and put my head down on my crossed arms on top of the table. Since my separation from Jim, I had been totally in control of my life. I decided for myself every detail, choosing which direction I would go and what path my life would take. For the past three years, I enjoyed everything life had to offer, living in paradise and following my dreams. I was content, happy, and satisfied. All of that had come crashing down around my head over the past five days. All because of my dead ex-husband. He was at the core of every one of these situations and his being, whether physical or ethereal, was in control.

I lifted my head and looked toward the beach. I stood up and wandered toward the boardwalk, feeling a little woozy. I needed to clear my head. I stepped onto the beach and felt the grains of sand hug my toes, embracing them with warmth. A throb of energy began pulsing up through the soles of my feet, just a tickle at first but gaining strength with every step I took toward the water. I splashed into the waves just far enough so the water covered my ankles. The vibrations grew stronger, as the strength of the ocean combined with the force of the earth. The air around me seemed to buzz with power and the sun directly overhead blazed down on me like a spotlight. I was being recharged, revitalized.

In that one moment, I understood with a clarity so crystalline and so sharp that I could feel the edges cutting through the frustration that seemed so oppressive a few minutes earlier. The real issue wasn't that I had lost control of what was going on in my life. It was that I had allowed it to happen. I needed to focus on what I was going to do about it and how to get control back. There had to be a way to stop this madness and damn it, I would do it.

CHAPTER TWENTY-THREE

Feeling renewed and more sure of myself, I marched back into the house with a purpose. I hadn't written anything in my journal for a couple of days and I needed to update it to the events of this morning. My intention after that was to skim through all my entries for the past few days and see if there were any common elements or patterns I could determine that might help me figure this out.

On the way to my desk, I checked my phone. I had two text messages, one from Jimmy and one from a number I didn't recognize. I clicked on Jimmy's message. I would read the other one later.

"Just landed in Providence. Checking in. Everything OK? Anything new?"

I paused for a moment, trying to decide how much to say before I typed back, "Glad you arrived safe. All is well here, no news." That was enough for now. There was nothing else he would believe if I told him anyway.

As I put the phone down, I noticed the package of photos from Jim's desk still on the kitchen counter. Although I doubted there was much in there besides photos of Jim and the kids, I really hadn't looked through it all. Anything might be a clue to unraveling this mystery. I detoured to the desk to get my journal and a pen, then back to the kitchen where I picked up the large, heavy package. It had to be the largest manila envelope I'd ever seen. I headed outside to sort through it.

I placed everything on the table and settled into the chair. Except for the tear across one corner, the rest of the flap remained sealed. I slipped my pen through the opening and sliced it open the rest of the way, then dumped the contents out on the table top. There was a bunch of loose photographs along with two smaller envelopes, one a ten-by-twelve manila and the other a letter-sized white that had a thin blue ribbon tied around the middle of it. I picked up a handful of the loose photos and started flipping through them. Most were snapshots of different family events—Jim's niece's wedding, Thanksgiving dinners, opening Christmas presents, a family vacation at a New Jersey theme park. They were all good memories but, as I suspected, Jim was in every one, several by himself and most with the boys.

If you didn't know any better, you'd think he was a great father by looking at these. I sputtered, followed by a sarcastic little snort. I did know better. I was the one who arranged all these events and always insisted Jim be there. Otherwise, he would have blown them off. The only reason he was in so many photos with the boys was because he always made me handle the camera. He claimed it was because I took better pictures. Really, it was because he wanted to show off the photos of him and the boys to all his friends, so they would say what a wonderful dad he was. I put those photos aside in a separate pile as I went through them. I would give them back to Jimmy and he could do what he wanted with them. I had my own collection of pictures of the boys at various ages that didn't include their father.

As I continued to sort, I came across one that was of Jim and me. It was the only one of us together in the pile. It looked like we were at a cook-out. We were standing together and he had his arm around my shoulders. At least we were both smiling. I couldn't remember exactly when it was taken but it was at least twenty-five years ago. I turned it over to see if there was anything written on the back. I flipped it over and threw it across the table like it was on fire. Scrawled across the back in bold black marker was a demeaning sexually-oriented profanity, explicitly insulting to women. My brain wouldn't even let me process the word. It was an offensive disgusting epithet that I never even thought of, much less used.

"Well, that was gross," I said out loud. "Who would have done that?"

I never heard Jim use that word in all our years together and didn't think he would have defaced one of his precious photos that way. I turned the picture right side up and pushed it apart from the others. I wasn't going to let myself worry over it with my new vow to stay in control.

Moving on, I continued to sort through the rest of the pile. All the rest were the same, Jim and the boys. When I had gone through them all, I put them back in the big envelope except for the one of Jim and me. Jimmy didn't need to see that one. I looked at our smiling faces again. Clearly the profanity was intended for me. Maybe Jim had been incredibly angry with me over something but I couldn't imagine what might have moved him to that level of vulgarity. I'd throw it out later but I made a mental note to include it in my journal entry for future reference.

That left the other two envelopes that had been inside the larger manila. I picked up the white letter-sized one and untied the ribbon. The flap popped open and I could see there was a stack of photos inside. I drew them out and looked at each one in turn, laying them face down in another stack on the table. There were about two dozen of them and they all were of Jim and Maria, the woman he cheated on me with, the one he left to move in with Janice. A few of them appeared to be at motorcycle club functions because they were both wearing their biker gear. Others seemed to be casual shots during different events.

I went back through them again more closely. It was evident from their changing appearances, that these were taken over the span of a few years. Some were obviously from their early time together, but others seemed to be later, perhaps even close to the time that Jim left her. At first pass, in every shot they looked like a loving couple having a good time. On closer inspection, I could tell that they were posed and maybe even contrived. In all of them, Maria beamed a smile that could have cracked her face. Jim, on the other hand, had only the faint trace of a smile and his eyes squinted, an expression I recognized after so many years with him as annoyance. Maybe the relationship hadn't been as harmonious between the two of them as Maria would have everyone believe. One would think that at some time during their seven years together, they would have been genuinely happy especially in the beginning but maybe not. After all, I figured out his motive for moving in with Maria very quickly. She had the money to buy him all the toys he wanted, and he was eager to let her do it.

What I couldn't figure out was why Jim would have saved these particular photos of the two of them, not to mention tying them up with ribbon in an envelope. It didn't make any sense, but I had the feeling it would fit in the puzzle somewhere. I put them all back in the white envelope in the order they had been in when I took them out and tied the blue ribbon around it again. I slid it across the table next to the other photo.

That left the manila envelope. When I picked it up, it was heavier and not as flexible as I expected. That meant there must be quite a few photos inside and probably eight-by-ten enlargements. I lifted the prongs of the clasp, opened the flap, and pulled out the thick sheaf of pictures. I was right. They were eight-by-tens printed on heavy photo stock.

I looked at the first one and shook my head. It was a photo of my house with my car in the driveway and it looked like I was sitting in it. I moved that one to the bottom of the pile and looked at the next. There I was getting the mail from the mailbox. The one after it was of me with my back to the camera unlocking my front door. I flipped through the rest and realized they were all of me doing something in front of my house. Twenty photos of me all taken from the same angle and fairly close up. There was even one of me standing at the edge of the driveway looking directly at the camera.

"Damn it." It was obvious from the photos they were taken from directly across the street using a zoom lens. My ex-husband used that camera set up in front of the balcony to spy on me and photograph my every move. In his mind, I was sure, this surveillance must have made him feel he had control of me. Well, the joke was on him because there was nothing in any of these pictures but routine day-to-day activity. He hadn't caught me with a new boyfriend or doing anything illegal. Those kinds of things just weren't part of my life if that's what he had been anticipating.

Along with all this analysis, my intuition was working overtime. There was something about this package of photographs that I should be able to unravel, and my sixth-sense was telling me that if I did, the whole picture would come crystal clear.

I pulled my journal toward me and flipped the bookmark, turning to the next clean page. I started to write everything since my last entry, which was Lynn's Tarot reading for me yesterday morning. It was just over twenty-four hours ago, but with everything that had happened, it seemed like an eternity. I got everything recorded up to the point of looking at the photos. I jotted down a few notes about the pictures in general, and then wrote specifics about the particular ones that had commanded my attention.

I flipped back through the pages until I found my initial entry about the incidents that started on Friday after Jimmy told me his father was dead. I sat back in the chair and started to read. It took me an hour and I was absolutely astonished that all of this had happened in such a short time.

Most of the earlier incidents seemed separate and distinct, though I knew now they were related in the context of the bigger puzzle. Taken individually, they weren't harmful in any way. As I explained to Jimmy, I initially thought of them as bad practical jokes rather than any threat. There were episodes that were undeniably supernatural, like the spirit messages, but others that were purely physical, like the crushed fire agates. It wasn't until I got to the photos, however, that I understood for the first time I was the victim of some twisted cumulative plot. I was spied on and photographed. My privacy had been violated. With the appearance of the photos, I now anticipated danger.

It puzzled me why my ex-husband took these photos, and why he wanted me to have them. When he wrote my name on the outside of the package, he ensured that all these photos would get to me. That included the one with the two of us that had been defiled. There had to be some perverted reasoning behind it other than an egotistical need for me to know he had spied on me. He was dead, and it didn't matter anymore. He was never going to know what my reaction was. As well as I knew him, I couldn't figure out his reasoning.

One thing kept bothering me, though. Jim couldn't have done all these deeds. Some of the photos had been taken while he was sick, dying, and then dead. I had to presume the physical tasks were beyond his ability, even as a spirit. Then it hit me like a load of bricks.

The only other person who had the opportunity to take these photographs, as far as I knew, was Janice. She lived in the same apartment and could easily have taken them. She could have packaged them up and stashed the envelope with my name on it in Jim's desk drawer, thinking Jimmy would find it and give it to me. Once again, I couldn't understand what her motive could possibly be, especially with the pictures of Jim and Maria so prettily ribboned together.

There wasn't one photo of Janice in the bunch, not even together with Jim. She had no reason to be jealous of me. Jim and I had long been divorced when they got together and we had been friendly before he left me. It made no sense at all. Her disappearance didn't make any sense either. From what I remembered, she didn't seem like the kind of person who would just drop out of sight. If her disappearance was deliberate and planned, there had to be some motive behind it, and that motive could fit in with guaranteeing that I saw the photos. I sighed out loud. Logically, it had to be either Jim or Janice, though neither seemed right to me.

"Wait a minute." I held up the envelope with the photos of me in it. Maybe the two of them together had plotted some weird scheme for whatever crazy purpose they had come up with.

Janice could have done the physical parts. Either or both of them could have used the camera and they both could have put the photo package together. Besides that, it provided answers to a few other questions too. Even though it sounded morbid and crude, Janice could have cut off Jim's finger after he died. Plus, she had the opportunity to put it with the vest on the beach. If the two of them spied on me, they would know that I walked every morning and I would find it there. Janice could also have put that photo of Jim on my computer and on my desk. Of course, that meant that she had been able to sneak into my house. The thought of that made me shudder. If I allowed that the two of them were in this together, then maybe she followed me as well and later gone to Lynn's shop and taken the fire agates and a store bag. It all seemed to fit together.

I shoved the eight-by-tens back into their envelope and put the white envelope with the ribbon into the larger envelope with the pictures of Jim and the boys. I stacked them up with my journal and the defiled photo on top and tucked the bundle under my arm. I was already plotting what my next step was going to be as I put the stack on the counter. I took the scissors from the drawer and cut the photo of me and Jim into strips. I stopped myself as I was about to toss the pieces in the trash basket. Those might turn out to be important. I got a baggie from the cabinet and threw them in there. Zipping it closed, I shoved it in the large envelope on the counter.

If Janice and Jim had cooked up some scheme with me as the victim, I was going to be ready. Wherever she was hiding, she wasn't going to catch me unaware. I would be waiting and watching. And I was going to make sure that I had put it on record so that others were aware of what was going on and could intervene if it became necessary. I would make sure that nobody could hold me responsible for whatever was about to happen.

I picked up my cell phone off the counter to make the call. Then I noticed the little exclamation point on the screen that told me I had an unread message, the one I had ignored earlier after I texted Jimmy. I tapped the icon and the message came up on the screen.

"Your fault. You'll be sorry."

"Well, we'll just see about that, won't we," I sputtered at the message in a snarky tone. This time I wasn't afraid but I certainly was angry. I clicked off the message and looked at the phone number it was sent from. It had a Rhode Island area code. If this was Janice, she had just made her first real mistake. Ghosts don't send text messages. The phone number could be traced, and the location she texted from might be traceable too. For the first time, I was beginning to feel like there would be an end to this, and I was finally in control of the outcome.

CHAPTER TWENTY-FOUR

"Gulfside Police Department, this is Officer Scott." The young man's voice answered before the first ring ended. "Your call is being recorded. How can I help you?"

"I'd like to speak to Detective John Brandon, please." I kept my voice calm but my heart beat like I ran a marathon.

"He's not in the building at this time, but I can take a message and have him get back to you as soon as he is available."

"Yes, that would be good. My name is Sharon Coady. I spoke with him earlier today. Could you please have him call me as soon as possible? I have some important information that I think he'd be interested in regarding the case we discussed."

"I have the number you're calling from here on caller ID," the officer said. "Is that the number where you would like to have Detective Brandon return your call?"

"Yes, that's it."

"I'll relay your message and have him get back to you," he said. "Have a good evening, ma'am."

"Thank you."

Now I just had to wait for him to call back. I picked up my journal again to jot down these theories I was coming up with. It might help me clarify my thoughts for when I had to explain them to the detective. Although it all seemed logical while I was thinking about it, it might be a different story once I had to say it out loud to another person. Ten minutes later the phone rang, not the police department number but it was local.

"Hello."

"Good evening, Ms. Coady." Detective Brandon spoke with his usual matter-of-fact tone. "I got a message to call you."

"Yes, thanks for getting back to me so quickly," I said. "I hope I'm not interrupting anything important."

"I don't think you would have called unless what you had to tell me was important, Ms. Coady. Now, what can I do for you?" His tone seemed genuine and that was encouraging.

"I found a package of photographs at my ex-husband's apartment. It was in his desk and had my name on it. I thought you might want to take a look at them."

"I see," he said. "Is that all, just photographs?"

"Well, yes." I had to make him understand what an issue it was. "It seems as if I was being watched, spied on. I thought they might give you some clues about Janice's disappearance." I hesitated. "And... and they made me feel very uncomfortable."

"All right." A slight pause. "It's ten minutes past six. I can come by in about an hour and take a look at them if that's not an inconvenience for you."

"That would be fine," I said. "Oh, I almost forgot. I got a text message that might be from Janice."

"Oh, really?" A spark of interest.

"Yes, I can explain when you get here," I said, feeling reassured.

"Good. I'll see you in about an hour." With that he clicked off.

An hour to fill up. I made a cup of tea and sat back down with my journal. Writing it all down was my practice run. Hopefully, I'd have the story in some kind of order before the detective got here. I certainly didn't want to look like a fool. I was just about finished when there was a knock at the front door.

I peeked out behind the curtain at the side window and breathed a sigh of relief. I unlocked the door and stood aside to let Detective Brandon come in.

"Hello, Detective. Thanks for taking the time to come over."

"Good evening, Ms. Coady," he said in his usual formal manner. "I'm eager to see these photographs and the text message."

Apparently, he was still on duty as he wore the same uniform of gray slacks and light blue shirt that he had both times I had seen him previously. At least I didn't drag him out of his house on a night off.

"Have a seat." I waved him toward the living room. "I'll get them. Would you like a cup of coffee or tea? Or some water?"

"Thank you, tea would be nice." He sat on the sofa in front of the coffee table.

"It's herbal." I called from the kitchen as I filled the kettle. "No caffeine, but it's refreshing. It's a blend I make myself." I set up the mugs while the water heated, then picked up the stack of envelopes and carried them into the living room. "This very large one had all the photos and other envelopes inside it," I said as I placed them on the coffee table. "Most of them were loose family pictures of my ex-husband and his sons when they were kids. They're in there. This white one with the ribbon has a few photos of my ex and his former girlfriend." I pointed at the pile on the table in front of him. "And this manila envelope had the photos taken of me from across the street."

The kettle whistled as I spoke the last word, as if for emphasis. "I'll go get the tea. Feel free to take a look."

I started toward the kitchen while he lifted the largest envelope by the corner between his index finger and thumb and held it up toward the light to inspect it. It was heavy, full of the boys' photos and he put it back down on the table in short order. He held up the other two envelopes in the same way, turning them around to view all sides. He put the white envelope down when I returned with the two mugs of tea.

"Sugar or milk?"

"No, thanks. I drink it straight." He lifted the mug and took a careful sip of the steaming liquid. "That's pretty good."

"Thanks," I said. "I like to make my own blends for different purposes. This one is supposed to quiet your mind and help you focus on the task at hand. I felt like I needed that tonight."

"It can't hurt," he said with the slightest hint of a grin. "Let's see what we've got here."

He pulled a pair of blue vinyl gloves out of a pouch he had hung on his belt and drew them on before emptying the large envelope onto the table. The photos fell into a compact pile. I watched silently while he seemed to randomly pick up one after another, looking at each one intently on both sides and from different angles and distances. He looked at six different photos this way and seemed satisfied that he had seen enough of those.

"These all seem to be similar, of your ex-husband and his kids. Is that right?" he asked.

"Yes." I decided to let him see the other one despite how offensive it was. "There was one more in that lot." I retrieved the baggie from the kitchen and handed it to him without a word.

He peered at the contents for a few seconds, then looked at me but said nothing as he popped open the zipper. The cut-up scraps of photo poured out into his hand. He turned them all over to the picture side and began to lay them together on the table, fitting the pieces to-gether like a puzzle.

"You and your ex-husband, I presume." He looked at me. "Was it cut up in the package or did you do that?"

"I did it, but not because of the picture. I would have thrown it back in the pile for my stepson to have." I hesitated. "It was because of what was written on the back. You can flip over the pieces and see for yourself." I hated to even think of that word and I certainly wasn't going to say it out loud.

He did as I suggested and then let out a low whistle. "Somebody didn't like you, I'd say." He must have noticed how uncomfortable it made me as he scooped the pieces up quickly and put them back in the bag. "You said it was the only picture of you and your ex in the batch. Was there anything written on the back of any of the others?"

"No, only that one." I relaxed a bit now that it was out of sight again.

"Okay, let's see what else we have here." He placed all the photos on the table back in the manila and picked up the white envelope. He gave the end of the ribbon a hard tug. The flap flipped open, revealing the stack of photos inside. He carefully grabbed one corner of the bunch between his thumb and index finger and pulled them from the envelope. Again, he held the photos up toward the light, turning them so he could view the stack from different angles. Then he looked at each photo, lifting it by the edges in one hand and turning it over to look at the back before placing them on the table face down so they would stay in order.

"I recognize the man as your ex-husband. Who's the woman?" he asked as he put the last one down.

"That was his former girlfriend, the woman he cheated on me with and left me for." I answered matter-of-factly and was happy to note there were no pangs of emotion as I said it.

"Oh, really?" He sounded surprised. As he picked up the stack of photos, he turned them over and looked at the top picture again. "Do you have any idea when these were taken?"

"Not really," I said. "Sometime between when he left me, twelve years ago, and when he left her, which would be about three years ago."

"That's good enough," he said and looked down at the top photo again. It was one of them in their biker gear. "Interesting." He put them back in the envelope and tied it up again with the ribbon. Taking a sip of tea, he appeared to be absorbed by what he had just seen, his brow furrowed and his lips set in a straight line. He stood and pulled his notepad and pen out of his pocket. "Excuse me a minute," he said. "I'm going to write down a few notes, if you don't mind."

"No, go ahead," I said. "Take your time." I sipped my tea and patiently waited for him to finish.

"What was the woman's name?" he asked as he continued writing.

"Maria Benevides." I offered. "She was married four times, I think, and that was the name of her last husband. I don't know any of her previous names."

"Thanks." He put the pad and pen down on the end of the coffee table, apart from the collection of photos, and picked up the last envelope. He opened the flap and slowly drew out the 8 x 10 photos. Holding the stack by the edges, he studied each one, and slid it to the bottom when he was done. He said nothing as he worked his way through all twenty of them, taking time with each photo. Finally, he put them down on the table and looked at me.

"Ms. Coady, why do I have a hunch there's more going on here than you've been willing to tell me?"

"Yes." I sighed. "A lot of things happened that you don't know about. I guess maybe it's time for me to tell you all of it." I hesitated as I felt energy build up inside me. "Excuse me for a minute."

I rushed to the bathroom and pushed the door shut behind me. The whole inside of my body vibrated with a frenzied pulse. My hands trembled and my breath came in short bursts. I glared at myself in the mirror and forced my body back under control, scowling at my reflection while taking several deep slow breaths. In two minutes, I was calm again. It wasn't often I had these energy bursts, and I was never sure what might trigger them. This time, the thought of revealing my psychic abilities to the detective was probably the catalyst. I splashed some cold water on my face and dried it. I was as ready as I ever could be to face him again.

"Sorry." I apologized in a more normal tone of voice. "It's been a very difficult few days, and I've managed it mostly on my own. It's reassuring you're here and willing to listen to me."

The blue gloves were crumpled in a ball on the coffee table, and the detective was writing in his notebook. He stared me right in the eye with an expression that dared me to contradict him. "Why don't you start from the beginning and tell me the whole story. We'll figure out where to go from there."

I nodded, took a sip of my tea and a deep breath. "Detective Brandon, I just want you to know something. I'm a psychic, and there are some things that are... well... I'll just say not of this world. You probably won't believe me even if I tell you."

He opened his mouth to speak, and I held up my hand.

"I'll tell you the events that I know you'll believe and leave it at that. I can handle the psychic stuff myself."

"All right then," he said with a smirk as he sat back on the couch. "Go ahead."

I started at the beginning, the day when I met Jimmy at The Jolly Pelican and he told me his father was dying. Brandon let me speak without interruption as I recounted every detail, fresh in my memory from my journal. He scribbled a few notes on his pad as I talked. True to my word, though, I didn't mention anything of the psychic encounters.

Every now and then, I'd stop to see his reaction, but he waved his hand and encouraged me to continue. He nodded when I explained the theory I had come up with that Jim and Janice were in this together, but said nothing as the story went on. Lastly, I told him of the text message that had prompted my call to him tonight.

I exhaled loudly. "I think that's everything," I said as I sat back to wait for his response.

"That's quite a story." He tapped his pen on his chin. "You should have called me sooner."

CHAPTER TWENTY-FIVE

The detective smiled. "You might as well put the kettle on. I think we both could use another cup of tea." He got up and picked up the mugs from the table. "I have a feeling we're going to be here for a while longer." He carried them into the kitchen and set them on the counter as I filled the kettle. I saw him glance at his watch.

"I'm going to make a phone call while you're doing that." He pulled his cell phone out of his pocket and strode back into the living room.

I tried to hear what he was saying while I waited for the water to boil but his voice was too low for me to make anything out. I put the tea in the mugs and took a box of whole grain crackers out of the cupboard, emptying its contents into a bowl. It was a minute before nine by the kitchen clock. When the kettle whistled, I poured the water and turned to see if the detective was off the phone. He hung up, so I brought the mugs and crackers over and set them on the coffee table.

"You've been through quite a bit in the last few days." He slipped back into his matter-of-fact police voice. If he had any opinion about the supernatural piece, he kept it to himself. "Do you still have the photo of the Rhode Island license plate? I'll see if I can track down any other information."

"It's right here."

The picture was the most recent in my phone gallery, and I showed it to him. He copied down the plate number in his notepad.

"The theory about your ex-husband and Ms. Crawford is interesting," he said when he was done. "I want to spend some time going over these photos with you. Do you have a pair of gloves?" he asked.

I guessed I must have looked bewildered by the question.

"Any kind of gloves—vinyl, cloth, leather—so you can handle the photographs without getting any fingerprints on them."

"Oh, yes," I said, understanding now what he wanted. "I have a few pairs of cotton gloves that I use for gardening."

He nodded. "Those would work fine. Get a pair for yourself to use."

"I handled the photos when I looked at them. Won't my prints be on them already?"

"Yes, some. But if there are other prints on them, we don't want to smudge them."

I went out on the patio to the little covered box where I kept my gardening tools. I dug around a bit and found the bag of gloves I kept in there. There was a new pair in the bag and I grabbed those and headed back inside. The detective had put on another pair of gloves and stood in front of the kitchen counter laying out the photos. He looked up at me as I came back in and proceeded to place the last three on the counter top.

"We're both going to study these photos for anything that might give us a clue to determine the date or time they were taken," he said. "Be looking for anything you see that doesn't belong in the scene or might be a one-time occurrence. Mention everything, no matter how silly or insignificant it might seem. Let me decide." He looked directly at me. "Got it?"

"Yes, I understand." I flipped on the light over the sink to make it easier to see.

"Good." He thought for a minute. "If you have a pen and paper handy, you can jot down what catches your attention. Then we can talk about each one when we're done. It's better not to break your concentration, and if we talk about each item as we see it, we'll never get finished."

"That makes sense." I went to my desk and grabbed a pad and a pen. "Ready."

"Okay. You start at that end and I'll start down here," he instructed. "You can use a number for each picture, starting with one for that one over there on top at the end. The one below it will be two and the one next to it will be three and below that is four and so on. Got it?"

I nodded.

"Let's get started then." He bent over to study the photos at the far end from me.

I looked at the photo that was number one. It was a picture of me sitting in my car in the driveway. I squinted and looked more closely. I could just make out through the glare from the window that I was looking over my shoulder toward the back window. Interesting. I must have been backing out of the driveway. I wrote the number one on the pad and made a note about my observation with the comment, *When did I go out? To Lynn's shop?* I glanced over at the detective. He was staring intently at the photo in front of him.

I looked at the next photo. In this one I was getting mail from the mailbox. I didn't see anything in the picture that seemed out of the ordinary. If I considered the setting, however, I might be able to figure out the day and maybe the time. My mail usually got delivered late morning about eleven. I realized I hadn't checked the mailbox today and there would have been no mail yesterday on Sunday. So that meant it was sometime Saturday or before. Not much to go on but I wrote it on the pad anyway.

Photo three was of me unlocking the front door with my back to the camera. I didn't see anything special at first, but I got a sense there was something in this one. I squinted and stared intently, starting at the upper left corner and moving across the picture to the end and then dropping down an inch or so and repeating the process. It took a while but as I shifted farther down the sheet, the feeling that there was something there got stronger. Then I saw it, the image camouflaged in the bright sunlight against the wall of the house. It was the plain cardboard box that had my snow globe in it. I sucked in my breath when I saw it. So much had happened over the past few days that I had to think hard about when I found it. Finally, I realized it was Saturday afternoon when I got back from the crystal store. Excited that I had been able to figure this out, I quickly scribbled a note on my pad and then moved on to study the next photograph.

I peeked at the detective and saw him writing too. He must have sensed that I was looking at him, because he looked up at me and gave me a nod before going right back to the task at hand. I slid over to look at the next pictures. As we looked at the photos, we were working our way closer together toward the center of the counter. There was nothing unusual or particular about the next couple of photos and I started to feel frustrated. I hoped I hadn't missed something important.

Finally, the detective and I were standing next to each other. I glanced down at my next target, photo number eight. Immediately, my eyes focused in near the bottom of the picture. There on the step just to the left of the front door was the little paper bag from Lynn's crystal shop. I wanted to clap my hands for joy, but I managed to restrain myself. I knew exactly when that photo was taken. I remembered Lynn left at 11:15

because she had looked at the time and said that she had to get to the shop to open by noon. Detective Brandon had arrived at about noon just a few minutes after I found the bag outside the door. Jimmy had called in between to tell me Janice was missing, and I could check the specific time he called on my phone. I furiously wrote all that down on my pad.

When I finished writing, I looked up to see Detective Brandon watching me.

"You must have found something interesting by the look of all those notes," he remarked with a grin.

"I think so," I said. "Do you want me to tell you now?"

"No, hold on a minute," he said. "What was the last picture you looked at?"

"That one, number eight." I pointed to the photo.

"Good," he said. "I got through number nine." He walked back to the end of the counter and began to pick up the photos, being careful to place them back in the correct order.

I stepped back when he got to where I was standing. His hand brushed mine, and I felt that powerful energy pass between us again as I had when I shook his hand. He glanced at me briefly but then turned back to what he was doing. I was glad I had decided to call him and relieved to know that he was taking this seriously. His presence gave me some increased sense of security.

He turned back to me when he was done. "Let's go sit down and we can compare notes," he said. "I have a couple of questions for you."

As we sat back down on the couch, he put the photos down on the table. "Okay," he said, "You go first. What did you find?"

"Well, from what I can tell, these are in chronological order. I think numbers one through eight were all taken between Saturday afternoon and today just before noon." I looked at him for some acknowledgement that I was on the right track. "Number eight had to be taken only minutes before you arrived this morning." I went through the pile, carefully placing each photo face down and on top of the preceding one to keep them in order. When I came to the eighth one, I pointed to the shopping bag on the ground next to the door. "Somebody left this bag, and I found it only a few minutes before you got here. There was a knock and, since it was just about the time you said you were going to be here, I thought it was you. But when I opened the door, nobody was there and this bag was on the step."

"Good," he said as he nodded at me. "So, we'll go on the assumption that the photos were stacked in chronological order according to the time they were taken." He looked at his notes. "Number ten was a picture of you opening the front door to let me in, so that was about noon. Right?"

"Yes." I nodded. "But there's an issue with the timing," I said with a sigh. "Jim died Friday close to four in the morning, Janice disappeared early Sunday morning, and I was in Jim's apartment for several hours Sunday afternoon. If these were taken between Saturday afternoon and today at noon, neither of them were around to take the pictures."

"Good point." He wrote a quick note. "There's not much else here. Just shots of your front door." He sifted through the remainder. "I'm going to take them with me, along with your notes, if you don't mind. We might be able to find some fingerprints." He put the photographs back in order and put them back in the envelope. "Do you have a bag or something I can put these in?" he asked as he got all the envelopes together.

"Sure," I said as I started toward the kitchen.

He looked at his watch. "It's late, and I'd better get going. I'll get started working through all of this early in the morning. I might need to call you during the day if I have any additional questions. I'm also going to want to come by and collect as much of the evidence from the other incidents as possible that you might still have here at the house, if you haven't already thrown it away."

"That's fine," I said. "I don't have any plans for tomorrow."

"Good. Can I see the text message you got this morning?"

"Oh, sure." I went to the desk and picked up my phone, clicking onto the screen with the message. "I almost forgot." I handed him the phone. He already had his notepad open again and I watched as he copied down the message and the number.

"Thanks. And thank you for opening up with all the details of what's been going on." He handed me the phone. "Just so you know, I'll have a police cruiser swing by here on regular patrol until we resolve this. That's who I was on the phone with earlier, to notify dispatch."

"Thank you, Detective. I appreciate that." I walked with him to the door.

"Make sure to lock all your doors and windows," he said. "I'll be in touch with you in the morning." He walked outside and then turned to look at me. "And try not to worry. We'll figure this out, and you'll be fine. Good night, Ms. Coady."

"Good night." I called after him as I shut the door. I locked it, did the same at the back door and checked every window to make sure they were closed and locked. I felt like a prisoner in my own house. I reminded myself that this would all be over soon. Detective Brandon was now my partner, and we'd figure this out together.

I suddenly felt exhausted as the adrenaline that had pumped through me all day finally drained from my body. I looked at the clock. Midnight. I really needed to sleep, and I yawned as I headed for the bed.

CHAPTER TWENTY-SIX

My bedroom was gray when I opened my eyes, not the cheerful early morning sunshine I was used to. I rolled over and saw 7:56 on the clock. I felt a little lethargic after going to bed at midnight, and it took a few minutes to motivate myself as bits of the conversation with the detective the night before rattled through my sleepy head.

I yawned as I got up and padded over to the window. The shade was down, and I pulled the cord to raise it half-way. When I looked out, a police car drove by the house which was reassuring. The detective had kept his word.

Gray clouds moved swiftly across the sky. It looked like it would rain later. I grabbed my shorts and a tank top. A walk would clear my head, and a cloudy sky wasn't going to keep me from that. I needed to process the conversation with Detective Brandon from the previous night. I also wanted to call Jimmy while it was still early. I knew he'd be up, and I had to ask what might be a very significant question that had popped into my head just before I fell asleep. I didn't know why I hadn't thought of it before.

I walked into the kitchen to get my phone from the counter where I always plugged it into the charger at night. The charger cord was there but my phone wasn't attached to it. I looked around and didn't see it anywhere nearby. Then I remembered that I showed the detective the text message. It was still on the coffee table in the living room. The battery was only at ten per cent so it needed to charge right away. I couldn't take the chance of a dead battery. Not today. I'd call Jimmy later. I took the phone over to the counter and hooked it up to the charger cord.

I filled the coffee pot and turned on the switch. It would be done brewing by the time I returned. I stepped outside and was about to close the back door when the phone rang. I ran back inside and looked at the screen. It was Jimmy. I pulled the charger plug out of the phone so I could talk.

"You must have been reading my mind," I said. "I was going to call you in a few minutes."

"Everything all right?" There was a note of uneasiness in his voice.

"Yeah, I guess so," I said. "The police detective was here last night and I told him everything that's been going on. The package of photos in your Dad's desk was the last straw and I had to call him. I had no choice."

"Why? What was in it?" Now he sounded worried.

"There was another manila envelope inside the big one. It had eight-by-ten blow-ups of me in it, taken from across the street. I was being photographed and spied on."

"What? That's crazy. Do you think it was Dad?"

"I don't know, Jimmy," I said. I wasn't going into the whole thing with him now on the phone. "But it was scary enough that I called the detective. He came by and looked at them. Then I told him the whole story that I told you, except for the ghost parts, right up to the snake in the pizza when you were here."

"What did he say?" His voice betrayed the increasing level of his concern.

"He took it very seriously." I tried to reassure him. "He's going to be checking into all of it. He even has cruisers patrolling by the house to keep an eye on things. So, you don't have to worry so much. They're watching out for me."

"Well, that makes me feel a little better." His voice relaxed as relief took over. "Anyway, I called to tell you my two o'clock flight back to Florida is delayed. Apparently, you're going to have severe thunder storms rolling through the area, and they're holding all flights until it passes. I'm not sure what time I'll get there."

"I haven't checked the weather report but the sky's gray and overcast right now." I looked out the window and thought the clouds seemed a little darker. "It looks like it might storm. Oh, before I forget, I need to ask you something too. I thought of it last night."

"What's that?" he asked.

"What does Janice look like? I haven't seen her in years."

"Why? Do you think you might have seen her?"

"I don't know," I said slowly. "But I woke up wondering if she might have been the woman in the bar the other night."

"No, definitely not. Not from the way you described that woman to me," he said. "Janice is on the heavy side and looks husky. Her face is round and chubby. She does have long gray hair that she wears pulled back in a ponytail, but it's always neat. She wears bifocals and can't see a thing without them. She usually wears jeans and a t-shirt. You'd probably describe her as tough looking."

"Right, that doesn't sound anything like the woman I saw." I said thoughtfully. "Oh, well, it was worth a shot. I can rule her out."

"Okay. Well, I've got to go. Dad's burial service is at nine this morning at the Veteran's Cemetery, and I've got to pick up my friend on the way." He paused. "Please, take care of yourself. I don't want to lose you too."

"Don't worry about me. I'm going to be fine," I said. "Call me later and let me know what's going on with your flight when you find out. Love you."

"I will. Love you too. Talk to you later."

I went to my desk and pushed the power button on the computer. I wanted to check the weather to get a better idea of what to expect. Jimmy's description sounded terrible. I poured a cup of coffee while it was loading, and the NOAA national map was on the screen when I returned. I typed in my zip code for the local weather.

The screen switched to a map of Florida with a sweeping radar arm centered around Orlando. A massive area of bright yellow covered most of the state, surrounding a long strip of bright orange that hovered over a big section of the west coast, from Crystal River in the north near the bend of the panhandle to Marco Island in the south, not far from the western tip of the state. Tampa Bay, with Gulfside on the coast, was at the very center of a circle of intense red. According to the color key this meant moderate risk of thunder storms with widespread and severe storms likely. I clicked again for the forecast in text. The whole Tampa Bay area was under a severe storm warning that had started at six this morning and would last until midnight.

I had to make sure everything outside was secure and bring in whatever might blow around. I shut down the computer and finished the last swallow of coffee as I headed for the kitchen. No walk for me this morning, I decided. Checking the clock, I saw it was just after nine.

I opened the back slider and stepped out onto the patio. The usual morning breeze had freshened into a light wind, and the sky was darker than it had been earlier. It was muggy, and I could tell the humidity was rising. I walked over the boardwalk to the beach and down to the water's edge. Sand blew around a little bit and whisked against my ankles as I walked. The waves were already starting to kick up, and there were whitecaps breaking out in the Gulf. Black clouds were visible near the horizon to the west with what looked like a dark wall of rain that reached down to the water.

"They're not kidding," I said when I noticed the dark wall moving closer across the water. "I'd better get to work."

Outside, I checked the grotto first. I grabbed the singed labradorite crystal I had left on the table and stuck it in my pocket. As I looked around at the numerous potted plants, I decided they would probably be safer if I left them in the grotto. The storm was coming in from the west, and the trees and bushes in the ground should offer enough protection from the wind. The pots might get flooded from the rain, but it wouldn't hurt the plants, since they all had good drainage. Some extra water would probably be good for them anyway. I rearranged the pots around the largest and fullest bushes to give them what I thought would be the maximum protection from the wind. I pushed the table up against the bushes on one side and laid the chairs down on the ground next to it. That was all I needed to do there.

The patio was a different story since it was completely open to the beach with nothing to block the wind and rain. I ran in the house, grabbed a couple of small trash bags from the cupboard and jogged back outside. I surveyed the patio and picked up all the loose odds and ends that were laying around. A pair of gardening gloves, a few loose shells and pieces of driftwood, two wind chimes, a bird feeder, the grill utensils, and a dozen other small incidentals went into the bags until the patio was cleared of anything loose that might get thrown around in the wind. I brought the bags in the house and stashed them on the kitchen floor in the corner.

Back on the patio, the wind felt stronger already. The umbrella flapped around the patio table and looked like it was ready to take flight. I leaned it against the wall at the back of the house. The outside trash barrel went next to the umbrella. Then I pulled each of the metal-framed mesh chairs from under the table and stacked them together. I carried the stack over to the house and laid them down so the chair backs were on the ground. That should give them enough weight to prevent them from flying around and keep them out of the way of the sliding door just in case. The patio table had a glass top. It wasn't very heavy but it was big and wide enough that I couldn't carry it easily by myself. I needed to think about what to do with it.

In the meantime, I started to move potted plants into the grotto. I might as well put them all together in there. It was the most protected spot, and I was sure they'd be fine. When I got all the plants situated, I came back onto the patio and looked at the table. That could go in the grotto too. It seemed to be the safest place and having everything stored in there together would offer less free space for the wind to blow around and knock things over. It seemed to make sense so I dragged the table across the patio and pushed it up against the bushes on the other side across from the grotto table.

With all the furniture and potted plants taken care of, I headed for the back door. I carried the umbrella into the house and leaned it against the wall and then dragged the trash barrel inside. I shut the slider and looked out through the glass. The patio looked naked and abandoned. I could see partway into one side of the grotto, and everything appeared secure there. It was the best I could do, and I felt it all was as safe as I could make it. I locked the slider and turned away from the glass.

It was now past noon. I felt like I was ready for the storm though I wasn't too worried about it. I had been through quite a few storms since I had moved to Gulfside, several big thunderstorms and a couple of hurricanes. For some reason this area was usually grazed by severe weather but seldom suffered a direct blow-out hit. That wasn't to say it couldn't happen. Thunderstorms were not unusual here, especially in the summer heat, with the accompanying lightning, rain, and winds coming right in off the Gulf. They generally didn't last very long, no more than an hour or two with the peak of the storm passing by us pretty quickly. I had no reason to believe this one would be much different.

My stomach growled. I was hungry since I had done all that work and hadn't eaten anything this morning. I checked what was in the fridge. There was some left-over vegetable soup which would be good with a grilled cheese. I turned on the radio while I heated the soup and cooked the sandwich.

"A severe thunderstorm warning is in effect for Tampa Bay and its vicinity now through midnight. These storms will likely bring heavy rains and winds with gusts up to sixty miles per hour. Lightning strikes are expected. Street flooding is likely. Residents are urged to stay off the roads and remain inside for the duration of the storm. Power outages are possible and expected, especially along the coast where the winds will be strongest. Residents should be prepared with alternative lighting and power sources. Updates will be provided throughout the afternoon. Now back to our regular program."

Soft rock music filled the air as I finished making lunch. I brought it all into the living room and set it on the coffee table. Back to the refrigerator to grab a bottle of water, and I picked up the book I was reading from the end table near my desk. I settled in on the couch to eat and read. At some level of consciousness, I was aware of the wind getting stronger outside but I was engrossed in my book and paid no mind to it. Finally, after an hour or so, I realized the room had grown dark, and I was squinting to see the print on the pages.

I went over to the front door and opened it to look outside. A blast of wind grabbed the door and slammed it back against the wall before I could stop it. The sky was that sickly storm-gray color mottled with yellow and socked in with dense churning clouds. The air felt thick and electric making the hairs on my arms stand straight up and the smell of ozone zinged in my nose. The palms across the street were waving wildly in the wind. Gusts whipped my hair around my face. I could feel each blow thrust against my body as I struggled to keep my balance. I wrestled with the door and finally managed to slam it shut. I locked it and walked back to the living room. I switched on the lamp near the couch and blew out a long breath.

"They weren't kidding. It's going to be a rough one."

I settled down on the couch and picked up my book again.

CHAPTER TWENTY-SEVEN

I screeched and jumped up off the couch, jolted awake by a house-rattling crack of thunder. The book on my lap dropped to the floor. I must have fallen asleep while I was reading. The room was dark but infused with an eerie luminescence. I looked around and realized the salt lamp wasn't lit. I picked the book up and set it on the coffee table next to the empty dishes from my lunch. Then I stood still and listened.

The symphony of the storm had begun the first movement. Wind whistled around the roof with only short breaks between gusts. The windows rattled in a weird rhythm. I heard a faint *plink plink,* which I slowly realized was the sound of raindrops flicked against the window. The rain had just begun and, according to the forecast, would get much heavier. I heard a scraping sound coming from outside the back slider that I couldn't identify over the noise of the wind.

The salt lamp wouldn't turn back on. I had no idea if I had any spare bulbs around. I took my dirty dishes into the kitchen and placed them in the sink, then turned on the radio to get a weather update. Nothing. Out of habit, I tried a couple more times and, when I got no response, checked to see that it was plugged in. It was.

The power must be out already. I went to the cabinet to get a few candles. Sometimes I used them in my readings or meditations, so I kept them in a handy spot. A battery-operated lantern was stored in the spare bedroom closet, and I hoped the battery was still good. I didn't think to check it earlier when I battened down the patio. I got it out of the closet and clicked the knob to ON. A low bluish light broke through the dusky gloom.

I placed the lantern on the end table next to my desk and twisted the knob to turn the light up brighter. The shadows receded to the edges of the room. I walked over to the slider and peered out. Everything looked like it was holding up against the wind. The tops of the palms and branches of the bushes swayed frantically, but through the narrow opening, the plants and furniture inside the grotto seemed secure. I didn't see anything that could have made the scraping noise though. Looking farther out toward the beach, I saw the sand swirl and arch high into the air, like I was viewing the scene through a veil. The surf was high. Waves broke far from the beach and sprayed grayish-green water and white foam in their wake. Dark clouds churned and seethed as they scuttled across the sky. I shivered, reminded of my ominous vision. I felt the energy build as the storm's strength accelerated.

I watched the storm maneuver around the beach for a few more minutes then turned away from the door. A bright flash of lightening up the whole house, followed by another crash of thunder, this time much louder. The storm was getting closer. There wasn't much I could do with no power except somehow keep myself occupied until it was over. The battery-operated clock on the kitchen wall said 3:17, but it looked more like late evening.

I was surprised I hadn't heard anything from Jimmy yet. The service must have been over hours ago. I spotted my phone on the table and picked it up to check and see if maybe he had texted and I missed the alert. The phone was off, and it wouldn't turn on. It took me a minute before I remembered that the battery had been low this morning when I got up and I unplugged it when I talked to Jimmy. I obviously forgot to plug it back in, and now the phone was dead. There wasn't any alternate charging source except to start the car and plug it in there. I wasn't going out in the storm to sit in a running car for the hour or more it would take to recharge so I was stuck with a dead phone until the power came back on. If a problem arose, I could certainly run out to the car and use the phone from there while it was plugged into the charger. I didn't anticipate any emergency, but I still felt vulnerable being essentially cut off from the rest of the world.

"The storm isn't going to last forever," I said emphatically to the darkened room with my hands on my hips. I told myself that maybe the clouds would clear in time to watch the sunset from the beach.

The light from the lantern was bright enough for me to read so I picked up my laptop from the desk and settled down on the couch. Since I kept it plugged in when working from my desk, it had a fully charged battery. This would keep me occupied for a while and I knew exactly what I wanted to do. While the computer booted up, I got my old note-book from my desk drawer. When I worked as a social worker in Rhode Island, I had access to a number of government websites which were off-limits to the average person because of privacy and confidentiality laws. This notebook contained a list of those and all my passwords. I wasn't sure if my access to all of them continued after I retired, but it was worth a try. My plan was to track down Isabella Santos, the name listed as the owner of the pickup truck across the street when I searched the Rhode Island vehicle registration website. If my hunch was correct, she was the woman who lived in the apartment below Jim, and was somehow connected to Jim's former girlfriend Maria.

After an hour, I got up to stretch and grab a pen and paper from my desk. Most of the websites no longer accepted my password, but I found some that still allowed me access, including the Department of Vital Records. My search gave me one death record for a woman with that name. She died only few months ago, and I found her obituary on a funeral home site.

That one document solved the mystery. Isabel Santos was 85, single and lived in Providence until her death. Her survivors were a sister, Ana Gauthier, and a niece who was her caretaker, Maria Benevides. The sister's name was on the list of people who lived in Jim's building. The residents of Apartment 3, directly below Jim, were Peter and Ana Gauthier. It had to be the same Maria, not a coincidence. Now I knew for sure she was the one who stalked and harassed me over the past week. I didn't have a clue what her motive was, or her ultimate goal, but it wasn't likely to be a happy reunion.

The battery in the laptop was still half full. I couldn't call Detective Brandon on a dead phone, but I could send him an email. I looked up the Gulfside Police Department but there was only a general email address. I typed "For Detective Brandon" in the subject line. I kept the message brief and included only the facts and one line about my discovery of Maria's identity and her part in the week's incidents. I clicked the send button and hoped the note would find its way to him.

I wandered around the house as I thought about Maria's potential motives, looking out of the windows in each room. The rain poured down harder now and blurred my view. I could barely make out the tall palms across the street bent over in the wind as they bobbed up and down with each gust. The rain water overflowed the storm drains, and the road had started to flood. I saw one car drive by as I watched through the bedroom window. Although the driver was going no more than ten miles an hour, the tires sent up a two-foot-tall wake behind them as the car rolled down the water-covered street.

The rain was mesmerizing as I stared out the bedroom window. Suddenly, a blinding flash of lightning blazed outside the window and pierced through my trance followed almost immediately by an ear-splitting crack of thunder. When it ended, big black spots clouded my vision. I closed my eyes to clear the spots but instead an image appeared behind my lids. A shadow more than an image, really, with the wavering form of a human figure. I squeezed my eyes to keep them shut but try as I might, I couldn't make out any details. All I could see was the vague shape of the shadow figure, blackness burned into the reddish-orange on the inside of my eyelids. It appeared to have its back to me, but that's all I could tell. There was no perspective and no distinct outline as the figure undulated before me.

Abruptly the shaded image pivoted and looked at me straight on as it began to grow larger and larger in my mind's eye. All I could see in the place where there should have been a face was darkness. But it wasn't a static darkness. It churned and slithered like the dark storm clouds as they swept across the waters of the Gulf directly toward me. I wasn't physically able to open my eyes now even if I wanted to. Just as the dark face was about to slam into mine, it burst into a thousand snakes writhing around me in my vision. I felt their scaly skin scrape against my skin and heard their hissing in my ears as they wound their wriggling bodies around my head.

I screamed as my eyes shot open. I ran back into the living room, panting and gasping for breath. My legs were jelly as my whole body gave in to spasm after spasm. I held on to the back of the couch as I choked and coughed, trying to catch my breath and my balance. The shadow figure was gone, but I couldn't shake the residual terror of the vision. I quivered inside and out and couldn't stop.

Slowly, as minutes passed, I regained my composure. The coughing spasms eased and my breath was less labored. It took a few minutes before I felt steady enough to let go of the couch and stand on my own. I didn't know who or what the figure in the vision was, but one thing was certain. It was a negative entity with sinister intentions, and for those few seconds of the vision, it had a death grip on me. I had never encountered a being so dark in all my years of work in the spiritual realm. Not that I didn't know they existed, but in the past, I had always been careful to ground and protect myself against their entry into my psychic interactions, and I managed to keep them at bay. This one caught me with my guard down, emboldened and made more powerful, no doubt, by the intense and potent energy of the storm. Energy in its pure form was always neutral, so how it would be used depended on the force manipulating it. This force had highjacked the storm's energy for its own hostile purpose.

I wondered if I might be able to use this same principal to my own advantage. Considering everything that occurred over the past few days, I had to believe this negative spirit had targeted me for a particular reason and was involved in some way with all that had happened. Since negative entities of all kinds prey on the living, a psychic shouldn't make assumptions about their nature or identity. However, I was prepared to face the fact that this dreadful spirit might very well be Jim or some residual left by his passing. In fact, if I had to bet on it, I would say it was. We had our battles when we were married, but none of those were going to even come close to the magnitude of this one.

No matter the intent, I couldn't let it beat me. I had to retain control of my own space and aura, or I would always be vulnerable to its will, to the point that I might never be able to work with positive spirits again for fear of subjecting them to its power. I had to try to use the potent energy of the storm to root out this negative entity and either defeat it or send it to the far reaches of the universe where it could do no more harm.

I sat on the couch to think seriously about what I was about to take on and exactly how I planned to do it. I had never performed any ritual of this kind before. I never had any reason to, but I understood the basics. I had to be absolutely sure of myself and my methods. Otherwise, I could be in grave danger. The storm and its energy were going to be my primary weapons. As long as my intentions were clear and good, I should be able to use the storm's power to achieve my goal. I couldn't waver from my course one iota, or all could be lost.

CHAPTER TWENTY-EIGHT

I made a mental list of everything I would need and then hurried to gather them all. I already had the candles. I went around the house and collected a few crystals I needed—pyrite, obsidian and my tourmaline and lapis lazuli tree. Putting these down on the coffee table, I reached in my pocket and pulled out the singed labradorite. It had already withstood one onslaught, and I needed its strength, as well as its protection. I shoved it back into the pocket as far as I could, making sure it couldn't fall out. The wire spring cage with the other crystals still hung around my neck, boosting the protective energy.

I went to the herb cabinet and rummaged through the many jars on the shelves, as I thought carefully about what I would use. Many herbs offered protection from negative energy or entities, but I needed much more than simply protection this time. I needed to banish whatever was after me with no chance of its return. I picked up the jar of agrimony first. I never had the occasion to use it before, but I had always kept some on hand for just such a purpose as this, to banish evil spirits and deflect hostile magic.

I pondered over the array of jars with their labels and spotted the mullein. This was exactly what I needed to supplement the agrimony since it would also work to drive any negative spirits away. An idea popped into my head, and I walked over to pull the small jar of cloves from the spice cabinet on the wall near the stove. Though it was usually used for cooking, cloves were one of the most effective repellants of evil spirits. I gathered up the containers of herbs and brought them into the living room. An occasional lightning flash and peal of thunder accompanied me as I had worked, as if the storm approved what I was doing. At least that was what I sensed, and I hoped it was correct.

One more thing. I went to get a small heavy-duty cast iron pot out of the cupboard and a trivet. I placed them on the coffee table, the trivet under the pot to keep it from touching the table top. That was everything I thought I would need, and I began to arrange the candles on the table—five candles placed in a shape to define the points of a star surrounding the pot and a sixth in the center next to it. The tourmaline tree also went in the center, behind the candle. I placed the other two stones next to the candles at the end point of the arms of the star. I poured cloves from the jar into my hand and then put three at each point. The agrimony and mullein were sprinkled on the surface of the table within the outline of the star, all around the crystals and candles.

The last thing I needed to do was to create a sigil, a symbolic representation of the spirit I wanted to banish. I got a piece of paper and pencil from my desk . In the center of the paper I drew a wavy line to represent a snake and then a horseshoe shape around the snake like a hood. An *X* went on top, covering both the hood and snake to indicate they were to be negated. I traced a *J* on top of all those, just in case Jim was the entity. With the side of the pencil lead I shaded over the whole area to depict the darkness of the spirit. I stared at the symbol for several moments, charging it in my mind to become the characterization of the entity I intended to banish, and then placed it on the table next to the star.

Everything was ready. My heart pounded in my chest, and my body tingled with energy, vibrating from my toes to the top of my scalp. I took a deep breath, ripped a match from the book and struck it. I had composed a decree of intent in my mind as I worked on the layout, and now I recited the words carefully and emphatically, speaking each phrase as I lit each candle.

"You've sent me strife and caused me pain." I lit the candle at the left arm of the star.

"I now reflect it back again." I lit the candle at the right arm point.

"With the power of thunder and lightning and rain." I lit the third candle at the end of the left leg of the star.

"No foothold here will you gain." The fourth candle was lit at the point of the right leg.

"I'll not allow your strength to grow." Next was the candle at the apex of the star.

"By my command you must go." I lit the last candle at the center.

I stared at each of the burning candle flames in turn and repeated its corresponding statement twice more. Finally, I picked up the piece of paper with the sigil drawn on it. I held it by one corner and placed the opposite corner into the flame of the center candle.

"I banish you! I banish you! I banish you!" I intoned as the paper caught the flame.

"Begone! Begone! Begone!" The fire rapidly devoured the paper. When the flame got close to the edge of the sigil, I dropped the blazing remainder into the iron pot. At the same moment, a flash of lightning illuminated the dark corners of the room while a crash of thunder echoed through the house. A gut-wrenching howl followed a scream that reeked of anguish. I felt the energy of the ritual as it buzzed all around and all through me in tune with the power of the storm. My fingers tingled, and the hair on my arms stood on end. These signs should be an indication that the ritual worked. Cautiously, I opened my mind to detect any spiritual presence, but I sensed no residual negativity in the air.

Suddenly, my eyes were drawn to the candle in the center of the star. As I watched, fascinated by the light, the flame flared up and started to flicker as if being blown around by the gale outside. None of the other candles were affected, only the one in the center. The flame held my gaze captive as it danced around the wick. As I stared more intently, I saw an image begin to form in the white center of the flame, a dark form that refused to take on a definite shape. Suddenly I was worried. If I lost the battle after all, I had no idea what to expect.

A sudden glare of lightning startled me and I nearly lost my concentration, but I righted myself even as the thunderclap followed close behind. I heard that weird scraping sound again in the background, but I couldn't allow myself to pay any attention to it. I followed the dark image with my eyes as it writhed and danced around the core of the flame. It had no form or figure, just a dark smudge against brilliant white. My eyes fixed on the shape and refused to look away. If it was to be a battle of wills, I was determined not to give in first. Then I sensed something, a slight shift of perception, the flit of a half-formed notion. I waited for the initial move to be made. Eventually a message emerged, jumbled at first, but after a few seconds its expression became clear.

"Beware! Be warned!" The psychic voice in my head strained to speak. I waited for more.

"Not yet." This time the tone was pressured, like the spirit fought to maintain a fragile hold. "Will not... Spare you... Yet... Must finish..." The voice sputtered and there was silence for several seconds. "Beware..."

Then it was gone, not only the psychic voice of the message, but the dark shape in the flame as well. The candle calmed and burned as serenely as the others, without any indication of the spirit that had troubled it. The strange message was too incomplete, too incoherent. I believed the spirit's energy sustained some damage with my banishment attack. However, one thing was crystal clear to me. I may have demonstrated my strength, but the battle was far from over.

The thunder boomed from a distance now, and there was no more lightning. The storm was moving away. The rain still pounded the windows, and the wind blew around the house. The power hadn't come back on yet. The kitchen clock said it was 5:50, still a long way to go before actual night time. I snuffed out the candles and moved them to the end of the table, then gathered up the crystals. I walked around the house and put those back where they were originally placed, except for the labradorite which went back in my pocket. I needed to keep up my defenses and maintain as much protection as I could.

On the way back to the living room, I got the dustpan and a rag from the utility closet to sweep up the herbs on the table. As I emptied the dustpan, I heard the scraping noise once again. I looked through the kitchen window and glimpsed something out of the corner of my eye moving at the edge of the patio near the grotto but when I turned my head to look that way, it was gone. Through the steady rain, nothing looked to be out of place, although the few pots I could see in the grotto looked disarrayed, not quite how I remembered them being arranged. It must have been my imagination. There was probably a palm frond caught on something and scraping against the side of the house. When the rain stopped, I would have to go out and pull it away so it didn't keep me awake all night.

There was one final thing to take care of for the banishment ritual, but that couldn't wait until the rain stopped. The ashes of the burned sigil had to be strewn in the wind, but I wasn't looking forward to getting soaked. I had just pulled my rain slicker from the closet when I heard the scraping noise, followed by a loud crash against the back slider.

My heart pounded. I had to look, but I was uneasy about what I might find. I tiptoed to the corner of the short wall that separated the back half of the kitchen from the living room and cautiously peeked around it toward the back slider. There were no cracks or breaks in the glass. Feeling a bit more secure, I walked into the kitchen and toward the slider. Outside, about six feet from the door, one of my plant pots was lying on the patio floor, the pot shattered to pieces with dirt and leaves scattered all around it. As I got a closer look, my heart dropped. It was one of my prized Rhode Island beach roses.

I had no idea how this could have happened, how it could have flown into the slider and smashed that way. The pot was really heavy, and I couldn't imagine a gust of wind strong enough to pick it up and throw it all the way form the grotto. But there it was. I only hoped I could save my rose. The rain had let up and was no more than a drizzle. I unlocked the slider and stepped outside.

Something heavy slammed into the back of my head, and I went down in a heap.

CHAPTER TWENTY-NINE

As I came to, I heard someone moaning and reflexively raised my head to see who it was. Bolts of searing pain jabbed through my skull, and my vision occluded with starbursts of blinding light. I instinctively tried to reach up to keep my head from exploding, but I couldn't move my arms. Another moan broke through my misery. It hurt to think and every muscle in my body was agonizingly taut. Finally, I realized the moan came from me, and my survival response took over as adrenaline kicked in. I tried to speak but physically couldn't. My throat started to spasm. Something thick and rough pushed against my tongue, and as I focused through the pain, I felt a cloth stuffed in my mouth. The instant reality of it made me gag, and my whole body convulsed over and over. I couldn't catch my breath.

With my eyes squeezed shut as tight as I could and by sheer force of will, I calmed my jerking muscles. I forced myself to stay perfectly still and took slow deep breaths one after another around the obstacle in my mouth, counting with each breath to keep myself distracted. Slowly my senses came back into focus.

Though my eyes were still closed, the smooth coolness beneath me told me I was lying on the tile floor. My arms were hanging behind my back and, without moving my throbbing head, I tried to lift my right hand but could only manage a fraction of an inch. I could feel the tile against it, so it wasn't asleep or numb. I tentatively wiggled my index finger and discovered I was touching my other hand. They were somehow tied together. They felt heavy as I tried to lift them and something metallic clinked together. It had to be a chain with some kind of lock.

I slowly opened one eye, and, when my head didn't blow apart from the pain, I opened the other. My vision had cleared somewhat, and I could see that I had been correct about lying on the floor. I was in the living room on my side looking toward the kitchen, my lower body from the waist down between the couch and coffee table. Every light in the house was on, it seemed, and the brightness hurt my eyes. It took a minute for my sluggish brain to register that the storm must be over and power back on. I tried to think back to what happened. The last thing I remembered was stepping out onto the patio to check my broken rose bush when something smashed into the back of my head.

I instinctively moved my head to get a better look. The pain was immediate and excruciating. My eyes squeezed shut automatically, and all the muscles around my skull contracted to try and stop the agony. More deep breaths as I willed the pain to go away. Eventually, after what was probably just a minute or two, though it seemed like hours, every part of me began to relax, just a little at first. As the pain in my head eased slightly, the discomfort of the cloth stuffed in my mouth flared back into focus and threatened to start the gagging all over again. I bit down as hard as I could and tried not to set off the piercing daggers through my head. Any movement might trigger another chain reaction of spasms.

I quieted my aching body and kept as still and as physically relaxed as I could. I had no idea how or why I got in this position and couldn't stop the thoughts that flew through my pulsing head. The events of the last few days had become a true threat, not just a series of pranks. I should have known I wasn't going to be let off easily after all the warnings. This wasn't the work of a ghost, but I didn't know who did this to me, really, or why.

There was nobody to help me. Jimmy was in Rhode Island or on a plane on the way to Tampa. Because of the storm, Lynn was in her own house two towns away. Even if the police were driving by my house, they wouldn't know I was tied up and gagged inside. My phone was dead. Whoever tied me up could kill me and nobody would ever know for days.

My panic was escalating. I willed myself to stop and started with the deep breaths again. If I was going to get out of this alive, I was going to have to do it alone. I needed to keep myself calm and rational.

I slowly opened my eyes and tried to look around without moving my head at all. It wasn't easy, but I had no choice. I had a straight line of sight into the kitchen. Both the ceiling light and the light over the sink were on, so I couldn't see how dark it might be outside. Only the right side of the clock was in my field of vision and I could just make out the end of the minute hand pointing to the four. Nobody was in the kitchen that I could see, and nothing looked out of place. I couldn't see around the wall to the sliding glass door.

My eyes shifted downward, and the couch and the side of the coffee table came into view. My legs and feet were positioned between them. There was a heavy silver chain wrapped twice around one ankle with another loop around the center leg of the couch and a padlock securing the two ends together. Even if I could sit up with the pain in my head, I'd never be able to free my hands or my leg. The only thing I could do at this point was try to change the position I was lying in so I could see the other side of the room.

Ever so slowly, I started the painful process of lifting my head off the floor so I could try to roll over on my stomach. Each time I moved my head a fraction of an inch, the pounding began again and lights flashed in front of my eyes. Then I had to wait until my vision cleared and the pain became tolerable. After three attempts, I decided I might as well go for it all at once. If the pain was going to come anyway, why not deal with it, rather than punish myself over and over, inch by inch. I steeled myself for the worst, gritted my teeth, and tensed all the muscles in my body. Without another thought, I hoisted my upper body two inches above the floor and heaved to my right. I lay on my stomach, panting, with my eyes squeezed tight against the stabbing pain in my head. My right leg was caught under my body but I had no strength left to release it.

After a few minutes, the pain lessened, and I lifted my head an inch off the floor. I could see my desk. My captor had gone through the drawers and rifled through the papers I had stacked on the corner. My journal was lying open on the side of the computer and several pages had been ripped out and crumpled in balls on the floor. A tarot deck that had been in one of the drawers had been thrown on the floor too, the cards scattered all around the torn journal pages. Worst of all, that framed photograph of Jim, the one I had thrown in the trash, was back on the desk poised in a prominent position beside the computer monitor. I lowered my head again and rested my forehead on the floor to ease my straining neck muscles.

I bit my lip and refused to cry. The back slider opened and somebody stepped inside. I had no time or strength to roll back over so I lay still and kept my breathing even. Footsteps padded around in the kitchen and something dropped on the counter. The steps sounded light, from a small person rather than a heavy one, and they were slow. I strained to listen and thought I heard one leg step down harder and then a little drag from the other, maybe a limp. The steps came closer and then stopped. I could sense being stared at, and as much as my eyes wanted to open, I kept them shut. Silence for a few minutes, and then the footsteps receded, back toward the kitchen. The slider opened and closed and then silence returned.

After a few seconds, I thought it was safe to take a look. I opened my eyes, and carefully turned my head to the left toward the kitchen. Nobody was there. The minute hand of the clock was out of sight, so at least ten minutes had passed. I moved my head a little to see farther into the kitchen, wincing at the pain but pushing it to the back of my mind. A dark blue plastic tote-bag sat on the counter with what looked like a folded up black garbage bag next to it.

The back door slid open again. I lowered my head back to the floor and closed my eyes halfway so I could peek through. A pair of sneakers and jeans covered the lower legs and ankles. The person walked to the kitchen counter and I could hear something else being put down there. The feet turned around abruptly and headed in my direction. I closed my eyes all the way.

"Don't think I didn't see those eyes of yours open," a raspy woman's voice said as the footsteps came closer.

I didn't dare move, and I kept my breathing steady.

"You're not fooling me, you bitch." The raspy voice was angry.

I shrieked as she grabbed a handful of hair and yanked my head up off the floor. My eyes were wide open now but she stood far enough behind me that I couldn't see her face or what she was doing.

"Don't try to play games with me." The woman cackled as she unexpectedly let go of my hair, and my forehead slammed back down into the tile.

Jagged bolts of pain shot through my head. Flashes of light flickered in front of my eyes. I was sure my head was split open like an over-ripe tomato. I heard myself whimper but couldn't stop it.

"Aw, you didn't like that?" She mocked me. "Well, you'd better get used to it. There's worse than that coming before I'm through with you."

I heard her walk away toward the kitchen. Despite the pounding inside my head, a little poke of memory tried to tell me something. I took deep breaths to minimize the pain as much as I could. The voice was vaguely familiar, but I couldn't place it. I wanted to lift my head to look at her, but I physically couldn't do it. Then I heard a thwack and a howl.

"You're as bad as the other one," the raspy voice said. "You're not fooling me either." Another whack and another yelp of pain. "The two of you disgust me. I don't know what he saw in either of you."

I wasn't alone with this madwoman. Somebody else was in the house and, from the sound of things, that person was as much a captive as I was.

Suddenly the significance of the photo on the desk dawned on me. The "he" she mentioned must have referred to Jim. In spite of the pain, I had to take a chance and look. At first, I couldn't see the raspy-voiced woman or the other person she taunted. I bit hard down on the gag in my mouth and raised my head in one quick motion, hoping to keep the pain to a minimum.

CHAPTER THIRTY

As I turned my head, a woman came into view with her back toward me. She was short with arms skinny as sticks poking out from the short sleeves of a faded black t-shirt with a hole near the hem. Pouches of loose old-woman skin hung from her bone-thin upper arms. She wore a pair of yellow plastic gloves that came up past her wrists like the old Playtex gloves my mother used when she washed dishes. The jeans and sneakers I'd already seen, but I hadn't noticed how worn and grimy they were. A long gray ponytail hung down to her mid-back and straggly pieces of hair stuck out from the band and hung loose around her head.

It was Maria. Once she turned to look at me, and I got a good look at her, I recognized her immediately, despite the extreme weight loss and how much she'd aged. When I saw the milky film of cataracts that covered her eyes, I knew without a doubt she was the apparition-like woman I'd seen at The Jolly Pelican and at Jim's apartment building.

I still didn't know why she was here in my house, holding me and someone else prisoner. And I didn't know who that other person was. All I knew for sure at this point was that somehow the three of us were connected by one slender common thread and that was my ex-husband. I wasn't going to let on that I had figured out her identity though. That bit of surprise might come in handy later.

Maria came back and walked around the other end of the couch. From my position on my stomach, I couldn't see what she was doing. Suddenly she grabbed my chained ankle and lifted it. I heard a low click, and the weight of the chain was gone. My first reaction was to kick out with my leg, but I was in an awkward position and it would have little effect. I waited to see what she was going to do next. She grabbed my left arm with her two hands and hoisted my torso up off the floor. She was a lot stronger than she looked.

"Get up," Maria ordered. "And don't try anything funny unless you want me to smash in that ugly head of yours for the last time."

I struggled but managed to scramble to my knees first and then to my feet.

"Sit down."

She pushed me before I had the chance to stand fully upright. My head smacked into the back of the couch when I fell. My brain hammered against the inside of my skull again. I wanted to scream but bit down on the gag instead. She bent over my legs and wrapped the chain around my ankle. A little click told me she'd fastened the ends with the padlock, and I knew she chained my ankle to the couch leg once again. She straightened up and peered directly at me.

"Now you just stay there and be a good girl while I take care of your buddy over there," she said, scoffing.

I didn't have much choice, and I didn't want to provoke her into any more physical abuse. There would be plenty more of that, I was sure, without causing it myself. I heard more clanking and figured she was doing something with the chains of my fellow captive. I could hear a wheeze in her breath as she panted with the exertion of her task. Although she might be physically strong, she was old and didn't have much weight on her. All this physical effort would take its toll. Another point I'd keep in mind when the opportunity to act arose.

"All right, bitch, stand up," she said to her other captive.

I heard a whimper and a scuffle on the floor along with a couple more thwacks which sounded like kicks to the person's body.

"Over there. Get going." Maria yelled at her captive who only responded with more whimpers.

As the two of them came into view, Maria shoved the other woman across the floor as she tried to walk. When they got in front of the couch, Maria pushed the other one down on the seat. I looked over at my fellow prisoner and gasped. I recognized Janice right away.

"Well, then, say hello." Maria sneered. "It's been a while, hasn't it? I'm sure the two of you have a lot of catching up to do. Don't let me interfere." She cackled as she bent over to chain the woman's ankle to the leg at that end of the couch.

All I could do was stare and, if I wasn't gagged, I'm sure my mouth would hang open. Janice hadn't changed much since I'd last seen her over twelve years ago, other than a few more wrinkles. Except now there was a trail of dried blood down the right side of her face and her left eye was swollen shut, surrounded by a huge black and purple bruise extending up her forehead to her hairline, over the bridge of her nose and across her left cheek. Janice looked at me and tried to smile. I gave her what I hoped was a reassuring nod in return. I certainly owed her an apology for thinking she had a hand in this.

Maria stood up slowly, apparently stiff and in some pain. She moved around to the other side of the coffee table and faced us with her arms folded across her chest. She stood there for a few minutes, looking us over but not saying a word, then laughed a couple of times with her lunatic's cackle. The last one triggered a wheezing spasm that took some effort for her to control. Both Janice and I sat still. I wasn't sure what to expect and apparently neither did Janice.

"What's the matter, Sharon?" Maria addressed me finally. "Don't you recognize me?"

When I didn't answer, she got agitated. "Answer me!" she demanded.

"Nuh." I tried to speak the single word through the gag. I wasn't giving her any more than that.

"Well, maybe if you hadn't acted so high and mighty, you'd know who I am," she said angrily, spit bubbling at the corners of her mouth. "You wouldn't even meet me for a cup of coffee. You thought you were too special to listen to what I had to say." She snorted. "Hah! Look at you now. Not so special any more, are you?"

I sucked in my breath as best I could with the gag and opened my eyes wide while I stared at her.

"So, you finally figured it out, huh?" Maria paced back and forth in front of the coffee table. "It took you long enough. I'm disappointed in you, Sharon. I was sure you'd get it without me having to hit you over the head." She cackled. "Literally."

I really was surprised in one way. Maria had changed so dramatically, not only her whole physical appearance but her demeanor as well. When Jim left me, I remembered her being excessively overweight with enormous thighs and upper arms, rolls around her abdomen and a huge butt and hips. She used to waddle when she walked because her weight was so disproportionate to her short stature. I also remembered her being extremely conscientious about her appearance and her dress, maybe to compensate for her size.

Besides that, she was a professor with a doctorate degree and taught business and management at a community college back in Rhode Island. She had always maintained a professional manner. Of course, from the stories I heard early on, that started to change when she got involved with

Jim and the motorcycle club. Mutual friends told me she took to the outlaw lifestyle with a vengeance, and they speculated that was her way of keeping him interested in her. Whatever the reason, there was little left of the Maria I remembered.

"Don't you have anything to say for yourself?" she asked sarcastically. "Cat got your tongue?" She wheezed as she suppressed a cough. "Oh, right, I forgot. You can't talk with a sock stuffed in that pretty mouth of yours, now can you?" She stopped pacing and glared at me. "Well, we'll just keep it there for a little bit longer. I don't particularly want to hear you whining."

"And you, Janice, no words of wisdom from you either?" She taunted the other woman. "And don't start that whimpering again, or I'll stuff a sock in you too."

I could see Janice bite her lip and hold her breath. She looked scared to death, and I didn't blame her. I was frightened too, but my anger overwhelmed my fear. I was furious that Maria had done this to me, to both of us. I had no intention of giving in to her, no matter what she wanted. If I got the chance I would fight back, and I didn't plan to lose. For now, though, she had me at a significant disadvantage and there wasn't much I could do about it. All I could do was be on the look-out for any opportunity.

"You two sit tight now." She almost giggled. "I've got to get a few things ready." She shuffled toward the kitchen and the back door, her limp becoming more apparent as she walked across the room. "Why don't you both have a little chat while I'm gone. Get re-acquainted and maybe compare notes on how you got here." Her speech was punctuated by cackles and her wheeze. "Oh right, silly me. I guess it's going to be a one-sided conversation. Janice, you're lucky you don't have to listen to Sharon babbling." She snorted. "Be good, girls. I'll be right back."

I heard the slider open and shut, and Janice and I were alone.

"She's crazy," Janice whispered to me. "What do you think she's going to do?"

I couldn't answer, so I shrugged my shoulders. Janice's hands were chained behind her back too so there wasn't really anything either one of us could do to help the other get free. I grunted to let her know I agreed with her, and I hoped she understood.

"She picked me up Sunday morning with a van, and I thought it was the shuttle for the airport." Janice continued to whisper. "It was four o'clock in the morning and still dark so I didn't get a good look at her. I don't think I would have recognized her anyway. She hit me on the side of the head while I was getting in the van. I guess I passed out. I woke up in an apartment somewhere with a blindfold over my eyes and a sock in my..."

There was a noise from behind us and Janice stopped in mid-sentence. We both turned our heads and looked toward the kitchen, but there was nobody there. Maria must have still been outside but I couldn't see what might have made the noise.

"She's been ranting and raving about the two of us and Jim ever since I came to," she said. "Nothing makes any sense. I don't know how long she kept me there. She took my blindfold and gag off but she never turned any lights on and all the windows had the shades drawn. She kept kicking and hitting me." She sniffled and I saw a tear run down her cheek. She took a breath and then waited a few seconds while she regained her composure.

"I didn't do anything to her," she sputtered. "Jim said he already ended it with her and moved out when he called me. That was the first time I'd heard from him in years. She kept saying I stole him away from her. I didn't. Really, I didn't." She was on the verge of a full-on hysterical crying jag but, to her credit, she managed to keep herself under control.

"I don't know what she's going to do to us, but she's crazy." She choked back a sob. "I'm afraid." Two more tears escaped and ran down the side of her nose and into her mouth as she looked at me helplessly. "She's evil, just pure evil."

CHAPTER THIRTY-ONE

I knew Janice was asking for some kind of reassurance that everything would be all right, reassurance that I doubted I could give her at that moment. She had no idea just how evil Maria might be, if my visions were any indication. As if a curtain had been drawn, the full import of Maria's place in all this became suddenly crystal clear. I had no doubt now there really were two entities, as Lynn's tarot reading had revealed—Jim's spirit and the negative energy that was Maria. She owned at least some of the malicious force I had witnessed in my visions, and as such, she was a grave threat and shouldn't be discounted in any way. We needed to be very careful and alert to any opportunity to thwart her plans, whatever they were.

To Janice, I simply smiled through the sock and nodded my head in a way that I hoped looked sympathetic. We were both in this together, and I might need her help. I couldn't let her fall to pieces and become a liability. I straightened myself as much as I could so I was sitting more upright from the slouched position I had fallen into when Maria pushed me onto the couch. When I was sitting as straight as I could, I looked at Janice and winked, trying to encourage her. I could see she was thinking about it. Then she smiled and straightened herself up too. We both needed that symbolic physical boost as well as the boost in spirit. I nodded at her in approval.

"Okay, we can do this," she whispered emphatically as she nodded back at me. "We're in this together, and we're gonna beat her ass." The tough side of Janice had regained control.

The sliding door opened at that moment, and Janice and I looked at each other. I winked at her, and she nodded back. Neither of us turned around to look. The door closed again, and Maria's footsteps limped across the floor toward us.

"You girls having a nice visit?" She looked us over as she scrunched her forehead to peer at us through half-squinted eyes. If she noticed our change of position, she didn't mention it. "I think I've got everything ready now so I'm going to tell you both a little story. You're going to love the surprise ending." She snorted and cackled at the same time, sending herself into another wheezing and choking fit. It took her a few minutes to get her breath back. "I just crack myself up," she said in her raspy voice as she wheezed and heaved out one more choking cough.

She grabbed hold of my desk chair and rolled it over in front of the coffee table. When she sat down, her feet didn't touch the floor so she fiddled with the levers until the seat was at the lowest height. She continued playing with all the levers until she had the chair adjusted to her liking.

"That's better," she said as she twirled the chair around so she could look directly at Janice and me. "Now I'm going to tell you two a story. Some parts are sad and some parts are nice. There are some good people in it and there are some wicked people." She paused and glared at each of us in turn. "Unfortunately, there is no happy ending... for anybody.

That's just the way it is sometimes. It could have been very happy, if the wicked people hadn't screwed it all up." Her voice became more agitated as she spoke. "The moral of the story is that the wicked people have to get punished in the end." She pointed at the two of us. "They get exactly what they deserve."

She screamed this last pronouncement at us with such fury I thought she would fall off the chair. I wanted to look at Janice to see how she was holding up, but I didn't relish the idea of becoming the immediate victim of Maria's escalating wrath. I sat still and peeked at Janice out of the corner of my eye. From what I could see, she was doing all right, simply sitting still and not responding to Maria with any sounds or even with her body language.

Turning my view back to Maria, I could see she was working to calm herself down. She readjusted her position in the chair and sighed deeply. I considered that was a good thing for Janice and me. It would give me more time to figure out all the angles of our situation. Maria was mentally disturbed, there was no doubt of that in my mind, and if I studied how she acted and reacted, I might be able to come up with a plan.

"Now you both need to pay attention," she said, glaring at us. "I'm only going to tell you this story once, and you have to remember the details. Your life might depend on it." She barked out that cackling laugh, but this time caught herself and cut it short before the coughing started.

"Once upon a time," she began, "there was a very handsome prince who lived in a far-away land. He was a great warrior and fought in many battles. He always won against every enemy he faced. Finally, the war was over, and he came back home to his own country. All his people loved him and they were all happy to have him home again."

I guessed where this was headed and I knew it wasn't going to be pretty. I watched her carefully as she spoke. She took deep breaths between each sentence and paused often, as if trying to remember. It was obvious she rehearsed this speech over and over in her head for a long time.

"One day the prince was feeling lonely." She looked at each of us and then went on. "He tried to find a good wife and married twice before but both of those women had turned out to be gold-diggers who only wanted to show off that they married a prince. They didn't love him at all. So, the prince looked around his kingdom to find another wife who was worthy to be his partner." She got up from the chair and pushed it to one side as she renewed her pacing.

"Unfortunately, one day the prince met a woman who captured his attention right away. Little did he know how wicked she was." She halted and pivoted, sneering in my direction. "This witch..." She all but spit the word at me. "Enchanted the prince so he saw her as the most beautiful woman he ever met. He fell under her spell, madly in love with her. He couldn't help himself." She pulled the chair back over and sat. She hesitated a few seconds, as if trying to remember her lines.

My hands chained behind my back were starting to become numb. I wiggled around to adjust their position to get the feeling back.

"Sit still and pay attention!" she yelled, sending spit flying in all directions.

I sat up as straight as I could and focused my attention on her face.

"That's better. Now, where was I?" She looked over at Janice and then back at me. "Oh, yeah... The charming prince and the wicked witch were married, and she kept the good prince under her spell for thirty years. She was mean to him and did everything she could think of to make his life miserable." She started to rock her body which caused the chair to roll back and forth in little short bursts. "She brainwashed him with her magic so he never understood what she did to him."

The rocking and rolling grew more frenetic and she became more agitated with each word she spoke. I was disgusted with her ridiculous story. She made Jim out to be the good guy in our bad marriage. It was a good thing I was gagged, or I'd say something I'd regret.

Abruptly, she stopped rocking and leaned back in the chair. She sat perfectly still with her eyes closed. "One day the handsome prince met a lovely princess. She too had been very unlucky with romance during her life but she knew the prince was kind and good and she fell in love with him at first sight." She let out a raspy sigh. "She tried very hard to help the prince overcome the evil spell that his witchy wife had put on him. One day, she finally made him realize the truth. He ran away from the witch and went to live with the lovely princess." Another sigh that sounded more like a croak.

It finally dawned on me. She was still madly in love with Jim and was going to make everything all my fault. The operative word here was mad. I had no doubt she was clinically psychotic, living in her own world of delusion. And that made her very dangerous. Maria's eyes were closed, so I turned toward Janice. She looked at me and raised her eyebrows, shaking her head. I took that to mean she understood what was going on here, too.

"The witch was furious that the handsome prince had gotten away and was living with the lovely princess." She sat upright and her eyes flew open, though she appeared to be dazed. "She continued to work her evil spells. Even though the wicked magic wasn't as strong because the prince was no longer in her clutches, she still enchanted him with the illusion that she was beautiful. And so, under her spell, he continued to long for the witch despite all the love the princess showered on him."

I watched in disbelief as tears welled up in the corner of those filmy eyes and rolled down Maria's cheeks. She really believed this fantasy she had concocted. One thing was certainly true—she had deliberately and doggedly convinced Jim to leave me for her. She wasn't going to persuade me that she was guiltless in that matter. As badly as Jim behaved toward me and his kids, she was the one who pushed him over the edge. They were both motivated by greed and entitlement, hell-bent on possessing what they craved, no matter the hurt they inflicted in the process.

Maria hiccupped and resumed her speech. "Then one day, the witch sent her crony over to seduce the handsome prince and take him away from the lovely princess. The old hag did her best to woo the prince, and since he was still under the witch's spell, he fell for her lies and left the lovely princess all alone." This time Maria glared at Janice with an expression of pure hatred. "Between the witch and the hag, their evil ways poisoned the handsome prince and he fell deathly ill. In the end, he couldn't fight them off any more and..." She paused with a sob and pointed at Janice.

To her credit, Janice didn't flinch or verbally respond which angered Maria even more. The chair flew across the room as Maria jumped to her feet. Spit foamed at the corners of her mouth, and a flood of tears streamed down her cheeks. She was so furious she gulped air, triggering another choking fit. She staggered to the desk and held on tight to keep from collapsing with the violence of the attack. Her body heaved as she gasped for air like a beached fish.

Now would have been the perfect time to overpower her but the chains on my wrists and ankle prevented me from reaching her. Janice and I could do nothing but watch her suffer and struggle to breathe. After many minutes, Maria finally brought her spasms under control. She limped toward the kitchen, looking exhausted. I heard the clink of glasses and then the sound of water running. When she came back, she placed a glass of water on the coffee table.

"Don't think you're going to get the best of me that way," she sputtered at Janice. "I know how you operate. And you, too." She pointed her finger at me and then swung it back and forth between the two of us. "You two are the cause of all my troubles. You took Jim away from me," she growled at Janice. "And you...," she bellowed at me. "You made sure he could never let go of you. He held on to your memory until his dying breath."

She looked the part of every madwoman I had ever seen in the movies. Her lips were coated with white foamy spittle. Her forehead and cheeks were deeply wrinkled as she squinted to see us through her cataract-obscured eyes. Her hair flew in all directions at once. The wheeze in her lungs rattled every time she took a breath. She was so pathetic, I almost sympathized with her. I had been able to see Jim for the shallow, heartless abuser he was, but she would never acknowledge that. Instead, she thought herself the victim of a malicious attack by me and Janice. The fact that Jim was dead, and she could never win him back again didn't matter to her. She was determined to avenge his death and her own loss. She totally believed that Janice and I were responsible.

"So that's the end of the story, girls. What do you think?" She smirked at both of us as she stood with her hands on her hips across the coffee table. "Very sad, isn't it? It's about to get even sadder for the two of you, I'm afraid." She cackled as she came around the table and yanked the sock out of my mouth. "What do you have to say for yourself, bitch?" She threw the soggy wadded up sock in my face. "Or should I say witch?" Cackling still, she positioned the chair to face us and sat back down.

I could sense that Janice was looking at me, maybe waiting for a cue about what to do. I wasn't sure what direction Maria was going to take the situation next. I didn't want to do anything that might give her an advantage, or worse yet, any reason to physically attack either of us again.

CHAPTER THIRTY-TWO

"I think we should have a little talk, the three of us," Maria said as she leaned back into the chair and placed the tips of her fingers together in a steeple, acting every bit the part of a talk show host. "You both probably have some questions and there are a few things I think you should know. Sharon, go ahead, you go first. Ask me any question you want. Don't be shy." Her demeanor was the complete opposite of the raving lunatic she exhibited a few minutes earlier.

"Ummm… Did you load the photo of Jim on my computer?" It was the first thing that popped into my head, and I could see the framed print sitting on my desk.

"Oh, that's a good one." She snickered as she glanced over at the photo. "Yes, I did that. I thought that was a clever trick, and you had no idea what was going on. He was such a handsome man." She sighed.

"How did you get into the house?" I asked tentatively.

"Well, okay. I was only going to let you have one but I'll give you this one since it was like a two-parter." She seemed to be enjoying the game and being in charge. "You were stupid enough to leave the house wide open at first. Then when you locked up, you put the spare key where everybody puts it. No imagination at all. It took me one minute to find it under the plant pot outside the back door. I had another one made for myself, and I've been able to come and go pretty freely. There's not much of your pretty little house here I haven't explored."

The thought horrified me but I kept my facial expression as neutral as I could. The idea of her wandering around my house and rummaging through all my belongings gave me the creeps.

"Okay, Janice, your turn." She turned and pointed.

"How did you get Jim's leather vest?" she asked without any hesitation.

"Good question, and you're going to love the answer. Actually, you'll both be surprised at this one. The simple answer is that Jim gave it to me the week before he died."

I heard Janice suck in her breath, and I'm sure my mouth dropped too. I looked at the smug grin on her face and could see she was about to tell us how she had pulled off a great caper.

"Isn't that a good one?" She snickered. "You're won't believe it, Janice, but I live in your same building, in the apartment directly below you. You never had a clue, never saw me." She waited for Janice's reaction but got nothing and her tone turned sarcastic. "Where did you think you were when you woke up from that knock on the head?"

I looked over at Janice, and she just shook her head at me. She really didn't have any idea. I turned my head back toward Maria who now sported a cocky grin.

"Yep, I lived there for three months and saw everything that was going on. That's how I found out you lived across the street," she said to me with a sneer. "Jim ran into me one day in the lobby. He was so happy to see me," she said in a dreamy voice. "He wanted to make sure you didn't find out I was there. I asked him for a token of his feelings for me and he brought me the vest the next day." Her tone changed completely to one of disgust as she now glared at Janice. "He said he couldn't get rid of you no matter what he tried. He promised me we would be together again soon."

I couldn't stand it. "What you really mean is that you demanded he give you something in return for you leaving him and Janice alone and that's when he gave you the vest."

Maria's head whipped around to glare at me. "Shut up!" She screamed at me. "That's a lie. He was happy to see me. We were going to be together again."

I had started on this track and figured I might as well keep it going. "You're nuts. He didn't want you anymore, but you still wanted him so you made up this whole fairy tale."

"Liar!" She shrieked and then stopped herself abruptly. She sucked in her breath and closed her eyes as she made a physical effort to stay in control. "He loved me. He knew exactly what the two of you were up to, and he said he needed my help to get rid of you both. He told me you lived here across the street, and I knew you were trying to control him again. I took pictures so we would know exactly what you were up to. He took them from me and put them somewhere nobody else would find them. I didn't trust you, so I kept taking more pictures. After he died, I sneaked into his apartment when nobody was there. I found the envelope in his desk and put the new ones in with them. Then I put it where I knew his son would find it. Since your name was on the envelope, I was sure he would give it to you."

"That was you? And you did all the rest, too, I suppose. You were the one who delivered the snake in the pizza and stole my snow globe. You put the crushed stones on the front step. It was all you, wasn't it?"

"Yes, it was all me. I wanted to make you afraid, make sure you knew somebody was watching you. Pretty good, huh?" She stuck out her chest and grinned, proud of herself. "After Jim... was gone..." She paused and swallowed hard. "I had to carry out the plan we came up with to get rid of you two. I had to do it in his memory. It was all pretty clever, wasn't it? I had you spooked trying to figure out who was behind it all."

"You even cut off his finger after he died." I couldn't keep the undertone of revulsion from my voice while I goaded her at the same time. "Was that another attempt to scare me? You actually defiled the remains of the man you were supposed to love just to play a trick on me?"

She wasn't prepared to answer that. In an instant, her face contorted, her mouth and nose twisted, and her eyes crossed.

"I didn't mean it that way." Tears streamed down her face and she blubbered as she spoke. "He didn't feel it. He was already dead when I sneaked into the viewing room at the funeral home. I cut it off when nobody was looking. It didn't hurt him. He wanted me to do it, just like he wanted me to put an end to the two of you." She wheezed and gasped for air, then started to choke and cough. With more agility than I would have given her credit for, she lurched from the chair and stumbled her way to the kitchen and out the back door.

"I told you she was crazy," Janice said, taking advantage of Maria's absence but still whispering. "What do you think she's going to do to us?"

"I can't even begin to imagine," I said truthfully. "We just have to stay on guard and try to overpower her if we get the chance."

I heard the door open and the sound of Maria's footsteps as she crossed the kitchen.

"All right, you two." She shouted at us as she came into view. "I'm done playing games, and I'm sick of the both of you. It's time to get down to business."

She carried the blue tote bag from the kitchen counter and placed it on the coffee table. Whatever was in it clunked when she put it down. She stuck her hand in her pocket and pulled out a small key.

"I'm going to release the chains around your ankles, but don't get any ideas about trying to run away," she said. "You won't get far."

She walked to the end of the table and bent over in front of Janice first. I couldn't see what she was doing, but I heard the clinking of the metal chain.

"Okay, go stand over there near the desk," Maria commanded.

Janice did as she was told. Maria then came to my side of the table. Her expression was pure evil, and I had never felt such hatred from any person before.

"Don't even think of trying anything, or I'll kill you. And I mean it."

I didn't doubt her for one second. I sat still as she removed the lock and chain from my ankle.

"Now go stand next to her," she said and pointed to Janice. She picked up the chains and locks and dropped them in the tote bag.

I did as she instructed. I needed to find out what her plan was, so I would know how to fight back. Both Janice and I still had our hands chained together behind our backs so there wasn't much we could do yet. I had to wait. I realized as I stood there that Maria was still wearing the plastic gloves. She never took them off at any point. It made me nervous to think that she might be deliberately protecting herself from leaving fingerprints anywhere, even though it shouldn't matter. We knew who she was and could identify her as the person behind all this madness. She picked up the tote bag from the table and pulled something from it. Suddenly I knew why she had on the gloves. I was truly afraid then, as I watched her point a small handgun in our direction.

"Now let's go. Outside," she said. "I don't want to make a mess in here and leave any clues behind. I'm not going to stick around long enough to clean up."

She waved the gun toward the back door and gestured for us to walk that way. She picked up the tote bag, and I heard something else rattling against the chains. Keeping the gun pointed at us, she followed us into the kitchen. We had to stop at the door, and she took the time to turn off all the lights. When she got back to the slider, she came around in front of us and opened it.

"Out." She gestured with the gun. "Go stand over there."

Janice went first, and I stepped out onto the patio behind her. Maria had set up two of the patio chairs, and we walked toward them, not daring to disobey. At this point I knew Maria was completely deranged, and it didn't make any sense to attempt to reason with her. It was also useless to think about fighting back until I was sure I could win. That gun raised the stakes exponentially, and knowing her current state of mind, I didn't want to take any unnecessary chances. I had every intention of staying alive and hopefully keeping Janice that way too.

"You sit there, and you, over there." She pointed to the two chairs that faced the house as she dropped her tote bag on the ground. She was all business now.

Although there were no lights, the patio was bathed in shades of silver and gray. I looked up and saw the full moon shining down on us, blanching out the colors as if everything had been whitewashed. To most people it would have been an ominous sign, but I felt just the opposite. The energy reflecting from the moon filled me with a sense of power, a positive charge that I knew I was going to need before too long. The anxiety oozed out of me, replaced with a calm confidence. I would get us through this.

CHAPTER THIRTY-THREE

"I'm going to explain exactly what's going to happen here." Maria paced back and forth across the patio. "No funny stuff." She pointed at me. "I've planned this down to the last detail, and neither of you will interfere."

Her milky eyes were as luminescent as they looked that night at The Jolly Pelican. The moonlight reflected off the film of her cataracts and gave them a spectral appearance. Her hair was wilder than ever, more strands pulled loose and frizzed around her head during her ravings. Where she had swiped the foamy spit from the corner of her mouth with the back of her hand, a white band streaked across her cheek, dried there like a gauzy bandage. She truly did look the part of the lunatic she had become.

"In a very short time, the two of you will be dead. Tough luck for you, I know, but that's the way it has to be." She cackled and caught herself in mid-wheeze with a few breaths before she started to cough. "I'm doing this for Jim, to avenge his soul." She sighed with a catch in her throat. "You," she sputtered as she pointed the gun at me. "It was your fault. You were a bully, a mean and vicious witch. All you ever did was abuse and brutalize him. He didn't deserve that. He was kind and good. After what you did to him, he still wanted you. I know he loved me, but you cursed him so he couldn't see how evil you were. You never released him from the spell you put on him, so he could never love me like he wanted to."

She waved the gun around in the air like a conductor's baton, orchestrating her grand scheme. The bright yellow gloves she still wore stood out in bleak contrast to the silvery bath of moonlight. I was afraid the gun would go off accidentally. I didn't know how to calm her down without getting her more agitated.

"I'm sorry," I said softly. "Really, I didn't mean to hurt him or you. I didn't care that the two of you were..."

"Liar!" She screamed to cut me off. "I know all about you and your ways. You didn't want him but you weren't going to let anybody else have him either. You sent this one." She gestured toward Janice with the gun. "She took him away from me. And the two of you tormented him to his death."

A strong gust of wind suddenly wailed through the patio. We all looked up, and I glanced at the moon. There were no clouds and the sky looked serene. The palms and bushes closer to the beach were still. Janice's eyes widened as she looked around.

"Enough," Maria said. "Let's get this over with so Jim can rest in peace."

Another blast blew through and keened eerily as it passed. Maria's mouth hung open and her forehead wrinkled in bewilderment and alarm. She reached over and fumbled with the tote bag.

"One for you," she mumbled as she stuck her free hand in and pulled out another handgun. She shoved it in her pocket. "And one for you." She drew a third gun from the bag.

An image of the scenario she had in mind for Janice and me flicked through my mind. I hoped I was wrong.

"Now, you're going to do exactly as I tell you and no tricks. We're going to walk out onto the sand just at the end of the bridge there." She pointed to the boardwalk. "You're going to face each other and I'm going to put a gun in each of your hands. I'll stand next to Janice and make her shoot you," she said smugly. "Then I'll make it look like she shot herself. Once you're both dead, I'll take the chains off your wrists and pose you both just right. Brilliant, isn't it?" She let out her wheezy cackle. "I'll be long gone by the time they find you and nobody will ever suspect it didn't happen the way it looked. Janice killed you because of Jim and then shot herself because she couldn't live without him. A fitting end for both of you, and Jim will be happy and free at last."

"Jim's dead," I blurted out before I could stop myself. "And you're crazy."

She took two quick steps toward me, and I ducked, expecting her to hit me with the gun but she stopped.

"Nobody's going to believe it." I challenged her. "What are they going to think about Janice's black eye and the wound on the back of my head?"

"Not a problem," she said. "They're going to think the two of you were fighting and hurt each other. Nobody even knows I'm here. There's no way any of this will be tied to me."

"The police know all about what you've done over the past few days," I said. "I filed a report. They'll figure out there was somebody else behind this and they'll know it was you."

"They won't have a clue." She snorted. "You didn't even know I was around until this afternoon, so I know you didn't tell them my name.

Trust me, I've thought out every angle and there's no way they're going to connect me to your deaths."

With that, she put the two handguns back in the tote bag but left the third in her pocket. I had nothing left to try and stall her. Besides, I couldn't see what good it would do. She wasn't going to release the chains on our wrists behind our backs, so I had no chance to overpower her. The only chance I might have was to try and kick her down and knock the gun away. It was a slim hope but I would have to wait for the absolute perfect moment. Otherwise, it would be pointless and might make her put her plan into action sooner.

"Let's go." She waved her gun at us. "Walk to the beach."

I got up from my chair slowly and stood looking around for a few seconds at my house, my garden, and the grotto. I wanted to imprint the scene on my brain. My pretty little beach cottage in paradise, the place where I was the happiest in my whole life. I didn't want to think that I might lose it after such a short time. My throat tightened and tears welled up in the corners of my eyes. I finally earned my peace with the Universe, and I didn't want it to end so soon. I lifted my chin and clenched my teeth. This would not happen to me. I would find a way to stop her.

We were almost at the end of the boardwalk. Janice had kept silent, but now I heard her whimper softly. She slowed her pace, trying to postpone the inevitable, I supposed. That wasn't going to do us any good. As soon as my feet hit the sand, I kicked off my flip-flops, trying to make it seem routine, as if I did it instinctively. In reality, I wanted to have the best footing possible on the sand if I was going to try to attack her. Kicking was the only weapon I had. I wouldn't have my arms free in front of me to help balance myself. Maria said nothing, and I hoped she hadn't noticed.

"Okay, that's far enough." Maria put the tote bag down on the sand. "Stop here."

We did as she said. While Maria fiddled with the bag, I winked at Janice. She looked at me in surprise, and I mouthed *Shhhh* to her. She nodded back at me, and I hoped that meant she would follow my lead. She would have to help me take Maria down if we were going to get out of this alive. While Maria was still bent over with her back to us, I winked at Janice and pointed toward the ground with my chin. She got the message and looked down as I slightly raised one leg and made a kicking motion with it. She looked up and I wagged my head to the side toward Maria. She smiled and nodded vigorously.

A breeze started to blow the sand in little whirlwinds around our feet. Behind us, Maria seemed to be more bothered by it than we were. She slapped at her ankles and rubbed her lower legs. The keening noise started again, a subtle hum at first that increased in volume as the breeze slowly freshened. Maria shook her head, like she was trying to rid herself of a pesky mosquito. She let out a low growl as she straightened up and glared at me.

"I told you no funny business." She waved her gun in my direction. "Stand right there and don't move."

Maria must have thought I was responsible for raising the wind, but I was as bewildered by it as she was. I watched as she took one of the guns from the tote bag. She came around behind me and yanked my hands up by the chain around my wrists. She put the gun against my palm, but I had no intention of making this easy for her and refused to wrap my fingers around it.

"Hold it!" she yelled.

I wouldn't do it.

"No!" Janice yelled and ran toward Maria and me.

Janice plowed into Maria, but she wasn't quick enough. Maria slammed the gun against my ankle bone from behind before the force of Janice's blow toppled her to the ground. I was down in a heap with excruciating pain piercing my right ankle.

Maria scrambled to her feet and lunged at Janice. Janice was quicker, though, and hopped backwards out of her reach. Maria almost fell again but managed to keep her balance. She smashed the side of Janice's head with the gun, striking a glancing blow off her ear. Janice wobbled, stunned, and leaned her head into her shoulder.

"Don't try that again." Maria screamed at Janice, then turned to me. "You! Stand up!" She shrieked as she grabbed me by the crook of my elbow and hauled me upright.

I couldn't put full weight on my right foot. There was no way I could kick her down. I could barely keep myself upright. I peeked over at Janice. Her eyes were wide and her mouth quivered. She looked on the verge of hysteria. I winked to reassure her, but I was in need of some reassurance myself.

"Now take this and no more bullshit." Maria hissed behind me. "I've had enough of you two. You're not going to change my plans no matter what you do. There won't be anything tying me to your deaths."

I closed my fingers around the handle of the gun. I didn't have a choice now if I wanted any chance to save myself later. Maria plodded through the sand over to Janice. I thought about dropping the gun on the ground, but I didn't want to lose the only weapon I might have any chance to use against her. I wasn't steady enough on one leg to turn around and get a good shot at her backwards.

"Stand there," she said to Janice and pushed her toward a spot about ten feet away from me.

Janice did what she was told, watching Maria the whole time. Maria paced between us, waving her gun in the air. The wind strengthened to gusts and whipped blasts of sand around us. It seemed to be windy only on our stretch of beach. There were no clouds in the night sky and the moon continued to douse the scene with its colorless light. I felt the thrum of energy in the air and a barely audible hum. As I watched, the gusts dove into the sand and brought up little dust devils that raced around the perimeter of the area where the three of us stood. Maria squinted and stared, and then surveyed the beach. She shook her head as if trying to rid herself of something annoying.

"It's time." She brought her attention back to us. "Get ready to die."

Maria pulled the third gun from the bag and walked around behind Janice. She undid the chains from her wrists, then stood on Janice's right side. Janice turned her body away as Maria tried to put the gun against her palm.

"Hold still!" She grabbed a handful of Janice's hair and yanked her back to face forward. Maria put the gun in Janice's hand and tried to close her fingers around it, but Janice wouldn't do it. Maria slammed the gun against Janice's elbow.

Tears welled in Janice's eyes but she bit her lip and held them back.

"Don't fight me again, or I swear I'll shoot you right now." She shoved the gun into Janice's palm and put her own gloved right hand over it. Before Janice had time to react, Maria raised their arms together so the gun pointed at my head. She forced Janice's index finger onto the trigger and then moved her own left hand to cradle her right for support.

"No!" Janice cried and dropped her arms, ripping her hand and the gun from Maria's grip. The gun discharged with an ear-splitting bang as it fell to the ground and the bullet shot into the sand.

"Damn you!" Maria stumbled backwards from Janice's abrupt movement and the gun's recoil.

Janice lost her balance and landed on her butt. Maria scrambled to her feet before Janice could recover and grabbed her hand, jerking her upwards. I heard a distinctive wet pop and Janice let out an anguished howl. Her right arm hung limply by her side and I realized Maria had dislocated her shoulder.

"Good enough! Now take this and hold it. Don't try anything else stupid," Maria said as she slapped the gun into Janice's hand.

The gun rested against her right palm, but Janice had no strength in her arm to hold onto the gun. Her teeth were clenched against the pain and I could hear her whimpers. Maria wrapped her hand around Janice's and aimed the gun directly at my head.

"This is it," Maria cried out. "This is for Jim."

I didn't want to my witness own death, but I felt compelled to watch. As I anticipated the crack of gunfire, objects appeared to elongate and time itself seemed to stretch. I saw Janice lift her leg in slow motion and draw it backwards, ready to kick Maria's legs out from under her. Before she had a chance to swing forward and make contact, one gust of wind erupted into a full-force gale and heaved Maria ten feet in the air.

Her body flew in an arc and landed face down in the sand about thirty feet from Janice and me, at the edge of the beach where the soft sand met the line of palms and vegetation. She kicked her legs and her arms flailed. She tried to push herself up out of the sand, but it was as if something held her down and the weight was too much for her. Each time she tried to turn her head and lift it out of the sand to breathe, some invisible force pushed her face back downward. She managed to cry out one word that I clearly heard above the wind. "JIM!" Then I heard the wheezing and choking as every breath she took must have sucked sand into her damaged lungs.

Janice limped by me to get to Maria, but another blast of wind and sand shoved her backwards and she fell to the ground. I hobbled toward Maria too, but the wind kept me from getting to her. It pushed at me and drove me back. Janice got up and came to stand next to me, pressing her upper arm against mine for support. A barricade of wind prevented us from moving any closer. All we could do was watch as Maria's thrashing became weaker and weaker until it finally ceased.

CHAPTER THIRTY-FOUR

An ear-splitting wail ripped through the air and high-frequency energy buzzed around my whole body. Janice stared off into the distance toward the beach in a trance. Suddenly, her eyes rolled back in her head and she collapsed to the sand. Her chest rose and fell in slow motion, but at least she was still breathing.

My ankle throbbed where Maria smashed the gun against it but I didn't have time to worry about that. The wind keened around my body and swirling sand devils nipped at my feet. Fingers of icy air ran over my skin, and I shivered as they clamped onto my arms and calves. I closed my eyes and immediately sensed a vile and brooding presence. Bolts of negative energy infused the ether with dread as the spirit tried to draw its dark cords tight around me.

I knew this spirit. Jim had come to claim me, to take control of my soul once and for all. I would not allow that to happen.

The metal on the cage of crystals I wore around my neck grew warmer against my skin. The combined energy of the tourmaline, obsidian, kunzite, and labradorite inside the coil buzzed and vibrated against my chest. The heat increased as it spread up over my face and head and down my back and legs, melting the icy grasp as it slipped to my ankles. The warm wave slid down my torso and belly, over my hips and down my thighs and shins to my toes. Where the two waves of energy merged at my feet, a force field formed that surged and pulsed around my entire body. The energy wave drilled deep into the earth, grounding me with its strength.

A different and persistent energy vibrated on my hip. My hands were still chained but I managed to work my fingers into the pocket. The marred surface of the labradorite met my touch, the piece damaged when I fought the dark spirit yesterday. It thrummed against my fingertips and its waves of energy coursed through my body. The crystal was ready to fight with me again.

These crystals were my strength and support. Their potent energy provided a shield against the menace of my ex-husband's malevolent spirit and bolstered my own determination. I had rescued myself from his clutches once before and I would never let him possess me in any way ever again.

I looked out over the sand toward the waters of the Gulf. Ribbons of cloud skittered across the starless sky, ragged remnants of the storm. The night was clear and dark. I shivered, but not from a chill. The time had come to take on my greatest challenge. This was the test my psychic ability had been groomed to meet. The final round was about to begin.

Careful steps across the boardwalk brought me to the beach. I limped to a spot past the lifeless Maria, halfway between my house and the water's edge. My energy shield remained intact and surged around me. With my feet planted in the sand, the high-frequency waves pulsed and pushed deep beneath the surface to root me in place. I breathed in deeply to fill my lungs with air still charged with the electricity from the storm.

I could barely see the water, but the rhythmic sloshing of waves played a drumbeat in my ears. I dug in my pocket for the labradorite and drew it out slowly. I cradled the crystal between my two palms and held on tight.

"I'm ready for you," I said into the ether and closed my eyes.

The temperature dropped and cold air enshrouded me. In response, the energy from my crystals grew warmer. The spirit's presence surrounded me but couldn't penetrate the shield.

"Show yourself," I demanded.

Instantly, an image appeared behind my closed eyes. It was from a photo of Jim and me on our honeymoon in Cancun over forty years ago. We were smiling, standing in front of a fountain with our arms around one another.

"Nice try, but those days are gone forever." I felt the wind pick up again. "Forget the tricks and show yourself as you are."

A low growl quickly crescendoed to an enraged shriek that echoed off the water. The night grew even darker, and the sky seethed with roiling black clouds. Eddies of sand scratched against my feet and ankles. Long curls of hair blew into my face and tickled against my nose. I ignored them and kept my eyes closed. My field of vision was blank. No words or messages came through my senses. The psychic stillness was eerie. I stood my ground and waited for Jim to make the first move, ready to respond in whatever way was needed, defense or aggression.

The darkness behind my eyes started to move. Pools of the deepest indigo spiraled into themselves to create a vortex. Murky black tendrils curled up from its depths and undulated like smoke caught in puffs of breath. There was a pull from the depths of the vortex, a potent vacuum that would suck anything into its core. Virulent pressure tugged at my limbs as it fought to draw me into the maw. My energy roots resisted and held fast as I was buffeted by the opposing forces.

Then I heard Jim's voice, deep and commanding.

"You are mine."

"Never." My voice struggled against his will. "I am not yours to own."

"You can't resist."

His voice, the same voice I had loved for so many years, echoed through my soul. A slight quiver fluttered in my breast and my heartbeat quickened. My mouth curled up in an involuntary smile. I stopped myself and breathed in deeply. My pulse slowed and I clenched my lips shut in determination.

"I can, and I will."

The vision behind my eyes changed and softened. A dozen images slipped through my mind in a slide show. The boys searching the yard for Easter eggs when they were little. A sunset in Hawaii where we vacationed for our tenth anniversary. A car trip through the New Hampshire mountains in the fall leaf-peeping season. Once again, my heart fluttered, and a smile threatened at my lips. There were so many times we'd been happy together.

Or rather, that I was happy being with him. I didn't know if he ever truly experienced happiness. His motivation was always control. I steeled myself against the onslaught and made myself think about the full story of each memory. Jim yelled at the boys not to get dirty as they searched through the yard for eggs, then took away their Easter baskets because they did. Their tears were a sad contrast to the delighted laughter at finding each treasure. In Hawaii, we went to a local restaurant after that sunset. Jim disappeared and left me to find my own way back to the hotel. I was frantic that something happened to him until I found out later he was in the bar with another woman. It was the same with every incident, ruined by Jim and his self-centered behavior.

The crystals around my neck pulsed against my skin. An image appeared of the courtroom where our divorce hearing was held. Jim's words echoed through my brain as he described me as mean and selfish, a faithless wife. A pain pierced to my core, deep within my heart. My breath came in ragged spurts. All the love I felt for him all those years bubbled up, sour and stinging in my throat.

A new vision came to me, one of me standing alone on my beach looking out over the Gulf's horizon. My heart beat a calming rhythm, and a gasp puffed from my lips. Finally, I realized I had never truly let go of Jim or my marriage. In my mind's eye, the image of my love for Jim popped like a balloon into a thousand flaming pieces of ash that blew away on the wind. I shuddered and shook my head.

I raised my head and straightened my shoulders. I was done. No more shreds of hope that he still loved me. No more games of hard-to-get to make him want me. The last cords that bound me to him broke. I was free. I was over him once and for all. The smile this time was genuine and serene.

"It won't work, Jim." I opened my eyes and drew in a deep breath. "I'm done with you." At last, I meant those words with my whole being.

A roar erupted from the depths of the Gulf waters. Fluorescent white foam spattered into the air in glowing plumes of froth, flying in all directions. Drops landed on my skin and spread rope-like across my arms and legs. The labradorite clenched in my hands grew hot, and its fiery power coursed up my arms and into my heart, its energy melding with the energy bubble that still surrounded me and grounded me to the earth. The ropes of sea foam dripped to the sand.

"Maria would have killed you. I saved you."

He sent waves of emotion that pushed against my senses, but they no longer had any impact.

"You manipulated her to do what you wanted." I smirked at this pitiful attempt. "You don't get any credit for saving me when you set the whole thing up."

"I will never let you go." His voice thundered through the air, and the sand beneath me quaked with its fury.

"You don't have a choice," I said calmly, my voice clear and strong against his wrath.

His negative force drove hard against me. My body swayed with the strength of the blows, but my protective field held fast against his anger. Hot wind blew the sand into cords that whipped around my body. The energy around me repelled the attack, and the cords of sand disintegrated into piles of grit on the ground. I took a deep breath and recited the spell I had used against Jim's dark spirit earlier.

"You've sent me strife and caused me pain."

The crystals around my neck vibrated and glowed.

"I now reflect it back again."

I clenched the labradorite within my two palms and tilted my head back to gaze skyward.

"With the power of thunder and lightning and rain."

White-hot rays of energy burst from between my fingers and the energy buzzed in my ears.

"No hold of me will you gain."

A low moan surged from under the water, and the sand around my feet swirled in a frantic dervish dance.

"I'll not allow your strength to grow."

The moan amplified as it erupted from the surface and hurled toward me, only to dissipate into shrieking fragments when it hit my shield.

"By my command you must go."

Blinding flashes of lightning crackled and thunder rumbled, spewing the pungent odor of ozone in my direction.

"I banish you! I banish you! I banish you!"

The energy at my feet rooted deeper into the earth as I cried the commands, my voice unwavering in its challenge.

"Begone! Begone! Begone!"

I shrugged my shoulders to my ears as an ear-splitting crack of thunder followed by a fierce shriek split the ether. Icy fingers dragged at my skin, but they melted from the heat of my body. Weakened strings of sand flicked against my ankles, no stronger than a blade of grass fluttering in a light breeze. I heard a faint whoosh as the last draft of wind trickled by me. Then all was perfectly calm.

He was gone, and I was free.

CHAPTER THIRTY-FIVE

The sand settled, and the trees were still. The buzzing ceased. The full moon reflected a silver aura on the peaceful beach. Janice sat up and shook her head.

"What happened?" Her wide-open eyes looked at me imploringly as she tried to make sense of the situation.

"I'm not sure I know how to explain it," I said.

We both stood there. She looked out over the waters of the Gulf, and I followed suit. I was exhausted. My ankle was throbbing, and I had a pounding headache at the base of my skull. Her face was dark purple with the bruise over her swollen eye, and her arm hung useless at her side. The two of us were a wreck.

At the same time, we both turned to look at Maria's lifeless body lying face down in the sand. I wasn't sure I could feel sorry for her, as much as I wanted to. She would have killed me with no remorse, despite the fact that Jim's spirit ordered her to do it. I only knew I was grateful I wasn't the one lying dead on the sand. At some point I would have to report the events that just occurred, but I had no idea how I would explain all that happened.

A strange sense of calm washed through me, though I probably should have been hysterical. I had been seconds away from death twice but instead I was alive and free, and I was going to stay that way. My life and my paradise were safe. I no longer had any attachment to Jim or our marriage. There were no tears and no words. I simply knew in my heart and soul that the ordeal of the past week was over forever. I was at peace.

"Come on, Janice, let's ..."

A siren broke the stillness and blinding red and blue strobes ripped through the silver moonlight. Car doors slammed.

"Sharon!" I heard a male voice yell.

"Sharon!" A different but familiar voice shouted. "Sharon, where are you?"

I nudged Janice and we hobbled over the boardwalk as the sound of running feet came around the side of the house. Jimmy was the first one I saw. He caught up to me and grabbed me in his arms.

"Are you all right?" He hugged me tight.

"A few bumps and bruises," I said as I pushed away from him to be able to breathe. "I'll live." He could have no idea how delighted I was to be able to say that. "You'd better check on Janice."

"What?" He looked beyond me, and saw her standing at the edge of the patio. "Oh, my God. What happened to you?" He let me go and hurried over to her.

"Ms. Coady?"

The voice came from a silhouette that approached through the flashing lights. I squinted and saw Detective Brandon trot toward me.

"Detective. I'm glad you're here." I let out a big breath. I really was happy to see him and a feeling of relief washed over me. "There's a body down on the sand that needs to be taken care of."

He gave me a strange look. "A body? Like a dead body?"

"Yes, exactly. Dead." I watched as he turned and started for the beach. "Oh, and can you see if there's a key for these chains in the plastic tote bag you'll find down there? My arms are starting to get numb."

I saw him grab his radio and heard the static as he requested reinforcements. Jimmy and Janice walked toward me, and I carefully motioned with my head for them to follow me into the house. Jimmy opened the door and turned on the lights in the kitchen. They followed me to the living room and I sank onto the couch.

"You guys look like hell," Jimmy said, shaking his head with a snort.

"Yeah, but at least we're alive." I chuckled back.

Janice nodded. "You have no idea what we went through," she said to Jimmy. "That woman was crazy. She was playing some kind of game, and revenge was the prize. It didn't make any sense."

"What woman?" Jimmy asked. "Who was it?"

"Maria," Janice said. "The one your father lived with."

Jimmy looked at me with an expression of total confusion.

"She really was delusional," I said. "She had this whole fantasy going on about your father and her. None of it made any sense, but she totally believed that I had him under some kind of spell and Janice was my accomplice. According to her, we were trying to take your father away from her, and when we couldn't, we caused his death."

"That is crazy. So how did she die? Obviously, you two didn't do it, being all chained up."

I had no idea what to say to him. I looked at Janice and she shrugged her shoulders. How was I supposed to report for the official record what I knew was the truth—that Jim's spirit had killed her. In the end, he couldn't stand not being in control of the whole show. That sounded as crazy as Maria's ranting and raving had been.

"I don't really know. We watched it happen but I don't know if I can describe it," I said. "It seemed like she was pretty sick with respiratory problems. All I can guess is that these strong gusts of wind blew her down, and she was too weak to get back up."

Detective Brandon walked into the room as I finished my explanation. He held up a key and came over to unlock and remove the chains from my wrists.

"Thank you." I smiled as I rubbed my hands, trying to restore their normal feeling.

"The coroner and the paramedics are out on the beach with the body," he said. "Uniformed officers are searching the area for evidence. They'll probably be here for a while."

"That's all right," I said. "They should find three handguns on the sand nearby and some chains and padlocks inside the tote bag. I'm not sure what else she brought with her."

"Do either of you want to go to the emergency room to be checked out?" he asked as he stared at Janice's swollen eye.

"I guess so," she said. "My shoulder is out of the socket and I should have my eye checked too. I can't see out of it."

"Absolutely." Jimmy nodded. "What about you, Sharon? I saw you limping. You weren't putting any weight on that right foot."

"She whacked my ankle bone hard with the butt of her gun," I said. "I think it will be better by tomorrow, probably just bruised. You can take a look at the back of my head if you want. She hit me with something heavy and knocked me out for a while."

I stood up so Jimmy could examine my head. I winced with the pain when he lightly touched it.

"You've got a great big egg back there. I don't see any blood though." He gently turned me around and sat me back down.

"That kind of head trauma can be dangerous," Detective Brandon said. "I think the two of you should be examined medically."

"The hospital's only a few minutes away. I'll drive you both over there." Jimmy had made up his mind, and I could tell there would be no arguing with him.

"Okay." I agreed, and Janice nodded.

"That sounds like a good idea. I don't think either of you are in critical condition, but you should be examined," the detective said. "I'll talk to the two of you tomorrow and get your statements. Take care of yourselves tonight first."

"I have a question," I said as I was getting up from the couch.

"What's that?" Jimmy asked.

"How did you two know we were in trouble here? You both showed up at the same time." I looked back and forth from one to the other, waiting for an explanation.

Detective Brandon chimed in first. "The computers were all down this afternoon because of the storm. Once I could get back online, I saw your email and ran down the number from that text message you got. Everything came back to Maria Benevides, the name you gave me for your ex-husband's girlfriend. I always pay attention to my gut feelings, and this time it was strong, telling me I needed to get over here right away."

"And I just got back to the apartment from the airport," Jimmy said. "I noticed that all your lights were out, but I thought I heard some kind of weird howling noise coming from the beach behind your house. I didn't like it, and a little voice in my head told me I'd better get over here pronto. I ran across the street just as the detective pulled up with the lights flashing."

"Well, thank you both. I can't tell you how happy I was to see you." I smiled. "It's nice to know I have people watching out for me."

"Enough gushing," Jimmy said as he held out one hand to me and the other to Janice. "Let's go get the two of you checked out."

"I'll stay until the officers are done, and then I'll lock up for you," the detective said. "If that's all right."

"Yes, that's fine." I nodded. "Thank you. And I'll talk with you tomorrow."

Hopefully, by then I would have figured out how to tell him what happened and make it sound believable. I shook my head and walked out the front door with Jimmy and Janice.

CHAPTER THIRTY-SIX

A sense of peace settled deep within my soul as I prepared to watch the sunset from my favorite booth at The Jolly Pelican. I took a sip from the frosty glass of Michelob while I considered everything that happened during the past week. My ankle was still sore. The bone wasn't broken, but there was a deep bruise, according to the emergency room doctor. I had to keep it wrapped with an elastic bandage for support for a few more days. I was starting to bear a little weight on it now but no long morning walks on the beach for a while. There was a nagging throb from the inside out at the base of my skull where Maria had slammed my head. I still didn't know what she hit me with. The x-rays didn't show any fractures there either, but the doctor said I probably had a moderate concussion. The lump on the back of my head was still tender when I touched it. These would heal, and I would be fine.

Most of yesterday was spent at the police station, giving statements to Detective Brandon and a couple of other officers. Janice was there too, with a patch over her eye and her arm in a sling. She said there was a tiny cut on the cornea, but they thought it would heal without any permanent damage to her vision and that her arm would heal in a couple of weeks. Jimmy was there for moral support for both of us. First they interviewed Janice and me separately, and then we had to meet with them together.

They had me sign an inventory list of the items they removed from my house as evidence. Looking over the list I could see they had taken Jim's framed photo that Maria had left there along with the rubber snake and a few other things. They took my fingerprints so they could eliminate them from any others in the hopes they could identify some that Maria left behind. I told them she had on those plastic gloves the whole time she was there Tuesday, but they thought she might have left some other prints on the previous occasions she entered with the key when I wasn't home.

I was exhausted by the time we were finished. My head pounded, and my ankle throbbed. Jimmy brought me home and offered to stay with me, but I told him to stay with Janice at the apartment. She needed him more. I would be fine, knowing that I didn't have to deal with Maria or Jim ever again. When I got in the house, I made myself a cup of tea and some toast and sat on the patio, trying to unwind. I went to bed early, about seven-thirty, and slept deeply all night, the uninterrupted and dreamless sleep that my body and spirit needed to begin their recovery.

I woke late this morning, after ten, but I felt much better. I puttered around the house all day, straightening up and putting things to rights. Outside, I put my pots and plants back in place as they had been before the storm. I found my poor beach rose still lying on the patio floor, apparently kicked into a corner during all the ruckus. Its root ball was still intact, and other than a few broken branches and missing leaves, it looked in good shape. I planted it in a new pot with fresh soil and put it out in its previous spot, feeling confident it would survive. It was as tough as I was. I hung my wind chimes back up and put my shells and other little trinkets back where they belonged.

Slowly as the day wore on, my house and my life got back in order. The remnants of Maria's rampage were removed bit by bit, and I stored away my pieces of memory of the ordeal as I dealt with each one of them. It was a day for healing. I gave myself about an hour of meditation time late in the afternoon, which was good for my soul. No spirits interrupted me or tried to get my attention, and I was grateful for that.

There was one more issue I had to deal with before I could have full closure, though. I walked to the beach and sat on the end of the boardwalk looking out over the water. I went back in my mind and relived what happened to Maria. I had no doubt Jim's spirit had killed her. No random gust of wind would have been strong enough to lift her off the ground and throw her thirty feet through the air. It was as if powerful invisible hands kept her head down and her body from rising.

Jim kept Maria from murdering me, but for his own selfish purpose. He used her to undermine my physical and psychic defenses so he could gain control of me. Yes, he saved my life, but not for love. He wanted to possess me. Despite what I wanted to believe, my heart had never truly let go of my love for him. Once I understood what bound me to him, I could break free and banish him from my life completely and forever.

I no longer felt any love for Jim, but I could wish him peace. We were finally released from whatever spiritual cord bound us together. We could move on, separately, with whatever the universe had in store for each of us. Once I banished Jim, the negative energy he directed at me was gone, and I hadn't felt any darkness since. That piece of my life was finally and utterly over. I was ready to embrace whatever might come next.

This afternoon, when I had everything back in order, I talked to Jimmy. He was taking Janice to the airport. She had a late evening flight back to Rhode Island, and he was going to stay with her to see her off. I promised I would see him tomorrow. By dinner time, I needed a change of scenery, and I decided The Jolly Pelican would be perfect.

I ordered my favorite fish tacos and discovered I was ravenous when they arrived. I realized I hadn't eaten much over the past two days and, as a treat, I ordered a piece of my favorite desert too, key lime pie. I ate every last crumb. Feeling sated and relaxed, I watched the changing palette of the sky as the sun eased closer to the horizon.

"Hello, Ms. Coady." A male voice broke into my reverie.

"Detective Brandon. Hello." I looked up and smiled. "Please, call me Sharon. I don't think you need to be so formal now that everything's over."

"Okay, Sharon." He smiled back. "And you can call me Jack. Can I join you?"

"Of course." I waved toward the seat opposite me. "I was just enjoying the sunset."

"It is beautiful tonight," he said as he gestured to Mike behind the bar. "Can I get you another beer or something to eat?" He picked up my empty glass and held it up.

"I just ate but I'll take a Michelob draft. Thanks," I said.

Mike came over to the table, and while he was taking the detective's order, I noticed Jack wasn't wearing his usual work clothes. Instead, he had on a pair of faded blue jeans and a Tampa Bay Rays t-shirt. He didn't look different, really, but he seemed a bit more relaxed in the casual clothes. Maybe it was my imagination, but his hair was a little rumpled too. My eyes dropped to his hand, and I noticed he wore no wedding ring.

The real Jack Brandon. Not bad at all.

"I hate to do this to you." He apologized with a grin. "But I thought you'd want me to bring you up to date on a couple of things. You probably don't want to think about it anymore, but I just need to tie up all the loose ends with you."

"That's okay," I said. "I don't mind. I'd rather deal with it all now and then put it away forever. It's not something I want to have to talk about for the rest of my life."

"Well, let's hope we can do that for you." He took his little notepad out of his pocket and flipped a few pages. "I told you that I traced the text message and, once I got your email, knew Maria was living across the street in the apartment below your ex." He looked at me and I nodded. "Somehow she had hooked up this wireless device so she could tap in to your cell phone. That's how she found out about the pizza you ordered. She did the same with Janice's phone for the ride to the airport which she canceled later, pretending to be Janice. You wouldn't believe some of the stuff we found when we searched her apartment. There were more photographs of you as well as some of Janice. The walls were covered with pictures of your ex. She really was obsessed."

He paused as Mike delivered our beers and a BLT and fries for him.

"Sorry, I've been too busy to eat all day," he said as he took a bite of the sandwich.

"No problem, go right ahead. I just finished mine." I looked out toward the beach and saw the sun sliding closer to the horizon now.

"The coroner finished the autopsy, and you were right. She had advanced lung disease." He paused to take a drink of his Heineken. "I can't give you any specific details but I can tell you that she died of suffocation. You knew that anyway. Her lungs were filled with sand. The coroner said she had never seen anything like it." He took another sip and then continued. "We found a few fingerprints on the photos, the picture frame, and the rubber snake along with a few partials around your house. The lab was able to match them with hers to prove that she had been inside."

"Is everything pretty much wrapped up then?" I hoped this story was almost at its end.

"Yes, I think so. Since she's deceased, there won't be any need for court involvement. Is there anything else you want to know about?" He ate the last bite of his BLT and followed it up with the one remaining french fry.

"No, I really have had enough."

"Look," he said as he pointed toward the water.

The sun was close to the horizon. It would only be a couple more minutes before it disappeared below the waters of the Gulf.

"Come on." He stood and gestured for me to do the same.

I walked ahead of him onto the back deck of the restaurant facing the beach. I felt his hand briefly touch the small of my back as he guided me toward the rail. We stood side by side and watched the glory of the sun's spectacle as it completed its evening journey. The gilded colors in the sky seemed more beautiful than ever, rose and mauve deepening to indigo and purple. Or perhaps it was just that I appreciated them more after the turmoil of the last few days. Finally, the last rays slipped beneath the blanket of the sea. A long sigh escaped before I could stop it.

"I'm pretty sure there's more to the story than just the physical events you've told me about," he said gently as he turned to face me. "In fact, I know there is. You might think nobody would believe you but, trust me, I understand more than you might think. Whenever you're ready..." He winked and grinned. "Come on, let's go back in."

The implications of his comment stunned me, and I was dumbstruck, not sure how to respond. I gulped and didn't say a word. His mouth turned up in a half-smile. As he guided me back toward the booth, the jukebox started to play "Nights in White Satin" by the Moody Blues.

"Would you like to dance?" He held out his hand.

I looked into his eyes as I reached out and placed my hand in his. Instantly, I felt that same surge of energy cross from his palm to mine, and from mine back to his. His gaze was welcoming and reassuring. I was definitely ready, and my intuition told me it was going to be very good.

ABOUT THE AUTHOR

Susan E. Rogers is a writer of speculative fiction. A genealogist with forty years' experience and a practicing psychic medium, she often twists these themes into her stories. In 2018, she published her first book related to her own psychic experiences and, in 2020, began her professional writing career with publication of poetry and short fiction. Since then, she's published five books, along with numerous short stories that have been published in magazines, anthologies, and podcasts. She lives with her partner Hardy in the Tampa Bay, Florida area, transplanted from a Social Work career in Massachusetts. Her move was the catalyst to begin her life-long ambition to write and she enjoys everything about her life in paradise.

Susan is a member of <u>WordSmitten Workshop</u>, <u>Pinellas Writers</u>, and <u>Florida Authors and Publishers Association</u>. She maintains a social media presence on Facebook, Bluesky, and Goodreads, and publishes a newsletter on Substack. A complete listing of her work can be found on her author website at www.susanerogers.com

ALSO BY

Susan E. Rogers

Non-Fiction, True Ghost Story series
<u>Uncovering Norman, Proving the former Life of a Ghost</u>
<u>Lady, Will You Hear Me?</u>
Fiction
<u>Death in the Cards</u>
The One in the Noose
Haunted in Paradise